Blue Bayou

JIFFY KATE

Jiffy Kate Books, LLC, www.jiffykate.com

Editing by Nichole Strauss, Insight Editing
Cover Design and Formatting by Juliana Cabrera, Jersey Girl Design
Proofreading: Karin Enders
Cover Model: Forest Tyler
Photographer: Wander Aguiar

First Edition: August 2018

Books by Jiffy Kate

Eventually, everyone comes back to the

Blue Bayou.

Maverick

"YOU'RE SO SPOILED...WEAK," **HE MUTTERS UNDER HIS** breath, running a hand down his face in disgust and frustration.

I grit my teeth and pinch the bridge of my nose in an effort to not respond. That's what he wants. He wants me to fly off the handle and prove I am what he says I am—a wild card, unpredictable, unfocused. And now, I guess, spoiled and weak should be added to his ongoing list, but what he's really angry about is that I'm not him.

My last name might be Kensington, but I'm definitely not like him.

Sighing, he collapses into his oversized, leather office chair and spins until his gaze is on the city in front of him. The shiny buildings of downtown Dallas are a backdrop to his soliloquy.

"You had one job today. Close on the McDaniels properties. That's all you had to do, but just like everything else, you fucked it up. Royally. Kensington Properties is not in the salvaging business. *We* buy. *We* filter out the shit. *We* resell. *We* make a profit." His voice rises as he goes and I'm sure, if I could see his face, it's probably an angry shade of red. But I want to laugh at his *we* because what he really means is *he*.

He buys. *He* sells. *He* makes a profit. It's all about him and it's all about money.

"You want to do things your way?" he continues. "Fine, but not on my time or my dime. When you have your own money, you can do whatever you want. For now, you work for me. You do what I say when I say. It's not up for discussion. You'd think after six years, you'd have that down, but I think I made a mistake by bringing you up the ladder too fast. I should've left you at the bottom and let you claw your way up."

He pauses for a second, his chair rocking slowly. I think he's done and I'm going to make my exit before things really get fucked up, but he starts again.

"Tomorrow, you'll go back to McDaniels and you'll get the fucking contracts signed. And you'll be there on demolition day. It'll be a good life lesson, showing you how things work. Your mother and grandfather coddled you too much. They made you into a bleeding heart, but that will get you nowhere in this life. It's a dog-eat-dog world out there, Maverick." Finally, he turns his chair and faces me, folding his hands in front of him on his pristine desk. "You should write that in your little journal."

I stare at him for a minute, wondering how I came from him. How is this man my father? I've always sought his approval. I went to the college he wanted. I got the degree he wanted. I came to Kensington Properties fresh out of school. I started in the mailroom, which was my favorite job thus far—it wasn't a dog-eat-dog world.

Who says life has to be like that?

Without a nod of my head or a word of agreement, I turn on my heel and walk out. When I get to the corner, on autopilot my feet head toward my office, but I stop. No. I don't want to.

I'm *not* going to.

What I want to do is tell him I quit. But I can't do that, not yet.

So, I'll stand up to him the only way I know how. Words don't work with Spencer Kensington. He can argue his way out of a brown paper sack. He should've been a lawyer. Or a fucking politician.

All he cares about is money. Simply put, he wants to purchase properties, demolish the existing structures, and turn them into shiny, high-rise apartment complexes. Today, it just so happened to be in the middle of a predominantly historic district and I couldn't do it—I couldn't close the deal. Scratch that. I didn't fucking *want* to make the deal. Work, for me, has become a soul-sucking rat race and I can't do it anymore. Today's deal was the proverbial straw.

Consider the camel's back broken.

Turning left, I walk toward the elevator and bypass it, going for the stairs. I need to blow off some steam before I get to my car.

I guess if I don't show up tomorrow, he'll have to close the McDaniels deal on his own.

When I pull into the drive at my house, I sit in my car for a minute, still forcing myself to cool down. Banging my head against the seat, I groan out my frustration. I've hated my job for a while. I knew a long time ago that I didn't want to be the next Spencer Kensington. Shit, I don't even want to be associated with him.

A few years back, I considered going out on my own or finding a job somewhere else. I have a fucking college degree. I can get a job. But in the real estate world, my father's word is golden. What he says matters, unfortunately. So, if I made a move, I'd literally have to make a move. I wouldn't be able to stay in Dallas. But the thing that keeps me here is the company. Even though Kensington is now on the side of the high-rise building, my grandfather built the company.

Maverick Johnson, the man I was named after, started in real estate more than fifty years ago. Unlike my father, he made an honest living buying and selling properties, while making a difference in people's lives. He found dream homes. He put people's businesses on the map by finding them prime locations. He was active in his community and was known as a philanthropist. The summers I spent on his ranch were some of the best days of my life.

But when my father took over after my grandfather died, everything changed.

I guess I've always hung on in hopes I could change things back.

In two years, I'll have access to the inheritance my grandfather left me. It probably won't be enough to buy my father out, but I could try. Regardless, I'll definitely have enough to open up a company of my own.

Twenty-eight is kind of late in the game to still be trying to decide who you are, but here I am: stuck in a job I hate, with a father who hates me and a life I'm not satisfied with.

Eventually, I get out of my car, pack a bag and lock up my house. I need to get away, clear my head, and there's only one place I can think of that'll get the job done.

Laissez les bon temps rouler.

Carys

"LAISSEZ LES BON TEMPS ROULER," THE DJ ON THE radio says boisterously, entirely too energetic for this early in the morning. I slam my hand down on the snooze button, needing just a few more minutes of sleep.

The good times are definitely not rolling around here.

As I close my eyes to try to squeeze just a little more rest out of the morning, my mind starts to drift to all the problems I've been facing lately. There's the water leak in room 204. The toilet that has been clogging up nonstop in 201. The A/C hasn't been running properly in one of the rooms on the third floor. My computers have been on the fritz. I have a mountain of paperwork waiting on me in my office.

My office. That still sounds weird.

A few years ago, if you'd have asked me what I'd be doing at the ripe age of twenty-five, I'd have told you I have no idea. That's the honest truth. I'm sure I would've been doing something; just not this, not running and operating a hotel by myself. Well, not technically by myself, but without my mom and grandpa.

It's weird how we think the people we love will live forever. It's also a harsh reality when they don't.

Rolling out of bed, I decide to forgo the extra minutes the snooze button would provide and go ahead and get ready. I need coffee.

I'm also hoping for some beignets from Mary. She stops and picks them up, hot and fresh, on her way into work sometimes. We tend to be on the same wavelength, even though she's forty years older than me, so I'm hoping she picks up my need of fried dough and powdered sugar.

Before I even get my clothes on and teeth brushed, my phone rings. "Hello."

"Miss Carys, I hate to bother you," George says, concern evident in his tone. "But these computers are on the fritz again."

I sigh, tucking in my shirt. "Sorry, George," I tell him, knowing he isn't incredibly tech savvy, so when things don't work the way they're supposed to, he gets flustered easily. "I'll be right there."

Tossing my hair up in a messy bun on top of my head, I run out the door and across the courtyard. In my world, problems concerning customers trump personal appearance any day. Without customers, I don't have an income. Without an income, I can't keep the lights on... or food in the pantry or pay George and Mary.

And let's face it, I'd be living in a van down by the river if it weren't for the two of them. Shit, I might not even have a van, more like a cardboard box, if I was lucky.

When I took over the daily operations of the hotel eighteen months ago, I knew it wouldn't be easy, but I had no clue exactly how difficult it would be to keep this place afloat. My mom, and grandparents before her, made it look simple. The hotel business was second nature to them and they ran this place like a well-oiled machine. But it's becoming apparent that the business-running gene skipped me entirely.

"Take a deep breath, baby," Mary urges when I come jogging in the back door. "This too shall pass."

"Ugh," I groan, but it sounds more like a cry. A cry for help. Because it's mornings like this when I ask myself if I'm really cut out for this job.

Can I run a hotel? Can I keep it open?

One look at the desk in my grandfather's old office has me following Mary's advice and taking deep breaths… lots of them, as I talk myself off the ledge.

Come on, Carys. Pull it together.

The surface of the desk is hidden with piles of papers awaiting my attention and causing me anxiety. All of this on top of today's computer failure might be what finally plunges me into eternal darkness.

Okay, that's a bit dramatic, even for me.

"I know you're letting that head of yours get the best of you this morning, but a little computer problem never stopped nobody."

"Right," I mumble, biting my lip while I try to get a grip.

"Your grandfather never used a computer."

"Nobody did back then," I add, rubbing my forehead as a slight headache begins.

"Well, still. He got by just fine without one." Mary walks up behind me and places a comforting hand on my shoulder that I quickly lean into.

"And he had a lot more people come through those doors than I ever have," I add with a sigh, not sure if that should make me feel better or worse.

"He did," she pauses, with a hint of hesitation. "But those were different times. People brought their families to the city, and they didn't need fancy pools and bars," she says in her deep Louisiana drawl. "They just wanted a nice room and a soft bed and familiar faces."

She sounds like I feel: nostalgic, sentimental, and on the edge of tears.

"I'm not sure if this is helping, Mar." I look to the ceiling, saying a silent prayer to keep the hotel running, even if just for another day.

"You're right." Mary brushes her hands down the front of her white apron, the same type of apron she's worn every day of my life. Literally. Mary has always been here. She worked for my grandfather and then later for my mother. She helped me learn to ride a bike and sewed my Halloween costumes. "I'm gonna find a ledger and the manual credit card machine. Those will get us by until we get this computer problem figured out."

"Thank goodness we didn't give into the keyless entry system that pushy guy tried to sell us last month."

"See, modern amenities aren't all they're cracked up to be," she says smiling at me from over her shoulder as she digs through a file cabinet in search of the old credit card machine that works on elbow grease and carbon paper.

"Tell that to all those travel websites and adventure bloggers."

Sitting down at the desk, I try to take a page from Mary's book and make a dent in the papers and bills while I wait to hear back from the computer guy. Before I can even get started, my attention is caught by a picture sitting on the corner. With the frame in my hand, I trace my finger over the faces of my grandfather and grandmother, then my mom's, and finally, my own. I was only a kid when this photo was taken, but it's always been a favorite of mine. My grandfather would show it off to anyone who'd give him a moment of their time, declaring he was the "luckiest man on earth to be surrounded by such beauty."

Anticipating the tears I've been trying to avoid, I put the picture back in its place and try to focus on the task in front of me. They didn't raise me to fail. If they didn't believe I could run the Blue Bayou, they wouldn't have left her to me. At least that's what I have to tell myself, and for the most part, it makes me feel better. So much so, I make it through the sales tax form and a few other important tasks in just a couple hours.

When I can't stand being cooped up in the office any longer, I walk into the lobby to stretch my legs and check on how things are going, hoping there are no new catastrophes waiting for me.

I find George sitting behind the front desk, working on the daily crossword puzzle.

"Hey, George. Everything okay up here?"

"Well, hello there, Miss Carys." He puts his newspaper and pencil down and stands, greeting me with the same broad smile he's had since I was a kid. Along with Mary, George has practically been here since the beginning of the hotel, and I can count on one hand how many times I've seen him without his trademark smile. Nothing gets him down and I love that about him.

"Don't stand on my account. I'm just taking a break from the office and wanted to see how you're doing." I motion for him to sit back down before pouring us each a glass of water from a pitcher I keep on top of a nearby antique table. We always have ice cold water for guests as they come inside or to anyone who needs it, really. It's always so hot and humid here in New Orleans that it's more of a necessity than anything. Plus, I just think it's a nice thing to do.

It's what my grandmother did. She started so many wonderful traditions here, some I continue, like the fruit infused water, and some that have fallen to the wayside.

"We've had two guests check out so far and that computer guy you spoke with yesterday called to say he'll be here after lunch."

"Oh, good. I was afraid he was gonna cancel on me. Was it a big pain to check out the guests by hand?"

"Oh, no," he says, grinning. "Miss Mary helped me with the first one, but it didn't take much for me to remember how we used to do it."

George is the resident *jack of all trades*, and even though he's in his seventies, he's still as sharp as a tack. But I have no doubt he enjoyed Mary reminding him how to manually check the guests out. Those two have always had eyes for each other and a sweet, flirty relationship. When I was a little girl, I used to daydream about being the flower girl in their wedding, even though they're both old enough to be my second set of grandparents.

"How many guests are scheduled to check out today?" I ask, looking through the ledger. "We had four rooms sold last night, right?"

"That's right. Besides the two that done left, we've had one request late check-out and one say they're gonna stay another night."

"Oh, okay. That's great." With it being close to the weekend, I'm hopeful we'll have even more rooms booked tonight.

"Yes, the lady who extended her stay said the hotel was very lovely, even though it's lacking in character." My eyes light up at his words only to come crashing back down along with my shoulders as he finishes his statement.

Character? I feel like the Blue Bayou has tons of character. I mean, if you looked in the dictionary under character, a picture of the hotel should be there. If we don't have character, what do we have? This place used to be the *bee's knees*, to quote my grandmother, and was always packed with guests.

While other kids my age were off at the pool or zoo or having sleepovers, I was here meeting people from all over the world. I adored this place. I still do, I just have to somehow help it get its mojo back.

And to be fair, business isn't always this dreadful. We have our busy seasons and our slow seasons, like any business in the tourist industry, but this particular season seems to be slower than a herd of turtles and it has me nervous. Summer is just around the corner, though, and I'm hopeful it'll be a great one for us.

The Blue Bayou is located just outside the French Quarter, sandwiched between Jackson Square and Bourbon Street, which is where most tourists want to visit. You'd think we'd be sold out most nights, but we're not. Before I inherited the hotel, it seemed like we were always filled to the gills with businessmen, as well as families on vacation. Now, we only seem to get late-night stragglers who've partied too hard to remember where they're staying, or those who wait too long to book elsewhere and have no choice but to stay here. We still have some of our regulars, but most of them are older and we only see them once or twice a year.

In days gone by, word-of-mouth was enough, but nowadays, you need a presence on the internet and paid advertisements. I know all of that but having the time and money to do it is another question.

I wish I could figure out how to get more customers, especially returning customers. I've thought about hiring a marketing firm, but I can't afford it right now. But without good marketing, I might never get this place filled back up.

It's a catch-22 if I've ever seen one, and a vicious cycle that keeps me up at night.

As the afternoon drifts on, my eyes begin to cross from looking at my computer screen for so long. The tech guy who came over to help only wanted to sell me a new computer, which I can't afford. I finally convinced him to fix the damn thing enough for us to get by, but we're still not able to run credit card payments, so it looks like I'll be putting in another call soon.

"How about I open the front door for a little bit and let some fresh air in?" Mary asks, already heading toward the door. She opens one side of the double door and a smile instantly spreads across my face.

There's a nice breeze blowing in, bringing with it the smell of Cajun food and the sounds of jazz music from down the street. It's faint, but it's just enough to soothe my mind and remind me how much I love my city.

"Watch out for Rusty," I warn Mary. "He's been trying to sneak in lately."

Technically, Rusty is a dog; however, he looks more like a long-haired baby goat, with about as much grace as one too. He's a sweet little thing, but I'm always afraid he's going to destroy this place.

"Did you tell Floyd he escaped?"

"I did, but I can call him again," I tell her. Floyd runs one of the horse-carriage tours around the Quarter, and when he works, he leaves Rusty at home, which is around the corner from here. No one can figure out how he escapes, but he does. Frequently.

Mary sticks her head out the door, looking for Rusty, I presume. When she's back inside, she has a sneaky smile on her face. "Oh, let me handle it. There's a cute young man walking down the sidewalk and I think he just might need a room."

I roll my eyes at her as I walk over to refill the pitchers of water on the side table. Cute young men are a dime a dozen in New Orleans, but without a gym or pool or bar, not many want to stay here, so I don't get my hopes up.

Still, I wouldn't mind catching a glimpse of whomever it is that turned Mary's head. I may be too busy to even think about dating, but I'm certainly not dead.

Peeking out the glass of the door that's closed, I nearly swallow my tongue when I see him.

Faded, slightly tattered jeans.

A well-worn t-shirt that's snug over his shoulders and biceps.

He's carrying a leather duffle bag that makes his arms flex as he continues down the sidewalk. The closer he gets, the more his features come into view.

Dark, messy hair.

Light stubble covering his well-defined jaw and chin.

Speaking of chins, I need to wipe the drool off mine and get back to work. He's a dreamboat, for sure, but Mr. Dreamboat is not going to help me get this hotel back in its groove. Although, he could get me back into mine, I bet. Just call me Stella.

I step away from the door and laugh at myself as I walk back to the table, straightening the water glasses on display. The sound of the bell jingling above the door catches me by surprise, but not as much as Mr. Dreamboat does when he walks inside. I'm so caught off guard by his presence, not to mention his blinding, white smile, I don't even notice Rusty rushing in behind him until it's too late.

"Rusty, no!" Trying to control the crazy dog does me no good. In fact, I only seem to excite him more, which causes him to run and jump on me, knocking me off-balance and into the table. When I fall to the floor, it's like I'm in the *Matrix* and everything happens in slow-motion. Thankfully, somehow, my typically clumsy self manages to catch the glass pitcher before it crashes to the floor beside me, but now I'm completely drenched.

Rusty runs back outside, leaving me alone with Mr. Dreamboat.

Maverick

WET.

I don't know who this woman is, but she's gorgeous. And wet. *Soaking* wet.

Did I forget to mention she's wet?

It takes me longer than I'd like to admit, to help her up. Eventually, the manners I was raised with finally click into place and I rush to the lady on the ground, offering to help her up. When I stick my hand out for her to grab, she just stares at it like she doesn't know what it is.

Did she hit her head? Maybe she has a concussion. I'm really out of my element here but I can't leave her lying on the floor.

"Ma'am, are you okay? Take my hand and I'll help you up."

Something about my words must grab her attention because she finally makes eye contact with me, setting the empty pitcher on the ground beside her. Now I'm the one stunned, because fuck me if she doesn't have the most beautiful eyes I've ever seen. I can't tell if they're blue or green or some color that hasn't been discovered yet, but they're incredible.

I watch as she tilts her head to the side like she's trying to figure me out, her eyes blinking a few times before going wide. I assume she thinks I'm about to harm her in some way, or maybe she thinks I'm the one who knocked her down instead of that dog. Suddenly, she takes in a large gulp of air bringing my attention back to her wet shirt, and I'll admit, her fantastic rack, and I brace myself for her scream. I mean, I don't blame the woman. Here I am, a stranger, standing over her, ogling her tits with my hand stretched out like I'm going to grab her. It's time for some fast talking.

Come on, Mav. You can do this. Just explain yourself. Quickly.

Before I can say anything, though, the woman busts out a laugh. Not a scream, but a laugh. Her belly-aching laugh soon has me relaxed enough to snicker at our situation.

"Holy shit, what a day I've had," she gasps out between chuckles. "Did you just call me *ma'am*? Please tell me I'm not older than you. That would be the icing on the cake, let me tell you."

"Umm, well, I don't know your age, but it doesn't really matter. I also don't know your name, so I had to call you something, and I was raised better than to refer to you as 'hey, lady'. Are you going to take my hand and let me help you?"

"What? Oh, right. Okay." She finally slides her hand into mine and I'm overcome with a feeling I've never experienced before. It's a mixture of calm and excitement and I know without a doubt I need to know more about her. I *have* to know more about her.

"So, what is your name?" I ask as she stands up. She's taller than I thought she'd be, and it's difficult not to imagine what it'd be like with her long legs wrapped around my waist. Or shoulders. I'm an equal opportunity kind of guy, you know.

"Sorry," she says, shaking her head, still trying to get a grip on herself. "Carys Matthews, and you are?"

"My name is Maverick, nice to meet you." As much as I'd love to hold her hand again, I don't want to scare her off, so I give her a little wave instead and she gives me a small one back. "Pardon me for being so bold, but are you staying at this hotel?"

Yeah, that's not creepy at all, dumbass.

Carys laughs again, thankfully. "No, it's worse than that, actually. I own and run this place. Are you lost? Looking for directions? You don't want a room, do you?"

I'm taken aback by her questions because, as a business owner, she should be encouraging me to rent a room from her, not talking me out of it. But, I'm not here for work. I'm on vacation or something like that, so I ignore that part of my brain and answer her instead.

"Actually, I do...want a room."

"Really?" Her eyes light up, but also look frazzled, just like her. "Well, you can have just about any room you'd like, including mine!" She laughs again before realizing what she has said and once she does, a deep blush covers her cheeks and it's fucking adorable. Unfortunately for me, she covers those cheeks with her hands and blocks my view. "That was very unprofessional of me, I apologize. It's just been an extremely stressful day." She clears her throat and looks down, obviously trying to get herself together.

"Don't worry about it—"

"Oh, shit, I forgot about my shirt," she hisses. Her comment forces my attention to her still wet, but very perky breasts.

When I look up, she meets my eyes and hers go wide with embarrassment. "Shit! I'm sorry," she says, apologizing again. "I'll be right back." Bolting through the door behind her, off to what I assume is an office, she disappears and leaves my head spinning a bit.

"Huh," I murmur to no one but myself, since the rest of the lobby and foyer are deserted. Smiling at the closed door, I try to wrap by head around this place and Carys Matthews. This girl is practically the poster child for the *hot mess express.* Not gonna lie, I want a ride.

Out of work-related habit and genuine curiosity, I start looking around the hotel lobby, cataloging things I notice that need repair or an upgrade. I can't help it. Fixing up properties is the part of my job I actually enjoy, so it's hard for me to walk into any establishment and not analyze it, looking for ways to improve it and make it better. Somehow, I need to find a way to relax, and hopefully, have some fun while I'm here. What's the point of escaping town and abandoning your job if you're not going to let loose and blow off some steam?

Speaking of fun...

I turn back just in time to see Carys step out of the office and walk behind the front desk. She's more presentable now with her clean shirt and hair pulled away from her face, but no less adorable than she was before.

"Is your name really Maverick?" she asks with another light blush creeping onto her high cheekbones.

"It is, in fact." I already know what's coming, so I wait for her next question.

"Were you named after Tom Cruise's character in Top Gun?"

And there it is.

Normally, I'd have bristled at her question because it happens nearly every time I tell someone my name, but she seems to be truly interested, so I want to answer. Of course, it could just be my wishful thinking that she's interested, but I don't care. Maybe if I share a bit about myself, she'll return the favor.

"No, I can pretty much guarantee my parents have never seen that movie. I'm named after my grandfather."

"Sorry for the stupid question. I bet you get that all the time, huh?" Her blush deepens, and she starts fidgeting with the pen in her hand. I swear, I could watch her all day.

Normally, girly behavior isn't really a turn on for me. I can't stand fake giggles and hair twirls, but this girl—woman—standing in front of me is anything but those things. Sure, she's a mess, in the most literal sense of the word, but she's also a breath of fresh air. It's like the universe drove me straight here and blew me into the doors of the Blue Bayou.

"I do, but I get it." I laugh slightly, shaking my head at the crazy turn of events. "I mean, it's not a very common name, is it?" She smiles as she shakes her head in response, her eyes locked on mine. But as soon as I place my forearms on the desk in front of her and lean in a bit, her eyes widen and the pen she's tapping starts moving in overtime. Apparently, I make this woman nervous. Interesting. "Carys is also a name you don't hear very often. Are you named after someone?"

"Ha, no. My mom was a bit of a free spirit and loved being different from everyone else. She thought it'd be cool to give her daughter a name no one around here could pronounce," she says, laughing. "Someone once told me it means 'precious' or something like that but I don't know if it's true."

"Precious, huh? I think that's fitting." I give her my best crooked smile, and she swallows audibly.

I swear, I'm not usually this much of a flirt but I'm really enjoying seeing her react to me. It makes me want to do less honorable things to her, so I can see *and hear* her reactions. Just thinking about what could happen if I were lucky enough to spread her out on my bed has my dick aching.

Thankfully, we have this tall front desk between us, so she doesn't seem to notice when I adjust myself.

"So, about this room you have available..."

"A room? Yes, of course!" She begins to shuffle things around on the desk in front of her. "I really should apologize for my verbal vomit earlier... and for not realizing sooner how inappropriate my shirt was. I'm horrible at first impressions on a good day, but I really raised the bar today."

"You have nothing to be sorry about. I think you were just stunned from being bowled over by that dog, and besides, you'll get no complaints from me regarding your verbal vomit or the wet shirt, for that matter."

I've really caught her off guard with that statement because her mouth is hanging open and her eyes are blinking in some kind of random pattern. Surely, this isn't the first time she's been flirted with. Surely, she knows how gorgeous she is.

"So, a room?" I remind her again.

"What? Yes, a room." She shakes her head a bit. "A room, of course." She turns to her side and grabs what looks like an old-fashioned ledger before pausing and asking, "Uh, are you sure you want to stay here?"

"Why? Are you trying to get rid of me?" I counter.

"No, of course not. I mean, I—*we'd* love to have you as a guest here. Lord knows we need to fill some rooms," she rambles nervously. "I just feel like I owe it to you to warn you about what you're getting yourself into."

Now, this should be good.

"What exactly am I getting myself into?" I quirk my eyebrow a bit to let her know I'm fine with whatever she wants to get me into. That is what quirking an eyebrow means, right?

"What am I doing?" she mutters, rubbing her forehead forcefully, obviously talking to herself. "Well, for starters, our computers are hit and miss at the moment, so I'll have to check you in by hand."

That explains the ledger.

"Not a problem. What else you got?"

She goes serious all of a sudden and swats at my hand, startling me and making me laugh. "Don't tempt fate like that!" she scolds. "Seriously, we need the business, so I shouldn't be trying to run you off, but today has been one for the books. I should change the name of this place to Murphy's Law because whatever can go wrong around here, will."

"Sorry to disappoint you, Carys, but you didn't scare me off. In fact, I'd love to offer my services and see if I can help with your computers. What do you say?"

I'm not sure why I offered to help with her computers. I'm much handier with power tools but I don't want to overwhelm her more than she already is.

Carys' eyes narrow at me and she puts her hands on her hips. "Are you some kind of salesman? Because, if you are, you can get right on out of here. I don't have the time or money to deal with any more salesmen today."

I've obviously hit a sore spot with her, so I need to make this right.

"No, I'm not a salesman, but I'm very familiar with the hotel industry and feel like I could be of some help around here. I know my appearance doesn't scream 'professional' but I swear I know what I'm doing. Trust me." I hope my face looks as legitimate as my words are because I want to help her just as much as I want to get to know her.

Finally, she lets out a deep breath and relaxes her stance. "Okay," she sighs and looks at me long and hard for a moment, not like she's checking me out again, but like she's trying to decide if my word is good. Once she comes to her conclusion, she begins again. "I'll let you stay here, and if you want to take a look at the computers, you can; but if you do, I'm not charging you for your room."

I start to protest but she holds her hand up to stop me. "That's the deal. It's the only way I can pay you for your services." Her voice goes quiet and even though I'm thrilled she's accepting my offer, I hate seeing her look so defeated.

"Well, don't put that in writing just yet because I may not be able to help at all. For all you know, I may make things worse." I give her a playful smile and after a few moments she returns it, oblivious to the relief coursing through my body as she does.

After filling out the ledger with my personal information, she hands me a key. Like, a *real* key, with a big, bulky keychain that reads *Blue Bayou*. I don't even remember the last time I saw one of these in a hotel. Carys catches me staring at it and jokes, "What can I say? I like antiques." She smiles and shrugs. "Room 304. Elevator is behind the staircase."

To say I'm smitten with this woman is the understatement of the year.

Carys

SO FAR, TODAY IS GOING MUCH BETTER THAN yesterday. I was able to enjoy my coffee in peace without spilling a drop, and the computers worked long enough for me to check out our departing guests. Granted, I've only been up for two hours and could, unknowingly, be facing a horrendous afternoon, but I'm trying to stay positive.

I even had time to brush my hair and put on a little makeup before coming into the hotel, something that did not go unnoticed by Miss Mary, unfortunately. She had the nerve to insinuate I was trying to look *more presentable* for Maverick, but I argued that I want to look professional for *all* of our guests, not just him.

She called bullshit, of course. I tried to convince her she was wrong, but we both know she's right.

How could I not want to make a better impression on him? I was a complete embarrassment yesterday, and yet somehow, he still got a room here. After the catastrophe he witnessed—and my full disclosure—I was sure he'd want to stay as far away as he could, but he seemed...happy, maybe even a little excited. All I know is I couldn't take my eyes off him as he walked up the stairs. Let's just say I was taking inventory of him while he was taking inventory of my hotel.

It seemed like an even trade.

Once he was in his room, I quickly exiled myself to my office for the rest of the day, telling George and Mary not to call me unless the hotel was on fire. I didn't want to allow for another opportunity to make an ass of myself in front of our resident dreamboat, so I spent the rest of the day sulking while researching hotel marketing trends instead of doing what I really wanted: watching my favorite cooking channel. It's one of my guilty pleasures, helping me to relax and forget about my troubles for a while.

But today is a new day and I will handle myself in a professional manner, dammit. This, of course, means I need to stop daydreaming of *handling* Maverick. He's just too freaking good-looking. And nice. I mean, how dare he be so perfect?

"What time is that young man comin' in?" George asks, effectively pulling me from my thoughts.

"How should I know? We may not have a lot of guests right now, but I don't feel it's my job to keep up with their itineraries. Maverick can come and go as he pleases." I don't make eye contact with George because if I did, he'd clearly see the guilt I'm feeling all over my face.

I *may* have watched Maverick through my office window as he left the hotel yesterday afternoon, and I *may* have noticed he didn't come back before I left the office at ten o'clock last night. Not that it matters. This is New Orleans, for crying out loud. Of course he was out all night. That's what you do here. Still, I feel bad for being such a creeper.

"Maverick? I thought his name was Jules." His brows furrow and he looks genuinely confused. "I don't know how I'm supposed to keep up with these new—what's the word— *trendy* names nowadays, anyway." George is so cute when he uses air quotes. As he does, realization strikes me and I smack myself on the forehead.

"Oh!" I exclaim, realizing my mistake and feeling my cheeks heat. "Uh, Jules, the new guy. He starts today and should be here any minute.

Sorry, George, I thought you were talking about some guy who checked in yesterday." The nervous laugh that escapes makes his lips quirk into a small smile.

"Why would I be askin' about him?" he asks.

"You wouldn't. I don't know what's wrong with me. There's absolutely no reason you'd ask about him or any reason I'd be thinking about him. Which I'm not."

George doesn't look convinced, much like Mary this morning. I must be losing my touch. I used to be able to convince them of anything.

"I'm most certainly not thinking about Maverick," I reiterate.

"Sure, honey. I believe ya," George replies just as a deep voice asks, "Did I hear my name being mentioned?"

Kill me. Just kill me now.

I watch as Maverick walks down the stairs, graceful as a model down a catwalk. His easy stride is confident, yet not arrogant. He seems like someone who is completely comfortable in his own skin. I envy that quality, seeing as though I'm in a constant state of unbalance these days, always adjusting my course to keep from crashing into something and sinking the boat, so to speak.

I feel a pinch on my arm and turn around to find George giving me a covert "thumbs up" before nodding his head in Maverick's direction. Narrowing my eyes at him, I mouth the word "stop" then turn to face the dreamboat heading my way.

"Hello, Mr. Kensington. How are you today?" Hopefully, if I ignore his question, he'll forget he asked it.

The gorgeous bastard smirks at me and I know he's onto my plan. But still, he plays along, thankfully.

"Please call me *Maverick*. My father is Mr. Kensington, and I'd rather not be mistaken for him at the moment."

He must notice the slight intrigue on my face because he adds, "I'm sure he'd tell you the same thing about me if you were to ask."

Interesting.

There's a strange vibe in the room and I don't like it. It makes me feel uncomfortable and when I feel uncomfortable, I do and say stupid things, and I vowed not to do or say stupid things in front of Maverick today, so I need to think of a way to clear the air immediately.

"So, how long are you in town for, Mr. Maverick?" George asks in his own usual lilt that always seems to set people at ease, saving us all with his question.

I blow out an inconspicuous breath and let my shoulders relax while turning my attention to the computer screen in front of me. I desperately want to know more about Maverick, but I don't want him to know that I want to know, so I'm trying to appear uninterested. Plus, I need to pull up the hotel's training software for when Jules comes in, which should be any minute now.

Maverick leans against the tall desk George and I are standing behind and geez Louise, he smells so good. I wouldn't even know how to describe what I'm smelling but it's enough to make my mouth water—woodsy, clean, manly. It's a heady combination and I'm struggling to keep my expression neutral. Inwardly, my eyes are practically rolling into the back of my head as I inconspicuously drink him in.

"Not really sure." He answers George, but I feel his heavy gaze on me. Normally, the attention would make me blush ten shades of red, but since I have the ruse of the computer to keep me occupied, I'm rather enjoying it. "I guess you could say I'm on vacation until further notice. Would you like for me to pay for my stay up front? I can pay a week at a time until I know for certain how long I'll be here."

"I told you, if you're serious about your offer to help with these computers, you're staying for free. And I hope you were serious because it looks like I need your help." I push away from the desk and cross my arms. "It's on the fritz again. It was working just fine this morning, but now I can't access the program I need. I have someone coming in for training today, so I really need it to work."

"Do you mind if I step back there and take a look?"

"Be my guest." I still myself, trying to come off business-like and unaffected. "I'll check the computer in the office, too." As I walk past George, he gives me a wicked smile, which I ignore. Walking over to the computer stationed on my grandfather's old oak desk, I give the mouse a wiggle, and nothing. Everything on the screen is frozen. "This one's dead, too," I call out before slumping in my chair, muttering expletives under my breath.

Maverick knocks on the door frame before sticking his head inside the office.

"Come on in," I tell him, feeling dejected and nearly at my wits end. Nothing freaking works around here anymore and I feel like simultaneously pulling my hair out and crying in the corner, not because it would fix anything, but because it would make me feel better. For like five minutes.

"You okay?" he asks, walking inside the room.

"I don't even know anymore," I admit, my frustration getting the better of me. "It's just always something, you know?"

I watch as he pushes a chair next to mine, then motions toward the computer. "May I?" I nod my approval and scoot back a bit to give him some space to work. He brushes my arm as he slides in closer to the screen, and once again I'm sniffing him like a can of paint. A hint of oak mixed with honey and vanilla hits me hard, reminding me of another man who used to sit in this very chair. Strong, but sweet. My grandpa always smelled like that, often mixed with a little tobacco, not like cigarette smoke, but a delicious cherry scent. He used to love lighting up his pipe in the evenings and sipping a glass of whiskey. The combination would lull me into a comatose state as I'd sit beside him.

The memory makes me smile and without thinking, I take another deep breath and let out a small sigh. When I see Maverick biting down on his bottom lip to suppress a grin, I know he's onto me, but for some reason, I don't care.

I can always plead stress-induced insanity, right?

"Can I ask you something?" I ask, taking advantage of the shift in atmosphere. There's something I've been curious about ever since he checked in last night. Call it marketing research.

"Sure." He's typing and clicking away on the computer, in some black screen I've never seen before, but still glances my way, smiling. Always smiling.

Stupid, perfect teeth. The nerve of this guy.

"What brought you here? To this hotel, I mean."

He sits back in his chair, looking deep in thought. "I'm not sure, to be honest," he says thoughtfully, giving me another smile, that's different from the others I've received so far. This one is smaller, with a hint of sadness... "Yesterday was a rough one and I needed to leave, get away for a while. I didn't even know where I was going until I bought my plane ticket. But I've been down here many times, so out of habit I went to the hotel I always stay at. The driver dropped me off, I entered the lobby and was immediately recognized and greeted by the manager." He sighs, thinking for a second before continuing. "As soon as he asked about my father, I turned for the door and didn't look back. Seeing as how I'm trying to get away for a few days, the last thing I wanted was for him to track me down there. Instead of calling for another Uber, I just started walking and eventually made my way here. When I saw the sign that read *Blue Bayou* and yet, nothing here is blue, I was intrigued. I mean, not even the front door? It made me curious, so I walked inside and well, you know what happened next."

"Yep, you let that damn dog in and he knocked me on my ass."

His loud laughter warms my insides, and I'm mesmerized by the way his Adam's apple moves up and down. I want to make him laugh again just to watch him. He's fascinating to me.

Maverick wipes his eyes once he's calmed down and turns to me. "My turn. Why have I not heard of this hotel before? I mean, it's obviously been around for a long time, so why haven't I ever seen any ads for it?"

His question instantly turns my warm insides sour and my mood starts slipping back to where it was when he first walked into the office.

"I don't mean to be rude, I swear," he starts, obviously aware this is a touchy subject for me. "I told you last night, I'm familiar with the hotel industry and because I've visited New Orleans so much in the past, I'm surprised I've never heard of or seen this place."

"Well, since you were honest with me, I'll return the favor. The answer to your question is simple: I suck at running this hotel. This place is everything to me. I was raised here, and I always knew it'd be mine one of these days, but when the time came, I wasn't prepared. I never realized how hard it is. Every day is a slap in the face, telling me how much of a failure I am."

"Carys, you aren't a failure."

I don't know when it happened, but at some point during my confession, Maverick's chair moved closer to mine, which means his body is closer to mine. *Much* closer. Too close to be professionally acceptable, in fact, but my own body won't listen to reason. I'm leaning toward him, just begging for him to touch me. It's like that magnet-type of attraction you read about in romance novels really exists, but that can't be.

Can it?

Maverick cups my face with his strong hands, his rough fingertips brushing against the soft skin on my cheeks. It strikes me as odd that someone who claims to be a businessman would have calluses on his fingers, but I don't allow myself to overthink or ask. Speaking would ruin this moment and I just want to feel more of him.

Before I can, though, I hear the bell above the front door chime, followed by a loud and boisterous "Hey, y'all" alerting me to Jules' arrival. I'm glad to know he's punctual, but I would've been totally fine with him being late today.

"That would be my new employee." My voice is barely a whisper, trying like hell not to break the spell we're under.

Maverick looks up and down, from my eyes to my lips and back again, before sighing and dropping his hands. He clears his throat before asking, "Can I stay in here while you train the new guy?"

"Absolutely. Make yourself at home...or at work or whatever...I'll be right out here if you need anything."

"I'll be here," he says, staring at me intently.

Does he mean something else by that statement, or is it just wishful thinking on my part? He seems so serious and it's turning me on even more than when he's being playful.

Get a grip, sister, and get back to work!

I walk out of the office and close the door behind me to find Jules leaning over the counter, checking everything out.

Smiling awkwardly, I walk around the counter to greet him. "Welcome to the Blue Bayou." I hope he didn't witness anything between Maverick and me. I don't want to get off on the wrong foot with this being his first day. I need the help, so I really want this to go well.

His gaze is still on the door I just shut to the office as he leans in conspiratorially. "Girl, who is that fine hunk of man meat hiding back there? Is he yours, or can I call dibs?"

My laughter causes the tension to leave the room. Oh, I think he's gonna work out just fine.

"Jules, I think you just became my new best friend."

Maverick

As soon as Carys closes the office door, I palm my aching dick through my jeans, trying to relieve some of the pressure, however temporary it may be. Ever since I checked in last night, I've practically been a walking hard-on, but the last few minutes in this room alone with her nearly killed me. Why I thought I could work with her and keep my hands off her, I have no idea.

Two good things did happen, though.

One, she told me a little about herself and I get the feeling she doesn't do that often, especially to people she just met. Of course, it only made me want to know more about her.

Two, she seems to be just as affected by me as I am by her. I'm good at reading women, and her body language was definitely giving me the green light. Bonus points for her not noticing the tent I'm currently displaying in my pants. Otherwise, she might've kicked me out of her office instead of inviting me to stay. Once the spell was broken, I could tell she was rattled by our close encounter.

As much as I would've loved to kiss her, I'm glad I didn't. I'd never want it to seem like I was taking advantage of her, using her moment of vulnerability for my primal gain.

The fact she feels like a failure doesn't sit well with me. She's definitely not. From what I can tell, she keeps this place running with little help and there's no way she can be older than me. She doesn't look a day over twenty-two, maybe just barely legal to drink, but if I had to guess, I'd say she's a solid twenty-five.

In all other areas, a solid ten.

Focus, Mav.

Spinning the chair back around, I sit down and pull up to the computer. I can tell this is a huge area of distress for Carys, so if I can figure this shit out, it'd take a load of stress off her.

And maybe she'd consider going on a date with me.

Fuck. Seriously, I'm not doing this to get in her pants. I swear. I saw someone in need, and it's an area I can help with, so I'm helping. It's who I am. This has nothing to do with how gorgeous I think that woman out there at the front desk is. Nothing.

Growling, I scrub my face and run my hands through my hair.

"Okay, you fucking computer. What the hell is wrong with you?" I mutter, punching a few keys to pull up a diagnostic screen. Sometimes, a little trash talking will do the trick. It could also be as easy as cleaning up a nasty virus.

After what feels like an eternity, the scan completes and operational systems seem good. Internet is connected. Virus check came back clean, which is surprising. Usually, there's at least a few items quarantined on a routine check. Carys obviously doesn't watch much porn. At least, not on this computer.

Half an hour later, after checking everything I know to check and exhausting my repertoire, I come to the conclusion this is out of my area of expertise. It could just be the old-ass computer, but I feel like there's something I'm not seeing, so I pull out my phone and dial up someone who will definitely know what to do.

"This is Shep."

"Hey, it's Mav."

He doesn't say anything for a minute, probably excusing himself from a room so he can talk. "Where the fuck did you take off to?"

"How did you even know I was gone?" I ask, rolling my eyes at his nosey ass. "I've barely been gone twenty-four hours."

"I ran by your place last night to shoot the shit and you were gone. Then I stopped by your office this morning and Meredith said you were out of town."

I bark out a laugh. "Guess I never have to worry about going missing and no one noticing."

"So, are you gonna tell me where you took off to?"

"You've probably already tracked my phone."

He clears his throat and mutters something I can't hear.

"Listen, I didn't call for a heart-to-heart. I need your help with something," I tell him, getting down to business. The sooner I get this done, the sooner I can get back to day drinking my problems away.

"What's up?"

"I'm helping a...uh." I pause, not sure what to call Carys. She's merely an acquaintance at this point, but I can't help the feeling of wanting her to be more. "A friend. She's, uh, having trouble with her computers and I thought you might be able to help."

"A friend, huh?" Shep asks, picking up on my hesitation. "What's in it for you?"

"I'm shocked you'd assume such a thing."

"Actually, you're a fucking do-gooder, so it's probably some nun you met at confession."

A picture of a younger Carys hanging on the wall in front of me catches my attention and a slow smile spreads across my face. I'm thankful I didn't Facetime Shep and I can keep this to myself for the time being. Damn, she's definitely no nun, and she's certainly not innocent. In the picture, she's laughing with a woman who looks like an older version of her, and their wild blonde hair is blowing in the wind. Actually, it looks like it was taken just a few blocks from here at the river. She's younger, but she's still sexy as sin, in an unintentional way. It's so appealing.

"Mav?"

"Yeah."

"Thought I lost you there for a second. So, what's the problem?"

I begin to tell him everything I've checked so far, having ruled out all the easy stuff, and why I turned to him. "So, has to be her software."

"Where are you?"

"The Blue Bayou," I say without hesitation. Unlike my father, Shep gets me. He might be a trust fund baby, but he's nothing like the rest of the douchebags we went to school and now work with. Both of his feet are planted firmly on the ground. He's not afraid of a hard day's work or getting his hands a little dirty, even though on most days, he's rubbing elbows with all of the bigwigs in the hotel industry. His father is a lot like mine, trading million-dollar properties like kids trading Pokémon cards.

After telling me how outdated the software is, he finally agrees to take a closer look at it, but that requires him having remote access to the computer system. I don't feel comfortable granting him that without talking to Carys first. I trust Shep with my life, but this is Carys' life, so she gets to call the shots.

Hanging up with him, I head to the door.

Laughter coming from the other side makes me pause. It's hers mixed with a deeper, male laugh and my hackles are immediately up.

Get a grip. I laugh for letting myself be so affected by a mere... acquaintance. I just met her. We've shared names and a few bits of information about ourselves. That gives me no right to feel ownership over her or her laughs, but fuck if I don't love them.

"Carys." She turns her bright blue eyes on me and they sparkle with mirth. Her smile still on full display.

"Oh, hey. Is it fixed?" she asks, but then immediately laughs. "I'm kidding. Nothing around here is ever that easy." She turns back to the guy who I'm assuming is her new employee. "Hope I'm not scaring you off, Jules, but it's better you know now."

"Wild horses couldn't drag me away." Jules places his palm on his chest in a grand gesture as his eyes scan me from my head to my feet.

I smirk and shake my head at my ridiculousness. If anyone should be jealous, it should be Carys, because if I'm reading him right, and I think I am, he's inspecting me like a fresh piece of meat.

"Uh, it's not fixed, but I know someone who can fix it," I tell her, glazing right over the insinuation dripping off Jules' comment.

Her face falls, and she looks a little downtrodden. "How much?"

"Free, hopefully. But he's going to need remote access."

"So, *he's* coming here too?" she asks, a bit confused.

I hide my amusement and shake my head. "No, he'll just need me to give him online access to your computer. There's a program we use sometimes. Free," I assure her. "He'll use that and log into your computer. It'll be like he's sitting in the office. I'll be there the whole time to make sure he doesn't steal any family secrets." I wink, and she gives me a slow smile.

"You trust him?" she asks, going a bit serious again. "I mean, it's someone you know?"

"My best friend. He's on the up and up, I promise."

She purses those full lips and looks at me with an investigative stare. "Okay, Maverick Kensington. If you trust him, then so do I."

"Okay." I nod, unable to take my eyes off of her.

After a minute, or maybe a century, Jules clears his throat and breaks the spell, forcing me back into the safety of the office. Once I'm out of their sight, I groan. What is wrong with me? Maybe this entire place is under a spell, some voodoo shit. I mean, this is New Orleans, after all.

Exhaling roughly, I throw myself back in the chair and dial Shep back. "Let's do this, jackass."

"Talk sweeter to me or I'll make you pay."

"That's the bad word of the day, don't let Carys hear you say that," I tell him with a shake of my head. Maybe she'll let me take a look at her books once we've figured out this computer stuff. She's got a great place here. There's no reason she shouldn't be making money. I'm sure I could help her find ways to bring in more customers. Like I was telling her earlier, in all the times I've been to New Orleans, I've never seen an advertisement online or in person. That's one thing we need to fix. I wonder if she even has a Facebook page or website?

"Carys, huh? Is that the friend?"

"Yeah, I guess she's more of an acquaintance at this point, but—"

He barks out a laugh. "You like her."

"I didn't say that."

"You don't have to. I've been listening to you talk about the female gender for more than a decade. I know when you want to know one in the biblical sense."

"Let's get this computer shit put to bed first."

"You're such a sly dog," he says as I hear the clicking of keys in the background. "Did you pick this place out because of her? Is that why you're not staying at the Mont?"

I sigh. "No and no."

"Are you logged in?" he asks.

"Yep, waiting on you."

"I'm here."

About that time, I see his avatar pop up on the screen, letting me know he's online. After I upload the remote access program, he's in the system and in control of the mouse as I sit back and watch him work.

After a few minutes, the questioning resumes. "So, what made you go to the Blue Bayou?" He says the name of the hotel like it's foreign.

"Don't," I tell him.

"What?"

"Don't make it sound like I'm slumming it," I tell him.

"I'm not. But I've never known you to go to New Orleans and not stay at Hotel Monteleone."

Sighing, I rub my hand over my forehead as I try to decide how much I want to get into this with him right now. "Well, I went there originally, but when I walked in...I don't know. I guess, I was just looking for something different. I'm so sick of the Kensington standard, you know?" I can say that, because he does know. Without me explaining the specifics of this particular argument with my father, Shep knows the basics. It's something we've talked about a lot over the years. "When

I walked in and the doorman recognized me, I just bolted. I'm trying to get away from my father, not be in a place where people are going to ask me about him every day of my stay. Plus, if I'm being completely honest, I didn't want him to be able to track me down."

"How'd you find this place?" he asks, chuckling to himself. "Damn, this program they're using is ancient. One of the first hotels my father bought out when I started working for him after college was using this, or I wouldn't have a clue how to find my way around. Has she thought about upgrading to new software? That would take care of all of her problems, plus she'd have so many more options."

I laugh. "Well, this isn't really an option kind of place."

"Does she run a different program for keys?"

"You mean the extra-large bronze one that's currently poking into my ass right now?" I ask, pulling the bulky thing out and turning it over. Not only is the key large, the key ring is a large wooden fleur de lis with the Blue Bayou engraved on it.

"Real keys?" he asks incredulously.

"How did she put it?" I muse, smiling to myself. "She likes antiques."

Shep laughs. "Doesn't like change or spending money, collects antiques. She sounds like my grandma."

"She's definitely not your grandma."

"Send me a picture."

Standing out of the chair and walking over to get a closer look at the picture hanging on the wall, I take in even more details of Carys— her long golden legs, carefree smile, and a few freckles on her nose and cheeks. The frame next to the photo is of an older man and woman with a baby. On a second glance, I recognize the front steps of the hotel and realize they're standing in front of the doors of the Blue Bayou. A plaque on the bottom of the photo reads *"Blue Bayou—where folks are fun, and the world is ours."*

I want to know more about you, Carys Matthews.

"Fuck no, Shep. This one's all mine."

Carys

Hurrying down the street, I nearly drop my grocery bags. I spent too much time talking to CeCe, my friend at the nearby coffee shop, and I told Mary I'd be back to the hotel by noon so she could run her own errands.

I should've known better. CeCe and I always find a million things to talk about, and this morning I was so excited about how smoothly the front desk was running that I had to tell her about Maverick and his friend Shep and the magic they worked. It hasn't worked so flawlessly since I started running the hotel on the daily. I've always known it needed upgrading, but that word freaked me out. To me, *upgrade* equals money, but Shep knew about a hotel management software that's user friendly, current, and surprisingly cheap. It was more money than I had to spend, but an investment worth making because I can already tell it's going to save me days of frustration. With Jules coming on to help with the front desk, it's like I can finally see the light at the end of the very long, dark tunnel I've been walking down for the past year and a half.

"Shit!" Just as I make it to the breezeway leading to the front door, the handles of one of my bags rips and groceries start rolling everywhere. Quickly, I get down on my hands and knees and start collecting the items in my arms to save them from the street. Looking around, I realize they'll never fit in my other bag, so I stuff what I can in there and then take my cardigan off, laying it on the ground to use as a bundle.

I can make this work.

Just call me MacGyver. Carys MacGyver.

A low chuckle catches my attention and slowly I look up to see none other than Maverick Kensington standing a few feet away, arms crossed, leaning against the side of the building with a bag of his own hooked around one arm. The smile he's giving me makes my knees weak, so for that, I'm thankful I'm not standing.

And with that thought, my mind begins to spin, heading straight for the gutter like it always does when he's near.

"Need some help?" he asks, cocky grin still in place.

"Nope, got it covered," I tell him as I begin to tie the arms of my cardigan and stand, dusting off my pants.

"Mess," he says with another chuckle.

"What?" I heard him, but for some reason, I ask anyway.

He smiles, kicking off the wall and stalking toward me. "Mess," he repeats and then pauses as he looks down at my feet and then back up to my eyes. "You. Are. A. Mess." Each word is pronounced emphatically, and it makes my stomach flip.

Now I'm the one laughing, but it's the result of nerves because his smile combined with the stalking has my breathing labored. "Yeah, I've been told that before."

"A hot mess, emphasis on the hot, but a mess nonetheless." Without asking again, he frees me from the makeshift bag and we both begin to walk toward the front door of the Blue Bayou.

"What did you buy?" I ask, needing to say something to fill the space between us, or maybe in an effort to create some space between us, because it feels like he's coming on to me. I mean, I know he is. I might be blonde, but I'm not stupid. And I might be busy and preoccupied, but I'm not oblivious. At first, I thought it was just my wishful thinking, but last night, before he retired to his room, he asked me if the hotel had turndown service. It was a joke, but I could tell by the way he looked at me, he wasn't kidding.

The scary part is that I almost took him up on it. I had to force my feet to walk to my apartment, instead of upstairs to his room. I've never done anything like that before, never even entertained the thought. But I guess there's nothing illegal about it. So what if I own the hotel he's staying in? It's not like I'm his doctor and he's my patient, although I wouldn't mind giving him a thorough examination.

Not helping, Carys.

"Stopped at the hardware store down the street. I was at a bookstore a few doors down and thought I'd stop in there on my way back to see if they had a knob for the office door. I noticed it was missing."

I pause with my hand on the door and just stare at him. "You didn't have to do that...or don't have to do that. George has been meaning to fix it, but he just hasn't got around to it yet." I can't explain what I'm feeling because there's such a whirlwind taking place inside me. It's hard to decipher one emotion—fear that I'm doing everything wrong, shame that someone else is coming into my hotel and fixing problems, overwhelmed with everything that needs to be done, and last but not least, relief that Maverick wants to help.

"I know I didn't have to, but I want to. I saw that it was broken, and I'd like to fix it."

He smiles and opens the door for me.

He wants to.

I don't know why, but him fixing things in my hotel does something to me. It makes my insides warm. Since me and the hotel are a packaged deal, when Maverick does something as simple as fix a door handle, it feels personal.

Have I mentioned how perfect he is? He shouldn't be this perfect. He's making me want to do things that aren't good. I shouldn't want him like I do. He's a guest. He'll be gone in a few days, a week at most.

But I'm strong. I can resist. I know I can.

"Do you always have to fix things?" I ask, turning to face him once I'm inside.

He shrugs, his eyes fixed on mine. "I like to. My grandfather used to always have a project he was working on, and even though he had enough money to pay people to fix things for him, he wanted to do it himself. I think he must've passed that on to me. I like working with my hands, it's relaxing." With that last statement, he raises his eyebrows suggestively.

Was he coming on to me again? I think there was an innuendo in there.

Ignore.

Deflect.

Be strong.

"Well, I really appreciate it, but it feels weird letting a guest do a handyman's job."

"I want to. Think of it as an amenity—an incentive to stay here. You've said it yourself that the Blue Bayou isn't a hotel with bells and whistles, so let this be something that you let me do because it makes me happy."

"You're weird, Maverick. Has anyone ever told you that?"

His strong jaw flexes and I'm worried I've offended him, but then he breaks out in a loud laugh, tilting his head back and making me ogle his neck.

What? I don't even pay attention to guys' necks. So what if his is strong, without being too muscular? So what if my insides do funny things when his Adam's apple moves? So what if I've wondered if the scent—the one I can only describe as pure Maverick Kensington—originates there, right at the base, between his neck and his shoulder? So what if I'm now having fantasies about nestling myself right in the bend...right there in the perfect spot, where you can feel a person's heartbeat.

"Pot meet kettle," he says when he dips his chin and shakes his head.

"Please let me repay you, at least for the knob," I tell him, redirecting this conversation back to the matter at hand.

"Okay," he agrees.

"Good." I set the bag down and reach for the one he carried in for me, setting it behind the counter. As I'm going to the cash box behind the counter to get money, he stops me.

"I don't take money."

Pausing with my hand on the metal lid, I stare down at the bills and change, afraid to look up at him—afraid of what I'll see or what he'll say next...afraid of the resolve I'd made just a few minutes earlier. "Oh?" I ask, unable to think of anything else.

"Yeah, see I was thinking I'd take you to dinner," he says in a low, husky voice. "I'm sure there's a great place somewhere close. Jules comes in at six, so let's say seven?"

He's thought about this—taking me out to dinner—like before now. Maverick wants to take me to dinner for replacing my broken door knob. Shouldn't *I* be the one to take *him* out to dinner if it's to repay him for his help? This man has knocked me off my rocker, I swear. Nothing about this seems logical, but everything about this feels right.

"Okay." I actually can't believe the word leaves my lips. I planned on putting up a fight, forcing him to take the money and telling him I'm way too busy to go out to dinner, but the truth is I want to. I have to eat. Why not eat with Maverick? Also, something else, call it fate or the universe or whatever, brought him into my hotel. So, who am I to get in its way? Besides, it's just dinner. We'll eat. We'll have a nice conversation. We'll come back to the hotel and I'll tell him goodnight. My repayment will be made. No harm, no foul.

"It's a date," he beams. "I'll see you right here at seven sharp." Running up the stairs, he calls back over his shoulder. "Don't be late, Carys."

A date?

Is it a date?

How long has it been since I've been on a date?

"It's a date, huh?" Mary asks quietly, startling me so bad I nearly scream. I was so caught up in my mental deliberation I kind of forgot where I was for a second.

"Uh—it...it's not a date," I stutter, scooting past her with the groceries. "Just dinner. He wants me to go to dinner with him to repay him for fixing the office door knob." I say it out loud with heavy questioning in my tone, more for me than Mary. "So, it's more of a business dinner."

"Business dinner. He's taking you out for fixing your knob." She bobs her head with placating smile. "Whatever you say, honey. Sounds like you're definitely getting the long end of this stick."

My eyes go wide at her words. "Mary!"

She laughs, swatting at me. "Oh, hush. I just meant you're making out like a bandit—a fixed door knob and dinner with a fine young man. Can't complain about that."

I take a deep breath and clear my throat. "Dinner. That's all it is. And apparently, he likes to fix things, so—"

"Let him." Turning her back to the counter, she leans against it and crosses her arms, leveling me with her motherly stare. "You've been meeting yourself coming and going for the last year and a half, we all have. If Maverick Kensington wants to step in and fix a few things." She pauses for effect, tilting her head to the side. "Let him."

"No harm, no foul, right?"

"None that I can see."

"And it's not unprofessional?" I question, needing her approval more than I realized.

She laughs again, shaking her head. "Girl, the stories I could tell."

My eyes go wide again. "What?"

"Oh, honey. They're not my stories to tell," she sing-songs, but cracks a conspiratorial smile. "But don't forget how long Miss Mary's been around."

"Mom?" I ask, when she goes quiet. "Did Mom date guests from the hotel?" I try to wrack my brain, digging through my memory. My mother was never engaged. She always seemed like she was married to the hotel, like me. She spent her days and nights here, taking care of everything, even when my grandfather was still alive. They were quite the team. I sigh, wishing so badly I had that—someone to share the load with. Mary and George are wonderful, but they're getting older. The mere thought of something happening to either of them sends me into a deep, dark spiral. I don't know what I would do.

"Your mama was a beautiful woman, just like you. She had admirers. And she might have been all business, but she had needs."

"Mary!"

"What? Do you think she only had sex once, the day you were conceived?" she asks with a scoff.

"Oh, my God! How did this conversation go from dinner to sex?" I ask.

Mary laughs again. "Well, you weren't an immaculate conception, even though we all thought the sun rose and set with you." She smiles and swats in my direction. "All I'm saying is there's nothing wrong with going out to dinner...or whatever else Mr. Kensington might offer."

"Okay." I turn toward the back door. "Thanks, Mary. Good talk." I feel my cheeks heating up and I don't want her to see it, so I retreat to my apartment to put up my groceries and get ready for my *date*.

Yeah, I said it. *Date.* Because, damn it, it is. I haven't been on one in ages. The last time I was with a man was over six months ago on my birthday, when Mary and George covered the hotel while I went out with CeCe. She took me to a bar, and I ran into a guy from college while we were there. There was nothing special about it. We drank. We danced. We hooked up. I did the walk of shame five blocks back to the hotel at four in the morning, where George greeted me with a disapproving shake of his head. It wasn't my best moment.

So, even though I don't want to admit it, this is a date and I'm a little excited about it.

Maverick

WHY AM I SO NERVOUS?

I've been on plenty of first dates, but I honestly can't remember ever being this anxious, with the exception of my very first date ever. I took Amy Copeland to our sophomore spring formal and incorrectly assumed we'd be having sex that evening. We weren't really dating or anything, but I'd watched a lot of teen movies in preparation for the big night and it seemed as if losing one's virginity after a dance was par for the course. After casually placing my hand over Amy's knee at dinner, she abruptly shoved it off and told me not to ever touch her again.

Of course, she changed her tune when I took her to Homecoming the following fall, but I digress.

Come to think of it, maybe it's not nerves. Maybe it's just anticipation. I really like Carys and I'm dying to get to know her better. Whether or not this evening leads to anything other than a nice dinner, I'll be happy to just be around her.

She fascinates me.

It's kind of odd, though, to be taking her out in *her* city, when I've really only done touristy things on my visits to New Orleans. But I get the feeling she doesn't get out much, so I'm hopeful she hasn't tried the restaurant I'm taking her to, and if she has, I hope she likes it.

I also hope she lets me kiss her. And that she kisses me back. I'm not expecting things to turn physical, but I can't deny I'm dying to feel her plump lips against mine...to discover what she tastes like. It's all I've thought about since meeting her. Well, maybe not *all* I've thought about, but I'm trying *not* to think about that. If I did, I'd have to relieve myself and take the tension off, which would only make me late for our date and that absolutely cannot happen.

One last look in the mirror to make sure nothing is stuck in my teeth or my nose and I'm out the door, practically jogging down the stairs to the hotel lobby. I'm about halfway down the steps when I see Carys waiting for me. I slow my pace and try to appear casual, but the truth is my heart is hammering inside my chest so hard she can probably hear it. When she turns around and sees me, her face lights up and my breath catches in my throat.

Fuck me, she's gorgeous.

She's in a dress that hugs her curves perfectly, and her normally wild hair has been styled in loose waves cascading down her back, just begging me to wrap them around my wrist and pull.

Focus, Mav.

"Why, Mr. Kensington, are you late for our date?" Her glossy lips shine as she smiles, and I have to fight back images of her mouth doing other things in order to answer her.

I slip my hand around her waist and pull her against me. "I may be a few seconds late, but it's only because the vision of you took my breath away, and I had to collect myself before I stumbled down the stairs."

"Just as I suspected," she says, placing her hand against my chest. "You're quite the schmoozer."

I cover her hand with mine, pretending to be shocked. "You wound me, Miss Matthews. I'd never lie about a beauty such as yours." I know I'm playing with fire, but I can't help but place a soft kiss just in front of her ear, briefly lingering to inhale her sweet scent. When I pull back, Carys' eyes are dilated, and she seems to be searching for a comeback, but I believe I've left her speechless for once.

Taking a step back, I take her hand in mine because I need to be touching her in some way and nod my head toward the door. "Shall we?"

She clears her throat and straightens her shoulders, tightening her grip on my hand. "Yes, please."

We don't have to walk too far before we're at the restaurant I've chosen, and thanks to our reservation, we're immediately seated in a cozy table for two away from the larger parties dining inside.

"Have you eaten here before?" I ask her.

"No, I haven't but I've been wanting to," she says, her eyes taking in the low lighting and open ceilings. "I've heard great things about this place."

"I admit, I was intimidated by not knowing how to pronounce the name, Lagniappe, but George helped me out."

"My George? He helped you plan this?" Her expression shows surprise, as well as her appreciation that I'd seek her old friend's advice.

"He did, indeed," I tell her, a little pleased with myself. "And then I Googled it and checked out the menu. I like that they tied in the name of the restaurant with the menu by adding *a little something* extra to everything." I give her a wink when she seems a little surprised that I did my homework. "It's a clever idea."

"Seems to be working for them," she says turning her attention to the menu. "Everything looks amazing; I can't decide what to order."

I watch her for a second, noticing that she's fidgeting a little, and I wonder if Carys is nervous. She mentioned that she doesn't date often, and then George made a mention of it when I asked for a restaurant suggestion. "He loves you, you know." I'm not sure why I feel the need to tell her something I'm sure she knows, but it never hurts to be told you're loved, right?

"Who, George?" Her smile clearly shows she returns his affections. "I know," she says confidently. "He's like my second grandfather. I don't know what I'd do without him and Mary, which is why I worry so much about him working too much."

"Why don't you hire more people for the hotel? Maybe it's time for George and Mary to semi-retire. I mean, they could still be with you at the hotel, but they wouldn't have to work as hard."

Carys bristles at my question and I mentally kick myself for sticking my nose where it's not wanted.

"It's not that simple." I can tell she's trying to reign in her emotions. "They're all I have left of my family and I can't just let them go. Besides, I can't afford another salary. It nearly killed me to hire Jules with all the extra expenses I've had lately."

I slip my hand across the table and place it on top of hers, wanting to smooth things over so we don't get off on a bad foot. "I'm not meaning to sound insensitive; I only want to help. I really like you, Carys, and I think your hotel has great potential. It just needs a few upgrades to make business boom again."

"Firing George and Mary wouldn't be an upgrade. They're what keep the place going. They keep me going." She pulls her hand away and goes back to looking at the menu.

"I didn't mean it like that. And I would never suggest firing George and Mary."

"Well, I can't afford another salary. Besides, they both need their pay. The Blue Bayou is their livelihood too." She sighs, setting the menu on the table. "Sorry. I don't mean to be so sensitive, but I depend on them. I need them. They're the only people who know as much about the hotel as I do, probably more. If they weren't with me, I'd feel completely lost."

"They depend on you too." I take her hand back, forcing her to look at me. "You take care of them just as much as they take care of you. I've only been around a few days and I can see that you're a family. All I'm saying is that maybe with a few changes—a few upgrades..." I pause, holding up a hand so she'll hear me out. "You could bring in some more help and still make the ends meet."

"Upgrades always mean money, and we don't have that right

now. I know they say you have to spend money to make money, but what happens when you don't have the money to spend?" she asks, exasperation evident. I can tell she's thought, probably worried, about this very subject a lot.

I exhale, sitting back in my chair as the waiter comes up to our table.

"Welcome to Lagniappe, my name is Max. Have you dined with us before?" He smiles, eyes on Carys as he speaks. I can't fault him for that. She's a looker. I'd probably be doing the same thing, but my tone when I respond says: *Eyes over here, Max. She's with me.*

"Hello, Max. This is a first for both of us. What do you suggest?"

"Well, let's start you off with some drinks. Are we partaking this evening?"

I look over at Carys and she shrugs her shoulders as if to say *if you're game, so am I.*

We take Max's suggestion of the French Quarter—Jim, Jack, Johnnie, and Jose mixed with a splash of Coke, simple syrup, and a twist of lime. For our lagniappe, we opted for a sidecar shot of tequila.

"Go big or go home, right?" I ask with a laugh.

"Well, if I'm only having one drink, and I am only having one drink because it's my night to work the desk, I might as well make it a good one." She laughs and does this girly move of flipping her hair over her shoulder and I forget about the deep conversation we were having about the hotel. All thoughts not pertaining directly to Carys' gorgeous hair or her full lips or the freckle on her shoulder go out the window.

"You're so pretty."

"There you go schmoozing again."

"I can't help it."

She shakes her head and hides a smile. "I bet you've got girls in every city."

"Ha, no," I deadpan.

"Liar."

"You think I'm a player?" I ask.

Leaning into the table, she sighs as she contemplates. "I'm not sure what to make of you. Where are you from, by the way? I just realized I don't even know where you live."

"Dallas."

"So, if you're a city boy, where'd you learn to be so handy with tools and fixing things?" she asks, leaning in a little further.

"My grandfather," I tell her. "He owned a ranch about two hours from Dallas. I used to go there during the summers. He was a businessman, but he really loved working with his hands, building things. I think that's why he loved the business so much. He told me once if his parents would've been able to afford it, he would've gone to college to be an architect, but they were dirt poor. He was the definition of a self-made man."

"You admire him."

"I do...did. He passed away a few years ago."

"I'm sure you miss him," she says.

"I do." I didn't plan on our dinner conversation going anything like this. I wanted to get to know Carys, maybe make out with her, but I wasn't prepared to expose myself. I know I don't have to. I don't have to say another word. I can leave it right here and change the subject, but I want her to know me just as much as I want to know her. "My mother died six months before him. Sometimes, I think he loved her so much that he died of a broken heart. My grandmother died when I was a baby and my mother was an only child. So, they were really close."

Damn, Mav. Let's dig up all the bones.

"Do you ever dial her number and then remember she's not gonna answer?" she asks just as Max delivers our drinks, which we both definitely need now.

Carys and I both breathe out a thank you and immediately pick up our shots of tequila.

"All the time," I tell her.

"To our moms," Carys says.

"To our moms."

We both toss back our shots and chase them with a drink of our French Quarter.

"Shit," I groan. "They might need to change the name of this. Maybe Alcohol Poisoning?"

Carys laughs and then takes another sip of her drink. "Pretty sure that honor's already been taken. I vaguely remember drinking it on my twenty-first birthday."

"How old are you, if you don't mind me asking?" I know it's not appropriate to ask a woman's age, but I want to know.

"Twenty-five." She takes another drink, visibly relaxing—sinking into her seat, shoulders at ease, and a slight pinkish hue to her cheeks. Parts of her look every bit of twenty-five, but others, like her fresh skin and freckles, make her appear younger. "What about you?" she asks.

"Twenty-eight. I'll be one year closer to thirty next month."

"Meh, thirty-shmirty. What's thirty? Right?"

"I agree. I've always felt like age is just a number."

"So, what do you do in Dallas, Maverick Kensington? Such an important sounding name...Maverick Kensington." Every time she says my name, I like it a little more. I'd like to hear her say it under other circumstances...perhaps coming undone beneath me.

"I'm in real estate. Family business," I tell her, not really wanting to get into all of that tonight. My father has been blowing my phone up the last couple of days, but I'd like to ignore my problems for just a little while longer.

"Real estate? Really?" She scrunches her nose and leans forward, resting her chin on her hand. "I have to say, I didn't have you pegged for a real estate guy."

I laugh. "What did you have me *pegged* for?"

Shrugging, she looks away, thinking about it for a second. "Maybe an entrepreneur of some sort. I don't know. You seem very capable, but also... I don't know? Something I can't put my finger on, like carefree or spontaneous. Regardless, you don't seem to fit the stuffy, real estate mogul vibe."

"I never said mogul. That's my father. He's the buyer, seller, and disposer of dreams."

"Disposer of dreams, huh?"

"Yeah." I pause, exhaling a deep breath. "He buys large properties, usually from people who have no choice but to sell, tears them apart and sells the pieces. And I work for him, so I guess I'm a disposer of dreams by proxy."

"But these people want to sell, right?"

"Some do, some don't. Some have no choice and they've exhausted all other avenues. When they fail, my father swoops in and makes the kill."

"You make it sound so brutal," she says with a slight laugh.

"Because it is."

I look past Carys and see our waiter approaching. This time when I let out a deep breath, it's out of appreciation. We need a change of topic before I release all my demons and ruin our date.

"Have you had a chance to decide what you'd like to eat? Can I make any recommendations?" He looks at me and then smiles over at Carys, obviously finding her just as pretty as I do.

"What would you recommend?" she asks, her cheeks a little pinker. The French Quarter is definitely doing its job.

"The shrimp and grits with a side of fried crawfish is one of our best sellers. It's served with bacon, crispy jalapenos, and a drizzle of honey balsamic."

She smiles, closing her menu. "Sounds perfect. I'll have that."

"Make that two," I tell him, handing over my menu.

"Great. I'll get that turned in. Can I get you another drink?" he asks, pointing to my nearly empty glass. I hadn't even realized I'd drank most of it. Huh. Probably why I'm just a wealth of information. Liquor has always been a lubricant for my mouth.

"Not right now," I reply with a low chuckle, my mind going straight to the gutter.

Max dips his head in acknowledgement and flashes a quick smile at Carys who covers her glass and says, "I'm good too, thanks." When he's made his way to the next table, she gives me a lazy, slow grin that goes straight to my dick. "What's so funny?"

"You wouldn't want to know."

"Try me."

I toss back the last of my drink and clear my throat. "I was just thinking about how this," I say, holding up my now-empty glass, "has always been a lubricant for my mouth." I can't help myself, the last few words come out slow and pointed, dripping with insinuation.

"Oh." Her mouth forms a perfect "o" as she stares at me for a moment before darting her tongue out and swiping it along her bottom lip. Draining her glass and setting it down on the table between us, she never takes her eyes off me and I know her mind is now floating down the gutter beside mine. Shit, we're probably sharing a raft.

Briefly glancing away, I contemplate slapping a few bills on the table and walking out, taking Carys and finding a dark corner so I can make the rest of her body turn the same lovely shade of pink as her cheeks. I refrain, though. My mama raised me to be a gentleman and I'm gonna try my hardest to be one until Carys gives me permission to stop. Besides, I'm starving and if this night ends the way I hope it does, I'm going to need my energy and so will Carys.

For a long, charged moment we have a silent conversation. The way her eyes lock with mine and then travel down to my lips tells me everything I want to know. She wants me. I want her. She knows it. I bet the people at the table behind us know it and are probably getting off on the sexual tension permeating the air around us.

Carys

HOLY UST, BATMAN.

Thanks to Jules, I now know that "UST" stands for *unresolved sexual tension* and he says Maverick and I have it in spades.

When he mentioned it earlier, I told him he was out of his mind but he swore he spoke the truth. Apparently, he has a gift for detecting sexual desires. Now, I'm no stranger to gifts and special powers, but his seem a little convoluted. But, sitting here, feeling Maverick's stare like an extra set of invisible hands raking my body, causing my heart to race and my panties to melt, I'd have to agree with Jules.

It's a no-brainer that we're attracted to each other. Incredibly attracted, even. But my dilemma is whether or not to act upon it. Do we keep the sexual tension unresolved, therefore, keeping our relationship platonic and uncomplicated, or do we give into the sparks and see what happens after the ashes have settled?

Not gonna lie, I want to resolve the fuck out of this tension right here and now. Pun intended.

Maverick will eventually figure out whatever sent him running for

New Orleans. He'll go back to Dallas, to his job and life. I don't know if that's a reason to pursue the sexual tension, or run from it.

It's been a long time since I had a fling. Actually, I don't think any of my sexual experiences could count as a fling. Regardless of past experiences, this would be different. He's staying at my hotel. So, do I pursue it for as long as he's here? Then what? He goes back to Dallas and I forget all about him, going back to whatever it was I was doing before he showed up?

Existing.

Surviving.

Trying to make it from day to day, keeping myself and my hotel afloat.

That's what I should be focusing on, right?

Any time I ask myself that, I get the same tug on my heart. I think it's from my grandpa. I think he would say the hotel is important, but not as important as the people inside. I remember one time, when I was about ten years old, I asked him if he loved the hotel more than me. He'd been working long hours in the office, probably putting out a similar fire like I've been doing on a daily basis since I took over. He stopped what he was doing and picked me up, sitting me on his desk, right on top of all the papers and ledgers he had spread out. He looked me square in the eyes and told me the hotel was part of him, but only because of what it provided for his family. He said if it all burned down tomorrow, as long as he had me and Mama and Mary and George that it would all be okay. He said the hotel is like a body and we're all like the soul. We make the hotel.

He wouldn't want me to forget how to live. He wouldn't want me to lose myself in the process of keeping the hotel afloat.

"Deep thoughts?" Maverick asks.

"Sorry," I tell him, wiping at the corners of my mouth with my napkin. "I guess I was hungrier than I thought."

We've both been working on making ourselves members of the Clean Plate Club. The food here is amazing and I can't believe I've never tried it before tonight.

"This is the best shrimp and grits I've ever had." He sits back in his chair, letting out a content sigh.

"How is everything?" a deep voice asks, causing me to look up.

A guy dressed in a white button-down shirt and black jeans is standing there with a kitchen towel thrown over his shoulder.

"Great," I tell him.

"I'm glad to hear it." He smiles, clasping his hands together in a pleased gesture. "Is there anything else I can get for you? Dessert, perhaps?"

"Oh, I'm stuffed," I say, looking over to Maverick who is looking as full as I feel. "Y'all don't lie about the lagniappe."

The man chuckles, shaking his head. "That we don't. If you leave hungry, we haven't done our job."

"Well, job well done tonight, man," Maverick says, offering him his hand to shake.

Looking toward the back of the restaurant where two sets of large double doors swing constantly as the wait staff walks in and out, I ask, "Are you the chef?"

"Owner," he says, dipping his head.

I offer him my hand. "I'm Carys Matthews. I own Blue Bayou around the corner. Dinner was great. I'll be sure to send people your way."

"Micah Landry," he says, taking my hand. "It's nice to meet you. Maybe we could do some cross promo. I didn't even realize there was a hotel nearby."

"Funny," Maverick says. "I've been telling Carys she needs to advertise more, maybe social media to get the word out." He pauses, looking across the table at me with a mischievous gleam in his eye. "Carys is quite fond of antiques and struggles with keeping up with the times. Is, uh, Myspace still around?"

Without thinking, I swiftly kick him under the table causing him to yelp in surprise or pain, maybe both. For his information, we have a Facebook page. It's just seriously outdated and one more thing I haven't kept up with since my mother died.

Micah chuckles at the exchange. "So, how long have you been there?" The look he gives me says *"are you even old enough to own a hotel?"*

"Since 1963," I inform him with a hesitant smile, feeling the weight of this conversation sitting heavier than the food in my stomach. How is it that a business owner just around the corner from the hotel doesn't even know it exists?

Micah's eyebrows go up. "Wow, 1963." He nods his head, looking back over his shoulder. "Tell you what, drop off a brochure or something. We've got a bulletin board up front with local vendors. I always have people asking for recommendations, so I'd love to be able to tell them about your hotel."

"That sounds great," I tell him, even though inwardly I'm cringing because we don't have brochures. We used to, but I haven't seen a box of them in a long time. This conversation is making me realize how badly I'm sucking at promoting the Blue Bayou. "I love supporting locals."

Micah smiles, nodding his head. "Me too. We're already doing a lot of cross promotion with other businesses, like Neutral Grounds."

"Oh, I love Neutral Grounds. CeCe and I go way back," I tell him with a nod.

"Do you know my sister-in-law? Camille Landry, well, it was Benoit...I think she hyphenates now Benoit-Landry."

"She's an artist, right? I've seen her work in CeCe's shop."

Micah shakes his head. "Yeah, she and CeCe have been friends for a while, since she was here going to school. She's getting ready to open up a new art gallery down the street featuring local artists."

"Wow, small world, huh?" I ask, looking over at Maverick who seems to be taking it all in with a pleased expression on his face.

"Definitely," Micah agrees, clapping his hands together. "Well, Carys Matthews, I'm glad you came in tonight and I look forward to getting to know more about the Blue Bayou. Maybe my wife and I will stay there soon, get a first-hand experience."

"We'd love to have you."

Someone from the kitchen calls out for him and he dips his chin in departure. "Y'all have a great night."

"See," Maverick muses approvingly when Micah's out of earshot. "That's what I'm talking about. It's all about networking, getting your name out there. People need to know about the Blue Bayou. I like this."

I laugh, wondering, not for the first time, why this man is so invested in me—my hotel. I mean, don't get me wrong, I love that he is. I love that he seems to really care about the Blue Bayou. I wish everyone felt as passionately about it as Maverick Kensington. But you don't usually find complete strangers who understand the importance of your business from the moment they stumble in the door.

"Who are you, Maverick Kensington?" I ask, equal parts in awe and infatuation, but also cautious. I have to force the latter. My heart wants to jump in headfirst, but my head is putting up blockades, keeping me from pursuing what my body desires.

How did I get so lucky that it was my hotel he sought refuge in? I've never had someone besides my family, George and Mary being included in that, who care about the well-being of the Blue Bayou like I do, but Maverick seems to fit the bill.

He gives me a smile that is slow and easy and shoots straight to my core.

How can he be so nice, so handsome, and so business savvy? That's unheard of, some sort of magical trifecta. Usually, people are one or the other, maybe two of them, if they're lucky. The ones who have it all are taken.

"What do you mean?" he asks, leaning forward and placing a few bills in the black folder the waiter left at our table.

"I don't know. I just find it so hard to believe that all of this is just a serendipitous coincidence. You walk into my hotel at just the right time, fix my computers, and my door knobs," I add with a smile. "Now, you're taking me to dinner and putting me in the right place at the right time to make connections with people like Micah." I pause, shaking my head. "It just all seems too good to be true."

With a wry smile, he asks, "So, you're saying I'm too good to be true?"

"I didn't say that." I try to keep the smirk at bay but fail.

There's mischief gleaming in his eyes as he leans a little closer, lowering his words to a near whisper. "So, you do or don't think I'm good?" His gaze burns into mine, making me swallow hard. "I just need to know where I stand and how hard I'm going to have to work to change your mind."

I swallow, wanting to look away from his penetrable gaze, but being completely unable to. I'm under a spell, his spell. To answer my own question from earlier, I think I'm willing to take the risk—no expectations, just pleasure. If I'm not expecting anything, then there's no chance of heart break, right?

"Let's get out of here," Maverick says, standing and offering me his hand.

As we walk out of the restaurant, I try to make my heart stop beating so fast. I try to calm the butterflies in my stomach. I try to ignore the electricity that seems to be transferring from his hand to mine and the way my hand feels in his.

I fail.

Half a block away from Lagniappe, I stop in the shadow of a darkened storefront and tug his hand until he stops. Turning toward me, his eyes find mine, and in them, they find the answer they're looking for.

I want this.

I want him.

Maverick

CARYS' EYES FLASH WITH BLAZING DESIRE. SHE swallows hard and then jumps off the proverbial cliff by grabbing the front of my shirt and pulling me to her.

That's the permission I've been waiting for all night. The green light I've been needing.

Before my mind catches up with her sudden movements, her mouth is on mine and I'm groaning into her kiss. Wrapping one arm around her waist, my other cradles her head as my fingers tangle into her soft hair. I've spent the last few days wondering—what would she taste like, what would she feel like...is her hair as soft as it looks? Yes. Yes, to every question I've had about Carys Matthews.

She tastes like sunshine after a rainstorm.

She feels like heaven.

I walk us backward to the side of the building, away from the people passing by on the sidewalk, and deepen the kiss. The moan that escapes her mouth reverberates in mine and travels to my chest and then my dick. It's well aware a line has been crossed and there's no going back. I hope she plans on being in my bed tonight. If not, I'm going to have a *huge* problem.

Not that I mean to toot my own horn, of course. I'll gladly let Carys judge and toot my *horn* any time she'd like. Toot, handle, blow... you get the picture.

"And, now we come to one of the most famous stories of the French Quarter," a voice calls out. "The story of the LaLaurie Mansion."

Carys and I release each other's mouths and turn to see a large group of tourists heading our way.

Realizing I'm about three minutes from taking Carys against the side of the building, I look at her and see she's breathless. We need this distraction. "What's going on?" I ask, still trying to catch my breath.

Carys lets out a heady laugh, but then looks down the street and then up at the buildings around us, smiling as she gains her bearings. "Ah, yes, the LaLaurie Mansion. This must be a haunted ghost tour." She points at the crowd. "Have you ever done one of these? They're really good."

My cock is still telling me I want to do *her* and that *she's* really good. That kiss was possibly the best kiss of my life. I've never been that worked up over a kiss. Making out and foreplay are all means to an end, but not with Carys. I could kiss her every day and never get tired of it. It's both not enough and more than enough all at the same time.

"You mean, we're making out in front of a haunted house?" Thankfully, her information about the ghost tour is the exact distraction I need, because fuck ghosts. Not that I'm scared or anything. It's just creepy.

She giggles at what I'm guessing is a look of leery hesitation on my face. "Aww, are you afraid of ghosts, Mav?"

Her teasing effectively changes the trajectory of the moment and I fight back a smile as I clear my throat, looking around me. "Of course not."

Carys just laughs harder before standing on her toes and whispering in my ear, "Don't worry, I'll protect you."

She could've whispered *supercalifragilisticexpialidocious* and my reaction would've been the same. Her breath on my skin makes my dick stand to attention and remind me of how good her lips felt on mine. Pulling her to me, I claim her mouth again, not only to stop her teasing, but because she's so damn close, I can't help myself. I wasn't done kissing her. The way she immediately opens for me, swirling her tongue with mine, shows me she doesn't mind and she wasn't done either. Breaking away just far enough to get a few words out, I whisper, "Let's get out of here," before she starts walking backward down the sidewalk, pulling me by my waist.

It's hard enough to walk and kiss at the same time, but when you also add the bumpy concrete of the French Quarter, you're just asking for trouble. Tired of all the stumbling, which causes our lips to be apart, I begrudgingly free my mouth from Carys' and lift her up and over my shoulder. I probably should've just wrapped her legs around my waist, but carrying her that way would've still been dangerous due to not being able to see where I'm going. This way, I can see and keep a tight grip on her ass as I quickly walk us to the hotel.

I've witnessed guys throw girls over their shoulders a few times in the past and the girls always squirm and pretend to hate the experience but Carys doesn't do that. She simply laughs and allows me to carry her. I fucking love the sound of her laughter; it's free and uninhibited and I have a feeling she doesn't share this laugh very often. That thought makes me sad but also determined to make her laugh like this as much as possible. Carys' laughter should be shared with the world but I'm perfectly fine if she only shares it with me.

She's still laughing when I place her feet on the ground outside the hotel door, and when she looks up at me with her bright eyes and beautiful smile, I don't think twice. I press her up against the old wood door and kiss her once more. Eventually, she pulls back and catches her breath before reaching behind her and opening the hotel door. Her eyes never leave mine as she pushes the door open and slips inside. My thoughts turn dirty as I imagine what it'll be like to finally slip inside her. I'm practically salivating at the thought.

Unfortunately, as soon as we walk into the lobby, Jules cries out, effectively breaking our erotic spell.

"Girl, PTL, you're here!" He rushes from behind the counter to where we're standing and grabs Carys by the shoulders dramatically. "I was just about to call you. The bathroom in room 201 is leaking and I'm freaking the fuck out. I've moved the guests to another room, but I'd already sent George home for the night and I didn't want to wake him up at this hour to fix the leak. Can you do it?"

It's obvious Carys is caught off guard. Her head is probably still stuck in the haze of the kiss we just shared. I know mine is. Not knowing what to do, she begins stuttering, but I interrupt and answer for her. "I'll do it."

They both turn to look at me like I just grew an extra set of eyeballs, so I put their worries at ease.

"I can fix more than computers and door knobs." I laugh, trying to lighten this mood back to what it was before we opened the door. "I told you I'm good at fixing things. My grandfather taught me to be handy," I assure her with a nudge of my elbow to her arm. I turn to Jules. "Does George keep tools nearby?"

"Y-yes, he does. I'll grab them for you." He rushes off in the direction of the kitchen.

"Are you sure about this?" Carys asks.

"Of course, I am. There's no reason to wake George, or call anyone, when I'm perfectly capable of helping."

She lets out an exasperated, and if I'm not mistaken, disappointed breath. Rubbing her forehead, she looks over at me. "I hate this. I don't want to ruin your night." Pausing, her shoulders slump. "You're still a guest here and I just—"

Leaning over, I press my lips to hers again—a reminder and a promise—and then take her chin in my hand, forcing her to look at me. "Stop. I want to help. You know I do, right?"

Slowly, she nods her head.

"Let me help you."

Exhaling forcefully, she relents. "Well, I'm coming with you."

I spot Jules heading for us with a large tool box in his hands. "Come on, then." I grab the tools and wink at her. "Lead the way."

When we arrive at the room, we discover that Jules and Mary have already done a lot of the work. Thankfully, they were able to stop it before it flooded more than the bathroom, and it didn't reach any of the carpeted area.

Carys starts picking up the soaked towels and placing them in the bathtub so they're not in our way as we work. I can feel her watching me as I assess the toilet, lifting the lid off the back looking for clues. After a few seconds, I turn to her, wiping my hands on my jeans.

"I have good news and bad news. Which would you like first?"

"Good, please," she answers. Her worried expression tugs at my heart and I hope what I'm about to tell her lessens her stress.

"I'm fairly certain this will be an easy fix. See how the entire bowl moves when I push on it?" I demonstrate, and she quickly nods her head. "I think it just needs a new wax ring, which is what attaches the bowl to the floor."

"And the bad?"

"Well, it's unlikely George keeps wax rings in this tool box, so it'll have to wait until I can go to the hardware store tomorrow and buy one."

"That's it? It just needs a new wax ring?" She looks skeptical and tilts her head to inspect the toilet. "That sounds a little too good to be true."

"I'm ninety-nine percent sure that's what the problem is, but if I'm wrong, I'll hire a plumber to fix it, I swear." I can tell that this is one of those proverbial straws and she's the camel's back that's close to breaking. I mean, just since I've been here, she's dealt with computers that wouldn't work, having to manually check guests in and out of the hotel, and using an antiquated credit card machine. She probably lost business during those first couple of days, because we live in the age of credit card fraud and some people aren't comfortable letting a business have a carbon copy of the card. Her hotel management system had to be updated. Fortunately, Shep was able to find something that was reasonable and fit her needs. But it's all been an expense she wasn't expecting.

"There's nothing more we can do tonight?" she asks, chewing on her bottom lip.

I stand in front of her and move her long hair off her shoulder. "It would be very proactive of me to go ahead and take the toilet apart and clean up in here, but I'd much rather finish our date." Leaning forward, I place a lingering kiss just below Carys' ear, smiling when she moans and angles her head to make more room for me.

I kiss her jaw and gently bite her earlobe before whispering, "There's so much I want to do to you, but maybe this isn't the best place. You ready to go?"

Carys' eyes are hooded, and dare I say, a bit dazed as she looks up at me. "A place. Yes, yes, a different place. My place? Maybe your place. Any place, really. Yes, okay, let's do this."

Laughing, I grab her hand. "Come on, mess."

She rolls her eyes at my nickname for her, but still allows me to lead her out of the room and back into the lobby. Jules is still at the desk, looking genuinely worried, chewing on his fingernails. His *painted* fingernails.

Whatever floats your boat, man.

"What's the verdict?" he asks, and it makes me happy to see how concerned he is. Being a brand-new employee, he could've used this opportunity to bail on Carys, but he didn't. So, Jules has officially earned my respect, not that he needed to, but I appreciate loyalty when I see it.

"I'll have to go to the store tomorrow before I can fix it, but it's nothing I can't handle," I assure him.

"Halle-loo, that's a relief!" He raises his hands like he's in church and then hops out of his chair. "Carys, I hate to leave like this, but I'm already late for my other job. I can call in sick, if you need me to stay, though."

Carys lets out a gasp then turns to me. "I'm so sorry. I forgot that I told Jules I'd work the overnight shift tonight."

Disappointment, my old familiar friend settles like a rock on my chest. And my dick mourns that our time together has been cut short. I had plans, damn it.

Then I realize just because Carys has to work, it doesn't mean our time together has to be over. "That's cool. I'll just hang down here with you."

There she goes again, giving me that wide-eyed Bambi look. "You want to stay here in the lobby? With me?"

Her questions make it sound like it's an absurd idea and she wouldn't know why I'd want to do such a thing. She obviously doesn't realize how addictive she is and how I'm already a junkie for her presence. "Sure. Why not?"

"Well..."

Before she can finish her sentence, Jules walks past us, heading for the front door. "You cuties have fun! And be sure to clean up after you do...whatever you two plan on doing," he says with a wave of his hands. "George will be here bright and early tomorrow and we don't want to start his day off finding y'all *en flagrante delicto*, if you know what I mean. Toodles!"

I'm not sure how long Carys and I stare at the now-closed doors before we both crack up laughing. "En flag—what?" I ask, with a laugh as I shake my head at Jules. The dude is a crack up.

Wiping her eyes, Carys looks at me before apologizing. Again. "Oh, God. I'm so sorry."

"Why are you sorry?" I ask, completely entranced by her gorgeous face as it glows with amusement.

"This, me. You're right, I *am* a mess and our date was ruined. But at least now you know why I never date."

I grab her hand and kiss it. "Our date wasn't ruined. Different? Sure. But, that doesn't mean it was bad... in any way. I mean, that alleyway?" I quirk an eyebrow at her and she tries to hide her smile as I walk toward her. Grabbing her by the waist, I force her to look at me and listen. "Carys, you're different and that's one of the things I like best about you."

"You like me?" she asks, her eyes hooded once again and the

boldness from earlier back in full force.

"I like you a lot."

She hums, placing her lips to mine. We kiss again, but it's different from earlier. This one is slow and easy, like we've got all the time in the world. I breathe her in and let her take the lead, having control of every inch of my body. Her hands start at my waist and feel their way up to my chest and then my jaw, as she strokes her fingers through the scruff I've let grow since being here.

"Fuck," I whisper. "I'm not usually one to throw on the brakes, but if we don't stop I'm gonna have you laid out on this counter and everyone is gonna get more than they paid for."

I feel her vibrating against my chest as she laughs, her teeth grazing my neck.

"Carys," I warn.

The phone ringing behind the desk does the trick. In an instant, she removes herself from me and flies behind the counter. With a fake professionalism, she answers, "Blue Bayou, how can I help you?"

The thought crosses my mind to walk around the counter and have a little fun, paying her back for the hard-on I'm sporting, but I decide to find a quiet spot over in the corner of the lobby by the large bookcases and watch her work. That'll have to be enough. For tonight.

Carys

I CAN HONESTLY SAY MY DATE WITH MAVERICK WAS the craziest one I've ever been on, thanks to the leak in room 201, but it's also been the best. I've dated and had boyfriends before, but I've never experienced the same kind of chemistry I have with him. It's thrilling, overwhelming, and downright scary at times. And I want more.

Maverick refused to leave me while I watched the front desk last night, opting to peruse the bookcase in the lobby while interrogating me about my childhood instead. Even though I felt bad about how our date turned out, I was very thankful he stayed with me and kept me from falling asleep or becoming bored out of my mind.

Working the front desk during the overnight shift is my least favorite. After locking the front doors at one in the morning, I'm usually able to work in the office or even sleep a little until a guest presses a buzzer, letting me know they need to be let in. Because of this, I'm pretty grumpy when the shift is over due to my work and sleep interruptions. I'm hopeful that, one of these days, I'll be able to afford more staff to cover this particular shift, but until then, this is the only way I know to do it.

A deep, rumbling snore comes from the chair next to me causing me to giggle as I watch Maverick sleep. He's so stubborn but so flipping cute. Once the front doors were locked this morning, he followed me to the office and dragged my grandpa's old but comfy reading chair to my desk, so he'd still be close to me as I worked. I was surprised he actually let me work and didn't put the moves on me again. Surprised and a little disappointed, I'll admit.

I know, without a doubt, I would've slept with Maverick if given the opportunity—a *real* opportunity that didn't involve cleaning bathrooms or checking in guests—and I'm not sure what to make of that. Never being one for a one-night stand, I find the more I'm around Maverick, the more my walls come down and morals fly out the window. And I'm okay with that. Very okay, in fact.

Maverick sleeps for a while longer before my guilt forces me to wake him. It's almost four a.m. and there's no reason he shouldn't be in his bed. Even though I've napped off and on during my shift, I'm counting down the minutes until George comes to relieve me so I can crash in my own bed.

Leaning over him, I'm overcome with the desire to kiss him awake, but I refrain, running my thumb across his cheek and down to his chiseled jaw instead. He really is so beautiful. Beautiful, but temporary, I have to remind myself. There's no need to develop feelings for him when he could leave at any moment. I need to let myself be free and have fun, enjoy Maverick's company and anything else he'd like to share with me. Preferably, multiple times.

"Hey, Mav," I murmur, wanting to wake him but not scare the shit out of him. "You need to get up and go to your room."

His eyebrows furrow and I imagine he's trying to figure out where he's at before completely committing to waking up. "Wakey, wakey, eggs and bakey," I say a bit louder, giving his shoulder a little nudge.

Maverick smiles but doesn't open his eyes. "Does this mean you're ready to go to a *real* bed?"

"Yes, I'm ready for *my* bed but that won't be happening for a couple more hours. You should go to your bed, though, and get some real sleep."

His bottom lip sticks out in a pout and I laugh to keep myself from nibbling on it. "Go on. You have work to do tomorrow and there's no need for both of us to be cranky. Get some rest while you can."

The bastard has the nerve to open his eyes and give me a sexy, bedroom-eye look. "Get some rest, huh? Does that mean I'll be expending energy in ways that don't include fixing a toilet?"

"You wish."

"I do. Very badly." He licks his lips before continuing. "Come to bed with me, Carys. I want to do naughty things to you."

Tingles run up and down my spine and my mouth goes completely dry. I think I may be blushing, too. It definitely got warmer in here, that's for sure. No one has ever been so forward with me and I've never wanted to follow someone so badly.

Standing up, I manage to clear my throat before sticking my hand out to him. "As much as I'd love to take you up on your offer, and believe me I do, I still have two more hours to work."

He takes my hand and stands up, pulling me forward until our bodies are touching. He moves the hair from my face before cradling my jaw in his hands. "Thank you for tonight. I'll see you soon." He seals his promise with a firm kiss to my mouth and then leaves.

Even if I were in my bed right now, there's no way I'd be able to sleep. Maverick left me good and turned on, and if I had to guess, I'd bet he did it on purpose.

It's late in the afternoon when I make myself get out of bed. As keyed up as I still was when I got to my place, it took longer to fall asleep than I'd anticipated and when I did finally sleep, it wasn't the deep slumber I was craving. Instead, it was restless with dreams of

Maverick and his teases and promises. This is why I allow myself two cups of coffee before making my way back to the hotel.

I'm not sure what I was expecting when I walk into the lobby, but catching Maverick and Mary playing cards was not it.

"Gin!" Mary exclaims.

Maverick throws the cards in his hand down on the table. "You got me again, Miss Mary." When he sees me watching them, his face lights up and he smiles. Can I really be the reason for that kind of reaction? He sure makes me feel like I can.

"Did you know Miss Mary here is a card shark?" he asks, pointing my way.

"I sure did. How much did she get you for?"

"Enough to treat myself to a manicure," Mary answers for him. "And a pedicure, I believe."

"More like, an entire spa day," Maverick corrects her before winking at me.

"Well, she certainly deserves it." I lean over and kiss Mary's cheek. "Thanks for holding down the fort while I slept."

"Of course, dear. I'm going to put my winnings away, but I'll be back shortly so you two can fix the toilet in 201."

Maverick waits for Mary to be out of earshot before asking, "Did you sleep well?"

"Well enough, I suppose," I say with a shrug. "How about you?"

"Slept like a baby." He stretches his arms above his head, giving me a view of his tight triceps, as well as his defined chest muscles, thanks to his shirt pulling tight with his movement.

"Braggart," I mutter, referring to both his physique and his sleeping prowess.

"I mean, I didn't fall asleep immediately; there was...*business* to tend to first. But, after that, it was snooze city."

Is he saying what I think he's saying?

I'm equal parts turned on at his words and irritated with myself for not thinking to do the same thing earlier.

When I don't respond, he laughs and grabs a plastic bag off the floor. "Come on, boss lady. I bought what we need to fix the leak already. I was just waiting for you because you said you wanted to learn how to do it."

"Yes, I do...want to learn how to do it. The toilet. Fix it." I close my eyes and take a deep breath. Damn him for turning me into a blubbering, horny idiot. Once I've calmed down some, I look him in the eyes. "Yes, I would like to learn how to fix the toilet. Thank you."

I can tell he's trying not to laugh, which I appreciate. Instead, he holds up a room key and motions for me to step into the small elevator.

I'm beyond pleased to see the leak is as easy to fix as Maverick said last night. I'm even more pleased to be able to watch him work with his hands again. If I didn't know better, I never would've guessed he works in an office for a living. He's such a natural with tools and he's very confident in his knowledge and skills. My mind goes straight to the gutter with my last thought and I don't even feel bad. The man simply oozes sex appeal.

Cold water seeping through my t-shirt quickly brings me out of my thoughts. Stunned, I look down and see that my shirt is, in fact, soaked through and sticking to my skin. It's not until I hear Maverick's laughter and the water running in the sink, that I realize he's responsible for this.

"You looked like you were either deep in thought or about to fall asleep, so I thought I'd wake you up," he says, still laughing.

When I stand up and place my hands on my hips, bringing his focus to my now wet breasts, his laughter comes to an abrupt stop. The atmosphere around us is no longer relaxed or light; it's charged with excitement and desire. Maverick's eyes are hooded, and he licks his lips like he wants to devour me. And for the love of all that's good and holy, I want him to.

"Come here." His voice is gentle and calm as he takes my hand and pulls me to him. I am anything but calm as I allow my body to follow his lead. He picks me up and sets me on the bathroom counter, spreading my legs so he can fit between them. I'm the opposite of calm; I'm more like a fuse on a firecracker, just waiting for his touch to ignite me, causing me to explode.

I expect him to go straight for my chest. It's right there on display, thanks to my now see through shirt. Instead, his eyes move over my face as if he's cataloging every feature, every freckle. He whispers that I'm beautiful—so beautiful—before his lips finally touch mine.

Our kiss quickly escalates, my mouth greedily accepting his tongue and loving the feel of it tangling with mine. Maverick kisses me like I'm his lifeline and I let him consume me. I'm wound so tightly I'm sure I'll die if he doesn't touch me soon. I take his hand and place it over my breast, even though I really want it to be lower, and his response is a deep groan that I feel in my mouth and between my legs. He pulls his lips from mine and watches as my breast responds to his touch. He squeezes and rubs his thumb across my nipple, making it even harder than it already was. I try to pull my shirt over my head, needing to feel his skin on mine, but he shakes his head, denying me.

I wasn't prepared for how good it would feel to have his mouth on me, even through my clothes. His tongue and teeth expertly find my nipple through the cotton and lace, and when he sucks on it, my gasp echoes throughout the room. He repeats his actions on my other nipple and it's a struggle not to rip his shirt to shreds when my nails claw at his back.

Maverick kisses up my chest, over my collarbone, leaving a wet trail up my throat to my ear. He sucks my earlobe into his mouth at the same time he brushes his knuckles over my center, through the rough fabric of my jeans. On instinct, I thrust my pelvis and I don't care if it makes me seem needy. I am fucking needy; I need him to make me come before I lose my mind.

"Can I touch you here?" His voice is gravelly and strained, like he too is hanging on by a thread, as his knuckles press harder.

"God, yes," is all I can manage to spit out before I feel him unbutton and then slide my jeans down to my ankles, followed closely by my panties. Normally, I'd feel shy or embarrassed being so exposed, especially while he's fully dressed, but Maverick makes me feel beautiful, wanted, and empowered.

He uses his entire hand to explore before sinking a finger inside me. When he adds a second finger, I feel my walls tighten around him while my thighs begin to shake.

"I love how your body responds to me. You're so tight and wet." He pumps his fingers deeper, harder, as his other thumb rubs against my clit.

"Please, Maverick." I beg him for more, the need to fall apart greater than breathing at this moment.

"I got you, don't worry." He kisses me, swallowing my cries as my orgasm rocks through my body. His fingers never stop thrusting, and soon, I'm coming a second time, stars and white light exploding behind my closed eyelids.

When my body finally relaxes, Maverick removes his fingers and redresses me, pulling me into his arms. I love how perfectly I fit and forbid myself to think of anything but this amazing man, while removing the word *temporary* from my vocabulary.

Maverick

When Carys' arms slip from my neck, I assume
she's needing to get back to work, but instead, her hands go to the waist
of my jeans. The slight graze of her fingers on the sensitive skin on my
stomach causes me to jump and then groan. Her hot mouth is on my
neck, and for a split second, I consider letting her continue on the path
of least resistance, but not yet.

"Carys," I breathe, her name coming out like a plea.

"Uh huh," she replies, equally breathless and lost in the moment.

Squeezing my eyes shut, I force myself to think of dead puppies
and saggy grandma titties. It's a trick my best friend in junior high
taught me. Everyone has something that pours on the cold water,
pressing the brakes. Dead puppies and saggy grandma titties do it for
me. "Not here," I finally manage in a calm, controlled tone. "Not here."

Her hands halt as she backs away a few inches to look at my face,
her eyes still hooded and dreamy from her orgasm. And what a fantastic
orgasm it was. I could watch Carys come all damn day.

"You don't want me..." Her words drift off and I see the confusion turning to some sort of rejection and I don't want that, so I interrupt, wrapping my arms around her as I do.

"I want," I confess in a low whisper against her hair. "I promise. I want you sprawled out on my bed. I want to see you come over and over again. I want to own every orgasm. And I want your sweet mouth on my dick. I want to see you, hold you, taste you. I want it all. But not here. I need more than ten minutes in a bathroom."

When she pulls back this time, her eyes are wide and alert. I watch as her tongue darts out to wet her bottom lip. She takes inventory of my face, drinking me in and I let her get her fill.

"Okay," she finally says, standing on her tiptoes to kiss my cheek, letting her lips linger on my jaw and testing my resolve.

"Soon," I promise.

My phone in my pocket rings, filling the quiet that surrounds us, and we both jump.

As I retrieve it and slide my finger across the screen absentmindedly, my heart drops when I hear the voice on the other end.

"Maverick," my father says without waiting for me to say anything first. "I was wondering when you'd finally take my call." Add my father's voice to the list of instant boner-killers. It may work better than my go-to dead puppies and saggy grandma titties.

"Hello, Dad," I say, working to retain my cool—my calm state of mind I've found since being here at the Blue Bayou. Closing my eyes, I back away from Carys and take a deep breath as I lean against the bathroom wall.

When I open my eyes, I meet Carys' gaze and give her a tight smile. She reads me well and points to the tool box, quietly loading up our supplies. "I'll take these downstairs," she whispers, brushing past me, but not before leaving a soft kiss on my jaw.

"See you in a minute," I whisper back, pressing the phone to my chest in hopes my father won't hear. I don't want him to know about Carys or this hotel. This is my own little piece of paradise and I don't want him to taint it.

"Maverick?" my father asks, sounding a bit distracted himself.

"Yes?" I reply, albeit a bit tersely. I just want to get this call over with, so I can go on with my day. I want to forget about him and everything waiting on me back in Dallas, at least for a few more days.

"Son, when are you going to stop this juvenile behavior and come back to work? You have responsibilities here. You can't just walk away and think everything will be taken care of for you. It doesn't work like that. Not in the real world."

I roll my eyes, not in the mood for one of his teaching moments or lectures. "I needed a few days to clear my head. I'm sure I have at least a few weeks of vacation I can use."

"Most people request a vacation ahead of time. They don't storm out and not come back."

Taking a deep breath, I kick off the wall and walk into the hotel room and over to the window. "I know. I'm sorry. I should've called."

"Where are you? I called the Hotel Monteleone, assuming that's where you would've gone, but Henry said he hadn't seen you check in."

"How did you know I'm in New Orleans?"

"Shepard."

What the fuck? Shep wouldn't sell me out like that. He knows I'm here to get away from my father. There's no way he would've put him on my trail.

"So, where are you?" my father asks again, going on with business as usual. "I have some paperwork I need to send over for you to look at. If you're going to be out of town, you should at least make yourself useful."

"That's not a vacation," I grumble, hating his workaholic ways. One more thing I never want to acquire from my father. What happened to living life?

"I think it's the least you can do since you didn't call or let anyone know you were leaving in the first place."

Exhaling another deep breath to keep myself from saying something that would lead to a full-on fight, I finally cave a little. "I'm staying down the street from The Mont. If you'll send whatever you need me to look at there, I'll pick it up from the front desk. Ask Henry to hold it for me."

"How long are you planning on staying?" he asks.

The street below is bustling and so alive, culture and character oozing from every brick. I want to be down there, taking Carys for coffee or stopping on a corner to hear a saxophone player. To get him off the phone and keep him content, I finally respond with, "Give me another week."

It's his turn to sigh heavily into the phone. "Fine, but I'm sending over some properties I need you to take a look at. I'm particularly interested in tracking down the owners of the individual buildings. I was going to go there and do it myself, but since you're already there, I figured I could trust you with this simple task."

My hackles are up immediately, because I have no desire to be his beck and call boy. I don't want to do his dirty deeds.

"I have a contact who's looking for some investment property in the French Quarter area. If this deal goes well, I think he'll be interested in trusting us with larger acquisitions down the road."

Investment property. I guess I could do that. As long as I'm not handing over someone else's life so this guy can flip it and get rich, I'm willing to give it a shot. Plus, it gets me another week...another week of figuring shit out and another week of getting to know Carys. Maybe I can even draw it out a little longer. I scratch his back, he can scratch mine.

"Fine, send it over. I'll see what I can find out."

"Sounds good. Pick up the paperwork from Henry tomorrow and get back to me once you've given it a look."

"Okay," I finally say, ending the call a second later.

For a minute, I stand at the window, thinking about how it's so easy to fall into this city and forget a world exists outside of it. That's what's happened to me since I've been here. I stumbled upon this enchanted establishment and its enigma of an owner and I've forgotten about my job, my father, and any responsibilities I left behind.

It's been good for me.

Being here makes me feel like I can breathe again. The real Maverick has made an appearance and I'm not ready to let go just yet. If a week is all I have left of my time here, I'm going to make the best of it.

"So, one week, huh?"

Carys startles me from my thoughts. I didn't realize she'd come back into the room, but I don't have anything to hide. Honest is the only thing I ever want to be with her. From her tone, I can tell she's a little disappointed, but also not surprised.

"Looks like it," I reply pushing off the windowsill.

She quietly shuts the door behind her to give us some privacy as a couple guests make their way down the stairs.

Stalking toward her, I wrap my hand around her waist and pull her to me, leaning closer so I can breathe in her sweet, sultry scent—like a sugar cookie mixed with exotic spices. I can't put my finger on it, but I love it. "I think we should make the best of it, don't you?" I ask, grazing my teeth along her delicate collar bone.

"Couldn't agree more," she acquiesces, followed by a soft moan as her body melds to mine.

As much as I'd love to take her on the bed behind us, I know we can't, and when I finally do, I want to take my time. "Let's get out of here so Miss Mary can do her thing and this room can be ready for your guests."

"Right," she says, bringing herself back to the here and now. "How about I treat you to a late lunch at my apartment? A thank you for fixing the bathroom and saving me a plumber bill."

"A late lunch sounds great. I need to clean up and make a phone call. Can I meet you there in an hour or so?" I ask, needing a chance to call Shep and get a grip on what's going on in Dallas before the papers arrive tomorrow from my father.

She quirks her lips, fighting back a full-blown smile. "Sounds like a date," she says, then pauses. "I have to work the desk again tonight, so we won't have very long, but..."

"We'll take what we can get," I finish for her, giving her a wink.

"Yeah, we'll take what we can get." She smiles and it hits me down deep, causing warmth to radiate through my chest.

A week.

That should be plenty of time to have some fun with Carys Matthews.

At least, that's what I keep telling myself.

One more kiss for the road and Carys and I part ways. My room is on the third floor, giving me a little better view than 201. I can see above the building across the street, allowing me to see more of the cathedral when I turn one way and deeper into the city when I turn the other. Regardless, the vibrantly painted buildings across from the hotel are scenic enough. Every night I open my drapes so the colors are the first thing I see. Call me crazy, but I think it's a great way to start the morning. Maybe I got that from my grandpa. He was always an up-with-the-roosters kind of person.

"Always remember, you can sleep when you're dead."

That's one of the lines he wrote in the old, worn journal I carry around with me everywhere I go. He left me so many practicalities, nuggets of truth, and pieces of wisdom—each word reminding me of days on the farm, when my life was simpler...when my mother was still alive and I felt like I had purpose and choices. Since they've both died, that part of me—the wild and free Maverick who felt like he had the world by the tail—died too. Each time I open the cover of the journal and flip to a random page, I'm hoping a clear plan will jump out at me, like a light bulb going off above my head.

Since I've been in New Orleans, I've probably read it from front to back twice over, searching the pages for an answer to my current predicament—which way to turn, what step to take next. Part of me says: do what makes you happy, go where you feel alive, be who you want to be. The other part of me says: you have a job and responsibilities. That second part is my rational side, the side that also remembers my inheritance won't be available to me for two more years.

Two years doesn't seem long unless you're stuck in a job you hate and slowly feel yourself turning into your father, who you've never admired.

I have a small savings, but living isn't cheap, and that old adage—

the more you make, the more you spend—is true. I think my grandpa told me that too, along with: *live below your means, always allow room for your dreams.*

Sighing, I pull out my phone and dial up Shep. I need some answers.

"This is Shep," he says after a couple rings.

"Hey," I reply, falling back on the bed.

"Mav," he greets with amusement. "Got more computer problems for me?"

"Nope, but I did speak to my father today, and he said you told him I'm in New Orleans, so I called to say: What the fuck?"

"Whoa. Dude, not me. I haven't even talked to him since you called."

"Who else knows I'm here?" I ask, wanting to know whose ass to kick or who is no longer in my circle of trust.

"The only person I told was Rosalyn. She was in my office when I was on the phone with you. We've been working together on a project."

I let out a sigh, pinching the bridge of my nose.

"Right," Shep continues. "Ros is no longer in the circle of trust."

I laugh, because we're always on the same wavelength. Shep knows me better than anyone. He knows the real me—the part my father tries to ignore and the part I try to overcome. He was there when my mom died and again, six months later, when my grandfather died. Thanks to our similar upbringing, he understands me. It's reassuring to have at least one person in the world who gets what it's like to be a Kensington, but deep down want to be a Maverick.

Shep is a maverick too, maybe not in name, but definitely in all the ways that count.

"Fuck Ros," I add.

"You did."

"Don't remind me."

"Have you done the deed with Miss Blue Bayou?"

"None of your damn business."

"What?" he asks, shock evident in his tone. "Since when do I not get full disclosure? You really like this girl or something?"

"None of your business," I reiterate, visions of Carys playing through my mind and feelings of possessiveness following close behind. "But you can do me a favor and keep your ears open. My dad is sending me some properties he wants me to look into while I'm here. He says it's investment property for a new contact that could lead to something bigger. You know I don't mind finding someone something to invest in, but if there's something more behind it, I want to know. I'm tired of being his pawn."

"Ten-four. I'll keep my ears and eyes open. I'm going to the Tower Club tomorrow night for a fundraiser. Your father will be there."

"I'm sure he will be," I mutter. "Whatever makes him look good. Gotta keep up that pristine appearance so people won't know what a slimy bastard he really is."

"Now, now, Mav. It's all in the name of good business."

We both laugh this time because we both know that's total bullshit.

"I've gotta go," I tell him, pulling myself to a sitting position. "I've got a date."

"Date, huh?" Shep asks, insinuation dripping from his tone. "You know, you don't have to dress it up fancy for me. We can call it what it is. But I've never known you to be one for midday booty calls."

"Yep, talk to you later," I reply, hanging up before he gets another word in.

After a quick shower and a change of clothes, I'm out the door and headed down the stairs. When I get to the bottom, I realize I have no clue where Carys actually lives. Pausing in the foyer, I take a few steps back toward the desk, where George is reading a newspaper.

"Hello, Mr. Kensington," George says, folding his paper. "How can I help you?"

"Maverick, George. Call me Maverick."

He smiles, shaking his head. I know I'm asking a lot, because everyone else around here gets called by their last name. George is a stickler for manners and tradition.

"Maverick," he concedes with a dip of his chin.

"Carys," I begin, but stop because I suddenly feel nervous that I'm asking George, the closest thing Carys has to a father or grandfather, where she lives. He might not want to provide that information.

"Miss Carys is in her apartment. Out the back door and through the courtyard, small door nestled behind the ivy. It's blue, you can't miss it."

I smile my appreciation. "Thank you."

Making my way toward the back door, I pause for a second when I hear George whistling a familiar tune. I can't put my finger on it, but the melody is something I've heard before. Grinning from ear to ear, I take a second and inhale, letting everything about this moment—the place, the city, the people—soak deep into my soul. I'm not sure another week here will be long enough.

I might never get enough.

Carys

WHEN I LEFT MAVERICK EARLIER, AFTER FIXING THE bathroom, I walked downstairs to yet another catastrophe.

The A/C in room 301 was now leaking.

I contemplated going back up to Maverick's room and asking him to take a look, but I couldn't take advantage of his willingness to fix everything. I knew he'd do it in a heartbeat if I asked, but I keep reminding myself that he'll be gone soon and I'll be back to figuring everything out on my own. So, instead, I called Pete's Plumbing and Heating, and relocated Sam Jones to room 303 across the hall with a lovely view of the courtyard.

Not two seconds after I'd taken care of that, Mr. and Mrs. York called the front desk claiming their credit card had been charged twice. We're all still familiarizing ourselves with the new software, but it's pretty user friendly. Thankfully, after looking over their bill and the charges that had been made, I was able to credit back the amount with few repercussions, nothing free coffee from Neutral Grounds and complimentary parking couldn't fix.

With George at the desk until three o'clock and Jules coming in at three thirty, I locked myself away in my apartment for some baking. I know it sounds crazy, but when life gets the best of me and everything seems completely out of control, a few hours in my kitchen baking my grandmother's recipes helps ground me.

Sure, there's powdered sugar covering every square inch of counter space, and piles of mixing bowls and spatulas in the sink, but my insides are as happy and content as the macarons cooling on my counter.

Picking up the sugar-dusted recipe card, I smile and lean back against the countertop.

Just the list of ingredients written in her handwriting is enough to take a bad day and make it bearable.

2 cups almond flour, triple sifted...ALWAYS triple sift

1 ⅔ cups confectioners' sugar

About 5 large egg whites, at room temperature, it's even better to age them at least a day

Food coloring (optional)

1 cup sugar

¼ cup water

Filling of your choice, see the back of the card for my favorites.

Her favorites included Lavender Honey, Rose, and the Blue Bayou special, which is a family secret that was thankfully passed on to me from my mother: vanilla and salted caramel...*The salt is most important*, my mother would always say. The part you also can't forget when making The Blue Bayou, as my mother and I came to refer to it over the years, was the perfect blue of the cookie—4 parts blue to 1-part green. When I use the brand my grandmother always used, the color comes out perfect every time.

The final note on the front of the card is my favorite: *This recipe is enough for two cookies per room.*

When my grandmother was alive, she baked for the guests every day. It was one of her contributions to the hotel that made staying here so special.

The dampness on my cheeks doesn't come as a surprise. Even though I feel close to my grandmother when I bake her macaron recipe, I also often feel lonely. It's hard for me to wrap my mind around the fact that they're all gone—my grandfather, my grandmother, and my mother. Never once when I was a kid did I picture myself here, at the Blue Bayou, all alone. It's always been my home, and it always felt full and alive. Never once was I lonely or scared.

Not even after my grandfather passed away. We had expected that. He'd been sick and held on for as long as he could. I got a chance to make peace with him leaving. But my mother, I thought she'd be around for a long time, teaching me everything she knows about the hotel and how to keep it running successfully. I thought I had all the time in the world.

She was taken from me swiftly. I didn't even get to say goodbye. She was there when I walked out the front door, headed to my classes for the day, and later that evening, she was gone.

George is the one who broke the news. He met me at the corner and I could tell by his red-rimmed eyes something was wrong. I feel horrible saying this now, even thinking it, but I thought it was Mary. I thought something had happened to her, maybe a heart attack or stroke, things that happen to people when they get older.

Not a car accident.

Not my mother.

Those were two things I'd never considered.

The knock on the door startles me out of my memories and I glance over at the clock on the stove, realizing more than an hour has passed since I started baking.

"Carys."

Maverick's voice sends another jolt through me.

"Shit." Looking around at my mess, I panic and start throwing things around. Lunch. I was supposed to be making lunch. He's right.

I'm a mess—a hot mess express. "Shit."

"I can hear you cussing all the way out here. Just let me in."

Turning around once more, I cringe at the white powder clinging to every surface, and then look down to see that I'm wearing a good amount of it myself. Walking to the door, I dejectedly open it, wincing. "Hey."

He's standing with one arm braced on the doorframe and I can't help ogling him. At his full height, he towers over me and I love it. I've always been a sucker for the tall, dark, and handsome type, and Maverick totally fits the bill.

"Can I come in, or did I catch you at a bad time?" The smile on his face tells me he's only asking out of politeness.

"It's a mess, I'm sorry," I preface, opening the door wider so he can step inside. The door opens directly into the kitchen so there's no skirting around the disaster zone.

"I really wouldn't have you any other way." His voice is low and husky as he walks inside, doing a full 360 as he takes in the small space. Then, he turns to me and backs me against the now closed door. "Mess," he says in a gravelly tone that reverberates straight to my core, right between my legs. Dipping his head down, he captures my lips with his, kissing me slow and sure, taking what he wants.

Thank you, God, for this door.

I lean into the hardwood for support as my hands grip his shoulders, needing to touch him, anywhere and everywhere.

Just as I'm getting good and into the kiss, he ends it, pulling back enough I can see the satisfied smirk on his face. "You promised me lunch."

Clearing my throat, I try to get a grip and pull myself out of the haze Maverick seems to induce every time I'm with him, especially when he's standing this close and I can smell him. Damn, he always smells so good. My insides literally want to cry at how good he smells—woodsy, warm, and a hint of leather. I want to bathe in it—him.

"Is this why you always smell so sweet?" he asks, stepping out of my personal space and closer to the counter where the macarons have been cooling.

"Uh, no. I mean—" I stutter, brushing my shirt and shorts off, trying to make myself presentable, all while trying to remember how to use my legs, because that kiss left them feeling like Jell-O. "You think I smell sweet?"

"Delectable, like the most decadent dessert." His mouth curls to one side as he leans against my counter, probably getting powdered sugar on his jeans.

"Stop that," I admonish, pulling him away from the mess.

He laughs, letting me guide him where I want him, which is the small table near the window. "What?"

"Don't tell me I taste like dessert and expect me to make you lunch. It's not gonna happen."

The lunch. The lunch might not happen.

Sex, on the other hand, is totally possible.

I sigh, brushing my hair out of my face and cringing again at my appearance. I should go freshen up and make myself presentable, but I don't want to leave Maverick waiting. "Sorry, I should've already had lunch prepared. I got a little sidetracked."

"A little?" he asks, scanning the kitchen. "I'd say a lot." He smiles up at me with his perfect, white smile. The scruff that's grown on his jawline since he's been here accents the strong lines and sets off his blue eyes. He's really something. Also, the way he's looking at me like he doesn't have a care in the world or no other place he'd rather be does something to me. "What have you been baking?"

Instead of telling him, I decide to show him. Walking over to the counter, I pick up my pastry bag full of delicious icing and pipe some onto one of the cooled cookies. Placing another on top to complete the process, I return to him and ask, "Do you like macarons?"

"Can't say I've ever had one."

"Really?" I ask, thinking surely he's had one at some point. He seems like a well-traveled, cultured kind of guy. And lately, macarons are all the rage. My grandmother would be pleased as punch at their popular resurgence.

"Really," he deadpans, his gaze locking onto mine. It's moments like this—simple, carefree, everyday moments—when he looks at me with so much desire and depth, I have to force myself to remember he's only here for a while.

Don't get used to being looked at like that, Carys.

Don't make this into anything more than it is.

A fling.

We're just having a little fun.

I sigh. "Well, you're in for a treat."

"Will it spoil my lunch?" The way he waggles his eyebrows makes my stomach flip. He's so bad, so bad he's good. And all I want to do right now is spoil his lunch.

"Hasn't anyone ever told you to eat dessert first?" I ask coyly.

Maverick's gaze intensifies and I see his jaw twitch, the muscles flexing. "Well, then maybe I'll have you instead?" He stands and I take a step back, but he counters my move until I'm flush against the counter.

Swallowing hard, I place the cookie at his lips. "Bite."

He does, and I watch as one of his dark eyebrows arch in intrigue, devouring the rest of the cookie, making me squeal at his eagerness and earning a wicked grin. When he darts his tongue out and licks my fingers, heat shoots straight to my core.

Who knew eating macarons was so erotic?

"What the hell was that?" he moans, walking around the counter—looking for more, I'm assuming—leaving me melting right where I stand.

"Ahem." I clear my throat, trying to sound unaffected when I reply, "Macaron." After a few more seconds, I'm able to regain my composure and I follow him around the counter. "The, uh, Blue Bayou special, to be exact." I smile, happy he liked it. It would've been hard for me to not take it personally if he hadn't. I mean, it's my grandmother's recipe and I baked it. Come on.

"Make me another," he demands. And it's hot, like really, really hot.

What the hell is the matter with me?

"So pushy," I tease, squeezing between him and the counter to pipe more filling onto half the cookies and not missing the hardness of his body when I do.

Focus, Carys. Make the man a macaron.

"Where'd you learn to bake like this?" he asks, leaning over my shoulder, watching my every move, his scent and voice consuming all the oxygen in my space and making me feel a little lightheaded.

"Uh, well, my grandmother used to make them for all the guests. I remember being little and standing on my little step stool, helping her mix the filling. She'd never let me make the batter for the cookies, though."

With his chin practically resting on my shoulder, he asks, "Why?"

"It's not easy. Macarons are a very finicky cookie. You have to hold your mouth just right to get them to turn out." I laugh at my own joke. "But when I was older, my mother helped me perfect the art. I've baked them ever since. It's like therapy. I do it when I'm stressed and I need to take my mind off things."

"Hmm," he sighs. "I don't want you to be stressed, but I'm definitely going to need more of these. They're amazing."

After I finish putting each tiny cookie together, Maverick steals a few more, and I force myself to not watch every lick of his tongue. I try to not picture him throwing me on the counter and eating me with as much earnest as he did the tiny blue cookies. I don't succeed, but somehow, I manage to keep my clothes on.

Switching gears and having a proper lunch accompanied by great conversation helps redirect my thoughts.

"So, tell me about the books in the lobby." Maverick leans back in his chair and places his napkin on his plate, which is completely clean.

I push my own clean plate away, feeling satisfied and full and more content than I've felt in a long time. Between the baking and Maverick, I think I've found my perfect remedy. He's given me the distraction I needed to really clear my head, even if I did refill some of the empty space with thoughts of him.

"We've always had books in the lobby. When I was little, I had my own shelf. My grandfather would read to me in the afternoons when someone else was working the front desk." I allow myself to remember for a moment—his olive complexion and the smell of his pipe. Of course, he didn't smoke in the hotel, but he always had tobacco in his pocket for the smoke breaks he and George would take.

"Then," I continue, "my mother started buying books at estate sales and used bookstores and my grandfather kept adding shelves. After Hurricane Katrina, one of my mother's friends, who owned a bookstore down the street, left and never came back. So, my mom salvaged what she could, and that's how the collection got as large as it is now. We haven't really added much in the past few years."

Sighing, I think about that, along with the macarons, all the small touches that have been neglected.

"People love them. I've heard several guests comment on them as they pass through the lobby," Maverick says. "Stuff like that makes the Blue Bayou unique, memorable."

"Like a place people want to come back to," I add, remembering a long-forgotten conversation between my mom and grandfather. "That's where the name came from, you know?"

Maverick's brows pinch together and he leans forward, resting his forearms on the table. "Where?"

"Blue Bayou, it's an old song that was popular in the sixties, just about the time my grandparents bought the hotel."

I watch as a slight bit of recognition moves across his face.

When I hum a small piece of the verse it makes him smile.

"That's the song George was just whistling earlier." He points toward the hotel.

"My grandmother loved that song. She told my grandfather she wanted a place people wanted to come back to, so they named the hotel after the song."

Maverick's expression is thoughtful as he looks out the window into the courtyard. "This place is really something, Carys. I know things seem hard right now, like everything is a mess, but really, you just need to do a little maintenance and, in the meantime, get people here. Show them what they're missing out on by staying at the mainstream hotels. Join forces with people like Micah Landry and your friend CeCe, draw people to the Quarter. I promise, they won't want to leave once they're here."

I laugh, his words making me feel hopeful and a little nervous. It's kind of earth-shaking having someone believe in this place as much as I do. "Where does that passion come from?" I ask, unable to take my eyes off him—the way his face lights up when he talks about something he cares about. He obviously cares about this place. I don't know why, but I'm glad.

It's Maverick's turn to feel the spotlight on him, but I don't feel bad. I've answered a lot of personal questions today. It's only fair that the tables turn.

"My grandfather," he admits, shaking his head. "He was a true maverick, in every sense of the word—independent, unorthodox...a bit eccentric. Unlike my father, my grandfather was honest and forthright, always looking out for the good of everyone. If he believed in something, it didn't matter if it was going to make him money or not, he went for it—all in."

Listening to Maverick talk has quickly become one of my favorite pastimes. I love the cadence and smoothness of his voice. I love the way his eyes dance with expression, helping him tell his story.

"You'd make a good politician."

"What?" Maverick's face morphs to distaste. "No fucking way. I'm not a bullshitter."

"No, you're not a bullshitter, but you're very charismatic when you speak. People love that."

He huffs a laugh.

"Your grandfather sounds like a wonderful man," I tell him, bringing back the slight smile that makes his eyes seem to sparkle.

"He *was.*" His words are simple, yet strong—full of conviction.

"When did he die?" I ask, wanting to know everything about the man sitting across from me.

"About a year ago, nearly six months to the day of when we lost my mom."

"I'm sorry." Those aren't perfect words, but they're true. I am sorry. I'm sorry for any hurts that have ever befallen him.

"I'm sorry too," he replies with sincerity. "I'm sorry we have these things in common, but it's nice to have someone to share memories with. It's nice talking to someone who looks at me with understanding instead of pity."

We sit there in silence for a long moment. His eyes never leave mine.

"You know," Maverick finally says, thoughtfully, breaking the silence. "I think the reason I'm so passionate about the Blue Bayou is because I've seen the end game of places like this. Thanks to my father, I've been in on the demise of many businesses. I've watched as the light leaves people's eyes, as their dreams and lives are demolished, making room for someone else's. Usually, it's greed that wins out, and that's never settled well with me." He sighs forcefully, leaning back in his chair. "It's what sent me running here. I came here trying to figure out my life, trying to find a balance between who I know I am and who I'm expected to be."

"Have you found it?" I ask, completely enraptured by his honesty.

"I've found something," he says with a small smile. "I've found this place, and it's speaking to me like nothing has in a long time. I guess that's why I want to help you bring it back to its glory days."

I laugh, not because it's funny or silly, but because what he just said speaks to me—to my soul. Taking a deep breath, I reply, "I think you're good at this...taking something that's a little rough around the edges and seeing what it could be. Maybe that's your calling—what you're looking for—it could be a balance between what you've learned from your father and what you've inherited from your grandfather. Maybe you should start going in and helping people find ways to save their business."

Maverick's eyes literally shine as the corners crinkle in delight. "It's something I've thought about, dreamed about, really. But that requires money, something to invest with."

I nod, hating that reality isn't always as easy as our dreams.

"I keep telling myself that I'll work a little longer for my father—pay my dues, bide my time—and eventually, I'll save enough money or my inheritance will kick in and then I'll be able to do what I want," he adds. "Then, there's this part of me that says screw responsibility and logic. It tells me to walk away now before I lose any more of myself in the process."

"I'm sure it's scary," I tell him. "I know firsthand that it's terrifying to think about leaving what you've always known. I thought about it when my mother died. I thought about selling this place and cutting my losses, but I just couldn't do it. I couldn't lose my last connection to my family. So, no matter the cost or sacrifice, I'm determined to make this thing work. I don't need to be rich, I just need to make enough to keep this place afloat and get it back to a place where it's thriving."

We sit in a moment of silence again, while Maverick's eyes bore into mine, like he's reaching down into my soul and finding something there he likes, identifies with. It's unnerving, yet life giving. I've never had someone look at me like that—with their whole self, seeing my uncertainties and insecurities and appreciating them.

"Money isn't everything," he murmurs, almost to himself, yet loud enough for me to hear. "It's one of the things my grandfather wrote in his journal, on more than one page. So, I know it was something he really wanted me to hear. There's so much more to life than capital gain or status. This place—you, everything about it—is so much more than that."

"I couldn't agree more," I say, now focusing on his lips and loving the way they look as he delivers his words. I want to kiss them. I want him to kiss me. I want to take him to my bedroom and spend time learning what the rest of his body looks like.

A strange sensation settles inside my chest, a feeling of longing and want, but it goes beyond physical desire. In the short amount of time I've known Maverick, which totals about eight days, I've found someone who understands me and cares about the things I care about. Looking across the table at him, I'm left with the hope that he'll always be here—a permanent fixture—but I know that's not the case. This is all temporary.

He's temporary.

Clearing my throat, I stand up, breaking our silence and whatever moment we were having. As I begin to collect dishes and scurry around my kitchen, I still feel Maverick watching me and it unnerves me, makes my skin tingle and catch fire.

I want him, of course, I do, but what if a fling isn't enough?

Maybe I don't want that after all?

"You're thinking too much," a low, silky voice says in my ear, catching me off guard and making me drop a plate into the sink with a loud thud. His warm breath on my ear makes my knees weak and I swear my insides literally quiver.

I'm not sure I had a tangible definition of that word, until now.

"Uh," is my only response. Somehow in the last minute I forgot how to form coherent sentences. My body is giving me a green light, telling me to turn around and take this man on my kitchen counter, but my mind is throwing up caution. All sorts of bells and whistles are going off, some because I think I like Maverick more than I'm letting myself admit. So, maybe giving into my body would be easy and fun and so so satisfying, but it might also be the road to heartbreak, and I'm not sure if I'm willing to risk my heart.

It's fragile.

It didn't used to be, but one can only take so much disappointment and sadness, and I feel like I've reached my limit in this life.

So, instead of melting into Maverick and giving way to desire, I blurt out, "I forgot I'm supposed to help Mary this evening before my shift starts." The laugh that escapes is nervous and foreign, and I feel Maverick stiffen a little behind me before taking a step back. Finally, I turn to face him, trying to school my features into an expression that won't give away my innermost thoughts and fears, but it's too late.

Maverick is watching me with a contemplative look, mixed with a tinge of disappointment. Letting out a loud sigh, he runs a hand through his hair and scratches at the back of his neck. "Okay," he concedes. "Guess we better get this kitchen cleaned up."

"No, don't be silly. I invited you to lunch as a thank you, not to have you clean my mess."

He watches me for a moment longer, wanting to say something maybe, but refraining. Finally, he dips his head in acknowledgement and takes a step toward the door. "Thank you for lunch and for sharing your macarons." He says the last word slowly, like he's letting it play on his tongue or memorizing it.

"Oh, here." I scramble for a few of the cookies and quickly put them into a plastic bag. "Take some with you. My grandmother used to make them for all the guests," I add, for what reason I don't know, maybe to fill the awkward space that's suddenly settled around us. "But you already know that...because I told you earlier." God, I'm making a mess of this whole situation. Mentally, I'm smacking my forehead for being such an idiot and also praying Maverick just takes the cookies and leaves, to save me from myself.

He looks thoughtfully at me and then the bag, accepting them. "It is really clever, you know? You should consider bringing them back." With a tight smile, not like the ones I'm used to getting from him, he opens the door and walks out.

Frustrated with my brain and the fact I can't just let myself enjoy the moment, I let out a groan and kick the cabinet. Did I seriously just send him away? What the hell is wrong with me?

Maverick

AFTER THE DOOR SHUTS BEHIND ME, **I** TURN AROUND and glare at it. I'm not mad. Disappointed? Maybe. Confused? Definitely. I thought Carys and I were on the same page. I thought our conversation earlier when she walked in on the tail end of my phone call with my father was an understanding between the two of us about what we're doing. She seemed on-board and now, I don't know.

All I know is that I could physically feel her putting up a barrier between us. So, I'll give her some space. Shit, maybe it's for the best.

Not for my dick, but maybe in the long run, because I really like Carys Matthews. I don't know what that means or what I plan on doing about it. My plans lately haven't stretched further than the next twenty-four hours. I haven't thought a lot about leaving and going back to the real world. *That* was the plan when I came here—forget about work, forget about my father, gain some perspective and figure out what I'm going to do with my life for the next two years.

Carys was not in those plans.

Walking back toward the hotel, instead of going inside, I veer right and head down the alley that leads out to the street. I feel the need to clear my head and blow off some steam. One thing I know about New Orleans, there are plenty of opportunities for both.

I'm not feeling Bourbon Street, so I head toward Jackson Square.

With my head somewhere else, I nearly get run over by a horse and carriage. "Sorry," I mutter, pausing long enough for them to pass and then I cross the street.

One of my favorite things about New Orleans, even when I was younger and I'd come here with my mom and dad, is the colors. It's like a crayon box exploded. There's nothing drab or boring. I firmly believe if you're bored in New Orleans, you're dead. There are too many things to do to keep your mind, body, and spirit fully engaged.

Jogging from one corner to the next, I officially enter Jackson Square and step out of the shadow of the cathedral.

My mom loved this place. I think it's one of the reasons we came here so often. My dad was always looking for easy ways to keep my mother happy.

"*Beignets for breakfast* and *dessert*." I can hear her voice so clearly in my mind when I'm at places we shared together.

"Come," a deep female voice calls. "Let me read your palm." Her face is warm and inviting, making it hard to turn her down, but I'm not in the mood for any of that voodoo shit. I did it once, on a dare, while I was here with some of my college friends for Mardi Gras one year. Honestly, I was so drunk I couldn't even remember what the lady told me.

"No, thanks," I tell her politely as I keep walking.

Artists are set up along the fence line, selling their works. Some of it is too eclectic for my taste, but some of it is really great. I've never bought any, though. Since I always fly here, I never want to mess with getting a big ass painting home.

Without thinking, letting my mind wander as I pass people and shops, I end up at the busiest corner, right across from Cafe Du Monde. My mom loved coming here and I think about stopping in, if for nothing else than sentimental reasons, but the place looks packed, so I pass it up and keep walking.

Once I'm on the other side of the square, the buildings are just in the right position to block some of the sun, giving me a slight reprieve, and a small sign catches my eye: *Neutral Grounds*. I remember Carys mentioning this place the night we had dinner at Lagniappe, so I stop. Opening the door, a bell chimes and a voice from behind the counter greets me. "Hello! Welcome to Neutral Grounds."

A girl with brown hair tossed up on her head in a messy bun finally pops up and smiles at me. Well, not a girl, but a woman, probably mid to late twenties, Carys' friend, I'm assuming.

"Hi," I reply with a two-finger wave, checking the place out as I walk closer to the counter to peruse the menu.

"Any questions, just let me know." She's pretty in a girl-next-door, unassuming kind of way.

"I'll, uh…" I pause, taking one more look before ordering. "I'll have an iced americano." I decide to go with my standard when I'm trying out a new place. It's hard to mess up an americano, unless her espresso sucks, but I get the feeling it doesn't.

"Sure," she says, stashing a fresh sleeve of cups on the counter and scooting a box out of her way. "Sorry for the mess. I just got a delivery and if I don't immediately put it away, it'll drive me crazy."

I laugh at her candor and nod. "I get it."

"Are you visiting?" she asks over her shoulder as she starts pulling my shots of liquid gold.

"Uh, yeah…I've been here a little over a week, but I guess I'm still classified as a visitor." I laugh again, kind of disbelieving I've really stayed here that long already. I mean, I intended to when I left home, but I don't know if I really thought I'd go through with it. I assumed I'd be here for a long weekend and then head back home, letting guilt get the best of me.

"Oh, well, you're one of us now. After a few days, we claim as for our own." She smiles, filling the cup up with ice and securing it with a lid. "Anything else?"

"That'll be it."

As she's ringing me up, she continues with her questioning. "So, where are you staying?"

"Blue Bayou," I tell her, pointing over my shoulder.

Her eyes light up. "Really? My friend Carys runs the Bayou. Great place," she adds as she takes my money and makes change.

"She mentioned this place, that's what made me stop."

"Sweet, I'll have to thank her with free coffee." She smiles again as I stuff her tip jar with my change. "CeCe," she says, sticking her hand across the counter for me to shake.

"Maverick," I counter, appreciating her firm, no-nonsense grip.

"Nice to meet you. Don't be a stranger, and if you see Carys, tell her I said hello."

I nod. "I will."

"Feel free to stay awhile. Soak up all the free A/C you want."

"Thanks."

I walk around the shop, admiring the artwork on display. There are pottery and ceramic pieces placed among the various bags of coffee beans, mugs, and store merchandise, as well as beautiful, eclectic paintings on the walls. I assume every piece was created by a local artist and I think it's very cool for CeCe to promote them in her shop.

"I really like this one," I say, pointing up to a painting hanging over a shelf.

"It's my favorite too, painted by a good friend of mine who's really made a name for herself. She started out right here in the Quarter, though. Camille Benoit-Landry? Have you heard of her?"

A small pebble of recognition rolls around in my brain until I remember where I heard it. "Right, somehow related to the owner of Lagniappe?"

"Yes," CeCe says with a pleased smile. "See, you *are* becoming one of us. You already know the locals. Micah, the owner of Lagniappe, is Cami's brother-in-law. Well, she's opening an art studio across the square. You probably passed right by it on your way here, but it's not open yet." Her openness and willingness to share information and open her doors is something that reminds me of Carys. Actually, those are characteristics of a lot of people who live and work in this city. It's refreshing.

"He mentioned that when Carys and I had dinner there the other night."

"So, you and Carys had dinner, huh?" she asks, lifting her tone and eyebrows suggestively.

"Yeah, we did," I admit, realizing a little too late that Carys might not want me telling her friends about our time together.

"Well," CeCe says, suddenly becoming tight-lipped. I can see her mind churning as she looks at me with new interest, like I've become an item on her shelf and she's taking inventory.

"I, uh, fixed something for her and she wanted to thank me." Of course, it was me who requested the dinner, but CeCe doesn't need to know that.

CeCe nods. "I see."

Now it's my turn to nod and take a large drink of my americano.

"Carys is good people," CeCe adds, under the ruse of praising Carys for her hospitality and graciousness, but I'm good at reading between the lines. There's a warning—a friend looking out for a friend, telling a virtual stranger that he should tread carefully.

"She is," I agree, but with my own hidden message: I know how good Carys is, and I'm not here to take advantage of her.

"I'm sure she appreciates your help. The last year or so has been tough."

I nod again, wondering how much I should say. CeCe could be testing me, waiting for me to mess up or tell her how much I know. I won't be doing either.

"She seems to have it all under control," I tell her. "The hotel is great. I've really enjoyed my stay there. It's a nice change from big name hotels, you know?"

"That's why I send everyone I know there," CeCe says, finishing her restocking of shelves and retreating back behind the counter, dusting off her hands on her apron.

"Well, just know Carys returns the favor. She tells everyone about this place."

"We've gotta stick together. It's getting harder and harder to fend off commercial investors from buying up all of the property. They see it as a cash cow, but I hate to break it to them. People come here for the history and authenticity. If they come in here with their shiny, new buildings and chain restaurants and stores, they'll kill business, and none of us will be making a living."

Her words hit a nerve and send my hackles up.

"We can't let that happen," I tell her with casualness and fake levity, because I bet I can guess who one of those commercial investors is who's been knocking, trying to buy out the locals. That has Kensington Properties written all over it.

"No, we can't," CeCe agrees, her eyes on mine, like she's still trying to figure me out, but she's going to be keeping a close eye on me until she does.

"Thanks for the great cup of coffee," I tell her, dipping my chin. "It was nice meeting you."

For the next few hours, I walk the streets of the French Quarter, passing street performers galore, stopping to be entertained by a few. My favorites are the bands and singers, playing for pennies and dollars, but sounding soulful enough to be in the best jazz bars.

Well, not all of them. There's the guy standing on the corner of Chartres and St. Louis singing horrible renditions of 80's ballads. I gave him twenty bucks to not sing until I was far enough gone he could no longer see me. By the time I got to St. Peter, he was bellowing *The Greatest Love of All.*

When I turn the corner toward the Blue Bayou, the sun has set and it's not an embarrassing time to turn in for the night, but I still feel wound up. Even though my feet are tired, my body is still firing on all cylinders. Carys has me so twisted I can't think straight, and the last thing I want to do is walk back into the hotel and be surrounded by her—her scent, her presence—but I also don't want to be alone.

Walking up the sidewalk, I see a familiar face leaving the hotel.

"Dreamboat," Jules greets.

"Jules." I nod, smirking at the nickname he's given me.

"Why so forlorn?" he asks, full of dramatics.

"I'm not, just tired. I've been walking for the past few hours, checking out the Quarter."

Jules frowns, inspecting me from head to toe. "That's no fun." He pauses for a second, obviously contemplating. "But, you know what is?"

"I'm guessing you're going to tell me." I chuckle, scratching the scruff on my chin.

"You. Me. Revelry," he says, gripping my shoulder and waving his hand in the air with dramatic flair. "Come, the girls are gonna love you."

It takes longer than I'd like to admit for me to learn that when Jules says "girls", he does not, in fact, mean actual females. He uses the term to refer to his drag queen friends, and well, everyone else he introduces me to at Club Revelry. Not that I was hoping to meet other women, but a little heads up would've been nice.

My first trip to the bathroom was an eye-opening experience. Let's just leave it at that.

Jules, it turns out, is a multi-faceted person. Not only does he work at the Blue Bayou, but he also tends bar here and dabbles in drag, all while attending law school. I'm absolutely fascinated by his tenacity and work ethic, plus he's a fun guy. I can also tell how much he likes and admires Carys, which earns him bonus points in my book.

"Oh, Mav-y, I need you!" Jules claps his hands excitedly as he walks up to where I'm sitting at the table we procured when we arrived.

"What's up, uh, Jules-y?" Yeah, I'm well on my way to drunk town, also trying to fit in with my new friends.

"It's my turn for karaoke and I need a partner." He tugs on my arm, but I'm still not following what he's implying.

"Well, have you asked, um, Cherry Bomb or Emma Stoned yet?"

"No, I want you. Come sing with me." Jules pulls my arm hard enough that I stumble off the bar stool. I'm sure the alcohol I've been ingesting for the past two hours helped.

"I don't sing, Jules. You need to find someone else."

"Listen, it'll be a piece of cake. I'm Elton and you're my Kiki Dee, so just follow along."

He doesn't give me another chance to protest. He drags me over to a dark corner and places a feather boa around my neck and then covers his eyes with huge sunglasses. Before I can register what I'm about to do, I find myself on stage with a mic in my hand, lights blinding me. A song I haven't heard since I was a kid starts playing, and when Jules starts to sing, I realize I'm supposed to follow his lead.

It's a rough start for me, but the crowd is encouraging, and soon, I'm loosened up enough to start having fun. Jules and I make a great team, or should I say me, Jules, and Johnnie—Walker, that is...red, black... hell, I don't care. I'm friends with all of them. We're really getting into our performance when Jules moves to smack my ass. I don't know what comes over me. Maybe it's the booze or maybe it's the bright lights and energetic crowd? Probably the booze, but regardless, I bend over, offering up my backside on a silver platter, making the people go wild.

By the time our song ends, the audience is on their feet, dancing and cheering, begging us for more. We bow, Jules much more graceful than I, and I'm completely caught off guard when he spins me around and dips me before pulling me up and kissing me on the cheek.

After they realize we're not giving an encore, they start to boo us and call for the next performance. Jules helps me off the stage, and the fact I now need assistance to walk tells me it's time to call it a night.

"Jules, I gotta go. It's been fun and all," I slur. "But I'd like to make an exit while I'm at my peak. That's what's wrong with people...they always want to milk their fifteen minutes for more than it's worth. Like Kenny Rogers said, you gotta know when to hold 'em and know when to fold 'em."

As we approach the table I've commandeered all night, I'm leaning heavily on Jules as the room spins around me. He grips my sides, turning me to look him square in the eyes, but when I try, there are two of him. And I tell him so.

"Okay, dreamboat, let's go," he concedes, leading me to the door and then outside. Even though it's late, it's still humid as fuck, and I'm thankful for the slight breeze. I welcome it, turning my face up and letting it cool my heated skin.

"I'm fine, Jules. You don't have to end your evening for me."

"I'll come back, don't worry your pretty little head, but there is no way I'm sending your drunk ass back to the Bayou all by yourself. Carys would kill me if anything happened to you."

The sound of her name sobers me up a little. "Why would she do that?"

"Because she likes you, duh." He says it like it's so obvious, but I'm not convinced. "You're her friend and after that performance back there, you're officially my friend too, and we take care of our own." He pauses while we cross the street and then continues. "Now, tell me your intentions with my boss. You're too drunk to lie, so don't even try."

Stopping in the middle of the sidewalk, I force my eyes to focus until his face isn't blurry and I can tell he's serious. I think on it for a minute, but don't really know what to say, so I shrug my shoulders instead. At least, I think I do.

Jules loops his arm through mine and continues walking, leaving me no choice but to follow. "You like her, right?" he asks.

"Of course, I do. She's amazing." My words feel thick as they leave my mouth.

"So, what's the problem?" Jules asks, saving me from face planting when my foot hits an uneven part of the sidewalk.

"What makes you think there's a problem?"

"Oh, I don't know. You're out with me instead of there with her. Now, I know you had fun tonight, but I'm not stupid enough to believe, if given the choice, you'd rather be here than in her pants right now."

"Why would I want to wear her pants?" I ask, completely confused.

"For the love of Cher!" he exclaims with a laugh. "One night at a gay bar and you think I'm asking if you want to wear Carys' pants! I said, you want *in* her pants, Maverick. In. You know what I mean by that, sweetheart?"

"Shut up," I say, trying to sound annoyed, but my ability to display the correct emotion is eluding me, along with my ability to think straight or talk right. *Fuck, I'm drunk.* "Yes, I know what you mean. But I'm too drunk to have this conversation, so stop talking to me."

"Answer my question and I'll drop it. For now, anyway."

I stop walking as we approach the Blue Bayou and run my fingers through my hair, taking a sobering breath. I'm sweating my ass off, so I'm sure my hair is a wild mess. I also still have this fucking boa around my neck, its feathers sticking to my skin.

"I'm waiting." Jules has his hands on his hips and he's tapping his toes, a clear sign he's not letting this go until I answer.

"Fine, yes. Yes, I want her, but I also don't want to hurt her. I'm not here for much longer, so I'm just trying to follow her lead. You know? She seemed like she wanted me, but then today she threw on the brakes, and if I'm being honest, it threw me for a loop. So, I don't know, Jules. Whatever Carys wants from me, that's what I'll give her. Is that a good enough answer for you?"

He watches my face for a few seconds before he's satisfied with my response. Smiling, he turns me around and pushes me through a door.

Carys

A NOISE IN THE FOYER BRINGS ME OUT OF THE OFFICE just in time to see Maverick stumbling through the front door. His hair is disheveled. His clothes are askew. His eyes are bloodshot and lazy.

But the best part? He's wearing a boa...a big, pink and purple feather boa.

"Do I want to know?" I ask, feeling relieved.

If I'm being honest, I've been watching the front door for the last few hours. Every time it opened or made a creak, my heart hoped it would be Maverick and I would get a chance to explain my behavior from earlier. My stupid, childish behavior.

Since then, I decided I can be an adult about this. I can enjoy the time I have with Maverick, no strings attached. Even if we have sex tonight and he leaves tomorrow, I'd be okay with that, because as long as my stupid heart and my stupid brain are in agreement that we're only in this for some much-needed pleasure, everything will be fine.

But now, a hint of dread is joining my relief, because as I've been sitting here waiting for Maverick to come back, I've also let my mind wander to where he's been and who he's been with. It's obvious he's drunk. It's also obvious he's had a good time.

How ignorant of me to think he wouldn't go find pleasure somewhere else, with someone else.

"Short answer or long answer?" he asks, staggering toward the front desk and dropping his elbows down on the hard wood with a thud.

"Uh—" I begin, but I'm quickly cut off.

"I'll give you both," he says, his tone turning serious...like, seriously thoughtful and contemplative. Much too contemplative for someone who's been drinking. In my experience, booze equals truth serum, so I'm guessing, no matter what, I'm getting ready to hear the truth.

"The short answer is: Jules." One of his eyebrows goes up, practically to his hairline as he smirks, shaking his head. Damn it all to hell. He's so sexy, even when he's wearing a pink and purple boa and drunk off his ass. "The long answer: Revelry. Johnnie Walker. Elton John. In that order," he says, ticking off the list on his fingers. His long, capable fingers.

And just like that, my mind is lingering in the past, back to the bathroom in room 201 and Maverick getting me off on the counter. I'm honestly embarrassed to say, at twenty-five, it was the best orgasm of my life to date. Maybe that's why I threw Maverick out today? Because if he was capable of eliciting emotions like that from my body with a flick of his fingers, what is he capable of with his...

"Ahem." I clear my throat, shaking my head, piecing together his cryptic response and trying to gather my thoughts and turn them back to the present. I'm pretty sure I got the gist of it. "Jules took you to Club Rev and you drank Johnnie Walker and sang Elton John?" I ask, testing out my deciphering abilities.

The smile Maverick gives me is panty dropping and proud. An odd combination, I know, but somehow he's able to deliver. "Good girl."

Good girl?

Not usually something that turns me on, but coming from him, dripping in honey and rolled around in gravel, it makes my insides clench.

"Did Jules walk you home?" I ask, changing the subject and trying to judge how pissed I'm supposed to be at him for taking Maverick out and getting him wasted. I mean, I know Maverick is a big boy...man, definitely a man...and he can take care of himself, but still. Jules took him to a gay bar and dressed him up in a boa, for God's sake.

There's a level of responsibility here.

"Yes, he did," Maverick says matter-of-factly. "He was the perfect gentleman." With his hand over his heart, he sways on his feet.

I chuckle, walking around the counter to steady him. "Let's get you to bed," I tell him, putting my hand on his waist as he leans into me. Not too much, but more than I know he normally would, if he were sober.

"I was hoping you'd say that." Leaning his head over, he rests it on top of mine. I bear hug him, just to make sure I don't lose him. Sure, I could put him to bed on the pull-out cot in the office, but he needs a real bed to sleep this off.

As we're riding the slow-ass elevator to the third floor, he turns me in his arms, forcing me to look up at him. "You're so pretty," he mumbles. "Not like magazine pretty. You're real pretty. Not just here," he says, running a hand over my hair. "And not just here," he adds, softly brushing his thumb over my cheek and down to my lips. "Or here." His hand drops lower to my neck and then to my chest as he takes a full hand of my boob. "Or here," he continues, gliding his palm down my torso and around to my butt. "But here." Bringing his hand back up, he rests it over my heart. "You're good people. I told CeCe that today. We agreed you're good people. She's nice too and pretty."

My heart, that had stopped beating while he was talking, falls down into the pit of my stomach.

"You met CeCe?" I ask, helping him off the elevator and into the hall as I try to shake this feeling of something resembling jealousy. Why didn't I know he met CeCe? I was going to take him to meet her. And he thinks she's nice and pretty?

"Yeah, good coffee too," he says, his words getting more and more garbled, so I start walking a little faster, hoping we make it to his door before he completely gives out on me.

"Yeah," I agree, forgetting my words as my mind races with all the what ifs. I hate this. I hate my traitorous heart. We just had a conversation about not having feelings for Maverick beyond thinking he's sexy and wanting what he has to offer me, and here it goes getting jealous over him meeting CeCe.

A few more paces and we're at his door, I reach around and feel his pockets, checking for a key. Maverick's arms go all octopus on me and the next thing I know, he's pinned me against the wall. "You wanna feel me up?"

"I'm looking for your key," I say impassively, trying like hell to keep my voice from exposing me.

"Is that what you call it?" His words come out deep and raspy, barely above a whisper. "My key, your lock. I think they'd make a good match."

"You're drunk."

"Drunk, sober...I still know what I want. You. And you want me. I know you do. You're just trying to convince yourself that you don't."

He's absolutely right, but not like this. And not before I get more information about CeCe and him meeting her. And her being pretty. I need a sober Maverick for that conversation.

I feel the key in his front pocket and dig it out, making fast work of the lock and door.

A few minutes later, he's horizontal on his bed with his shoes off. It's the best I can do, because he's now passed out and his dead weight is a bit too much for me. Rummaging through his toiletry bag in the bathroom, I find some ibuprofen and leave two on his bedside table with a full glass of water.

Maverick

HOLY FUCKING HANGOVER, BATMAN.

What the hell happened to me last night? I don't even remember getting to my room and I sure don't remember where all these damn feathers came from.

Oh, wait, it's coming back to me.

Flashes of bright lights, a pink and purple boa, and loud music filter through my mind, helping me remember being at a club with Jules. There were a lot of drag queens...and some mild groping of my ass...and, oh shit, whiskey. Right on time, a burp I swear starts in my toes, makes its way out of my mouth confirming my drink of choice last night.

Fucking Johnnie Walker. You are no friend of mine, sir.

This is why I don't drink in excess. Sure, I'll have a drink with clients or go out for a few beers with Shep. I even had my fair share of binge drinking in college, but that was over the day I graduated. Actually, before that. I had my fill after living a couple years at the frat house. Twenty-eight-year-old Maverick knows when to stop. Except for last night.

Fuck.

I slowly roll from my stomach onto my back and peel the feather boa off my sticky skin. Someone definitely helped me to my room because I don't normally sleep in my clothes. Any clothes, for that matter. The fact that only my shoes are off means another person was with me, and either they couldn't or wouldn't undress me. Not that I'm complaining. I think it would've felt really strange to wake up like this and butt naked, as well. My first guess is that Jules helped me in here because he's the one who got me so fucked up. I mean, he didn't pour the whiskey down my throat, but he certainly didn't try to stop me.

Something catches my eye and I look toward the nightstand, finding a glass of water and pills.

Carys.

I vaguely remember talking to her last night, but I was hoping it was just a dream. She's never seen me drunk off my ass and there's no telling what I said to her. It must not have been too bad, though, if she helped me to my room. Jules might've done the same for me, but there's something about the gesture of leaving me water and medicine that has Carys written all over it. And, if she did that even after I upset her yesterday in her apartment, maybe that means she's forgiven me.

I'm dying to see her again, but not like this. Not when I feel like shit and have no idea what I said or did when we were together. I gingerly roll out of bed and swallow the pills, finishing off the water in record time, before turning on the shower.

Shower, first. Eat as much greasy food I can find, second. Third, coffee. All the coffee. It's the only way I can conquer this damn hangover. Then, hopefully, I'll feel human enough to find Carys and apologize for whatever I did to upset her yesterday afternoon, and for whatever I might have done last night before I passed out.

Feeling a good eighty-five percent better after standing under the hot water spray for a good while, I dry off and get dressed.

As I'm about to leave my room, my cell goes off in my pocket, alerting me to a text.

Dad: The papers are waiting for you at The Mont. Get to work.

I didn't even know my father knew how to text, but I guess it's a form of communication that doesn't slow him down, like a phone call would. My finger hovers over the middle finger emoji for longer than I'd care to admit before I resist temptation and slide the phone back in my pocket. Seeing his message does nothing to improve my hangover.

I need coffee and breakfast. Stat.

George is at the front desk when I get downstairs. I nod my head at him and give a slight wave before making my way out the front doors and onto the too bright sidewalk. If I'd stayed any longer, I would've started looking for her and I'm just not ready for that yet.

Even though it's technically out of the way from the Hotel Monteleone, I go back to Neutral Grounds for a large coffee and breakfast sandwich. CeCe is there, of course, and is much too chipper for me this morning.

"Rough night?" she asks.

I groan and massage my temples. "That obvious?"

"Kinda," she says with a laugh. "Plus, you're wearing shades inside and you're inhaling your breakfast like you haven't eaten in days. And you're also scruffier than yesterday, but don't worry. It looks good on you." She winks as she walks off, but it's not super flirty. It's just friendly and familiar—like CeCe.

"Thanks, I guess," I half laugh, half moan. "I went out with Jules last night and I can't even remember getting back to the hotel. I'm sure you hear stories like that all the time around here."

"Jules?" Her expression is one of surprise but then she fixes it. "I'm sorry, I was under the impression you and Carys were having a...thing. Maybe that was just wishful thinking on my part."

Oh? *Oh.*

"Oh, yeah, wishful thinking on my part, too, I'm afraid."

She doesn't look like she's very happy about my response, but instead of asking what she really wants to know, she asks, "So, who's Jules?"

"Jules works at the hotel."

CeCe crosses her arms over her chest. "Couldn't you go out with someone who doesn't work at the Bayou?"

"What? Oh, no, wait." I pause, taking a much-needed sip of my coffee and wondering if hair of the dog wouldn't be better. "You're misunderstanding. Jules is a guy, and he took me to the club that he also works at. Club Revelry."

Understanding dawns on CeCe and she relaxes her stance. "Ah, gotcha. Okay, then. Sorry for getting all up in your business, but I gotta look out for my girl."

I hold my hands up in a defensive pose. "I get it, and I'm glad Carys has you on her side."

"And to answer your question from earlier, yes, I do hear hangover stories like yours all the time. New Orleans queens know how to throw down."

Laughing, but also cringing from the added movement to my still throbbing head, I walk toward the door. "That, they do. I have to do some work, unfortunately, but I'm sure I'll see you again. Have a good day, CeCe."

"Stay out of trouble, Maverick," she hollers at me, laughing.

Making my way toward Royal Street, I walk at a leisurely pace, letting the combination of coffee, breakfast, and the ibuprofen do its trick. Even hungover, I can't help but appreciate my surroundings. There's a hustle and bustle that's common in cities, mostly food deliveries to hotels and restaurants, but the people here aren't frantic, as if they don't have a moment to spare. They still make time to stop and say hello to anyone who walks by, and laughter is usually quick to follow.

Even though it's technically still morning, the sun is already high and it's hot. There's no other way to describe it; it's just fucking hot, which doesn't help the smell of the city. I've been told the streets get hosed down overnight to get rid of everything the drunk crowds leave behind, but if that's true, the water's magic doesn't last long. I think I'll head to the French Market later, where the only smells are of delicious foods and spices.

Once I've stepped inside the Hotel Monteleone, I'm immediately greeted by an employee. I give them my name and explain that Henry has some papers for me and after a few minutes wait, Henry quickly walks up to me with a large envelope in his hand.

"Good morning, Mr. Kensington. I must say, I was disappointed to learn you were here in New Orleans and staying elsewhere. Is there anything I can do to make you reconsider your arrangements?"

"No, thank you, Henry. It was a very impromptu decision to come down here, and I thought it'd be fun to stay somewhere closer to the action."

"I see," is his response and there's no doubting the judgement in his tone. "Well, your father sent this for you." He hands me the heavy envelope and takes a step backward. "Have a good day, sir."

A few seconds later, he's gone through a door behind the counter and I'm completely dismissed.

Normally, we'd chat, at least about the weather.

Huh.

I admit, I'm a little surprised at the cold shoulder, but I just can't find it in me to care. I take a moment to pull out the papers and look over them, trying to get as much time in the air conditioning as possible. After typing the addresses of the buildings I'm supposed to check out into my notes for easy access, I make my way toward the door. Looking around the hotel lobby, I mentally wave a middle finger salute in the air as I leave.

Standing at the corner, I plug the first address into my GPS app and start walking.

It only takes me about five minutes, and when I look up, I'm on the same block as the Blue Bayou, just at the opposite corner. A flood of adrenaline and dread fills me, and I quickly type another address into the app, hoping like hell it's somewhere miles away.

Less than a minute walk. "Fuck." Every address on this list is within the block of buildings occupied by the Blue Bayou.

"Goddamn it," I mutter, turning sharply on my heel and heading back in the other direction.

Hitting redial on my call from yesterday, I wait for my father to pick up as I punish the sidewalk beneath my feet. Sweat is beading on my forehead when he finally picks up.

"Maverick, I'm assuming you got the papers I sent."

"What do you want with the Blue Bayou?" I ask, not beating around the bush or playing games. I have no time for that.

A long pause forces me to pull the phone back and make sure the call didn't drop, but finally he answers my questions with one of his own. "What's the Blue Bayou?"

I'm forced to tamp down my frustration, so this doesn't escalate to a full-blown argument, because if there's one thing I know about Spencer Kensington, it's that he does his fucking homework. He never leaves a stone unturned when he's trying to close a deal. *Don't play stupid* is on the tip of my tongue, but then he comes back with another question.

"What do *you* know about the Blue Bayou?" His tone is cool and calculated, and if I were a betting man, I'd bet he's piecing together this little mystery.

"I asked first."

He huffs his own frustration, never liking to be challenged, then sighs in concession, "It's a piece of property within a block of properties," he says, his words thick with sarcasm and bite. "I want it. The offers are in the paperwork I sent over. I need as much detail and contact information you can obtain. Face-to-face meetings would be even better. If we can close this deal within the month, I feel like we could negotiate a larger percentage, if not on this contract, then the next."

My mind is spinning so fast I can't even get my mouth to work. When I do finally manage to spit out some words, the only thing that comes out is low, muttered, "What the fuck?" Pinching the bridge of my nose, I lean my head back and try to keep my cool. Losing it won't help anything or anyone, especially Carys. If I show an attachment, it'll only make matters worse.

"I'm sorry?" my father questions, shuffling the phone.

"Why this property?" I ask calmly, trying to sound interested, but not invested. "What is the end goal? I need more information if I'm going to be able to negotiate with the land owners. And have you researched permitting and zoning? This is a predominately historical area of the city. I doubt they'll allow someone to tear everything down and build a high-rise." I'm not sure if those words are for him or me. All I know is that I want to think of a way to turn him off of this path. Like a hunting dog, I know I'll need a decoy. "How about I take a few days and check out some properties downtown. Are they settled on New Orleans?"

"I didn't ask you to scout new properties. That's been done for you. Take the locations, find the owners, make the deals. That's what I pay you for. The only property currently occupied is the hotel you mentioned, and I have it on good authority that the owner is in financial distress. A child could negotiate this sale. Don't be a child, Maverick. If you can't complete this simple task, your position at Kensington Properties will be terminated."

I swallow. Hard. Not because he threatened my job, I was already considering it, anyway. This just confirms it. But it's the hunger in his words, the fact that he'll do whatever's necessary to obtain these properties, which includes the Blue Bayou, that has me fighting to keep down my breakfast.

That and my still lingering hangover.

"I'll expect an update tomorrow," he continues. "I can probably delay for a few extra days, but I need this done. Now. If you can't do it, I'll do it myself."

"Yes, sir," I mumble, ending the call and shoving the phone in my pocket.

What are the fucking odds? The one time I find something that feels like it's me and I connect on a personal level, my father comes after it? If I didn't know any better, I'd think it's some sort of conspiracy, but he has no way of knowing I'm here, and even if he did, what's the punchline? I'm sure it's merely an outlandish coincidence, kind of like stumbling into the Bayou and finding Carys. Sometimes, shit happens and you have no logical explanation for it.

So, the better question is: what's my plan?

Stall?

Divert?

I'll buy as much time as I can until I find the right time to talk to Carys. I know she won't sell, but I also know my father won't give up. And what kind of financial distress? Not that she would tell me, but I feel like we've been open with each other and she knows how I feel about the hotel.

Suddenly, I feel sick and it's not the lingering Johnnie Walker. It's so much more than that.

Walking down the sidewalk, I make my way around the block. He's right. Most of the buildings on this block look like they haven't been occupied in a while. I wonder if the buyer would be willing to buy up everything, excluding the Blue Bayou? Also, what are their intentions? These are questions I need answers to.

The conversation I had with CeCe the other day comes to mind, so I decide to head back over there and pick her brain for a minute. She seems pretty forthcoming with information.

As I walk, I compartmentalize. It's how I work through problems.

Worst-case scenario: I lose my job and my father takes it upon himself to come down here and try to convince Carys to sell.

Carys won't sell. At least, I don't think she would. Opening the files, I scan the papers, searching the offers. The number listed for the acquisition of the Blue Bayou seems like a low-ball at first glance, and my blood boils hotter.

If I thought it was enough to give Carys a good life, I might consider telling her about it, but not until I have a better grip on the entire situation.

Worst-case scenario: Carys gets mad at me for butting into her personal life and business.

Regardless, I can't let her be taken advantage of, not by my father or anyone else.

That's not happening.

I'll make sure of it, even if I piss her off in the process. Somehow, I'll figure a way out of this. I'll even help her out of whatever financial distress she's in, if she'll let me. My father assisting in the acquisition of the Blue Bayou and its surrounding properties—and doing God knows what with it—is my own personal nightmare. It's what I've been running from and I won't let that happen, not here...not to Carys.

"Back so soon?" CeCe asks when she sees me.

"I wanted to ask you about what you were talking about yesterday," I tell her, cutting straight to the chase.

"Carys?"

"No, about the commercial investors."

CeCe's eyebrows furrow and she finishes off a drink she's making and hands it to the customer. "Have a nice day," she tells them, before turning back to me. "What about them?"

"I was just wondering if you know who they are and what they might be looking for."

She thinks for a moment and then walks over to the cash register, pulling out a card. "This is the last guy who stopped by here. He told me he was looking for a considerable amount of space. That's all he said."

"And you told him to fuck off, right?" I ask, taking the card from her. The name on the card is different from the one in the file that's tucked securely under my arm, but it doesn't mean they're not working together. Often, one company acquires property under a different name, or there's a chance a parent company is involved.

She fights a smile and nods. "Basically, but maybe I was a tad more diplomatic."

"Have they been to any of the other businesses around here?"

"Uh, yeah, I know he stopped by the cooking school a few doors down. Oh, and Micah Landry said he'd seen him snooping around his place and the building next door that he recently purchased for an event venue."

I breathe in deeply and let it out. "Thanks for the info."

"Why are you so interested? What's your MO, Maverick?" One of her eyebrows arches and she crosses her arms.

"I'm on your team," I tell her. "Promise." I look the card over once more. "Can I keep this?" I ask, holding it up.

"Sure, I was just saving it for kindling."

I smirk at her smartassness. "Thanks."

When I turn to leave again, she stops me. "Maverick."

"Yeah?" I ask, one hand on the door handle, the other still holding up the business card for further inspection.

"Does this have anything to do with Carys and the Bayou?"

"Let's hope not," I tell her, walking out the door and back into the sweltering heat.

When I get back to the Bayou, Jules is on duty at the front desk.

"You've seriously gotta stop walking your fine ass around the Quarter. You're gonna sweat your balls off," he mutters, turning his attention back to the glossy magazine in front of him.

"Have you seen Carys?" I ask, knowing I need a shower and time to collect my thoughts, but I also need to see her.

"George said she went to her apartment after she finished helping Mary with the rooms. I'm sure she's beat, she worked most of the day yesterday and all night last night."

I nod, looking around the lobby. I need something to do, something to take my mind off this stupid property shit. My father. Finances.

"You need a drink," Jules says.

"No. No, I do not need a drink."

"Not that kind of drink." He leaves his post at the counter and walks over to the cart where the delicious fruit-infused water is kept, pours me a glass and sets it down in front of me. "All that sweating is a good way to detox, and baby, you needed it."

"No thanks to you," I mutter, downing most of the water in one gulp.

"I didn't pour Johnnie down your throat. You did that all by yourself."

"You did make me sing backup on karaoke," I accuse, with a

pointed finger. As I've been walking around town, most of last night's activities have caught up with me.

"And you were brilliant...a total piece of cake. The ladies loved you."

I smirk. "At least someone does."

"Still haven't talked to Carys?" he asks, closing the magazine.

"No, well, I sorta remember talking to her last night, but not about anything coherent," I smirk, wondering exactly what I said to her. "But she wasn't around this morning and I've been busy all afternoon."

"How long are you planning on staying?" His expression is thoughtful, yet guarded. I know him and Carys have really hit it off, so I'm guessing this is him feeling me out.

"At least another week. My father put me to work on a... project."

"Well, if I were you, I'd hold off on any heavy talk with Carys today. She had quite the morning."

"What happened?" I ask, my heart rate increasing at the thought of anything bad happening to her. I'm telling you, less than a week and this girl has gotten under my skin. Normally, I'm a casual relationship kind of guy. She does her thing and I do mine. I wouldn't go so far as to say no strings attached, but not many strings and they're usually easily snipped. My last long relationship was with Rosalyn, but we mostly just enjoyed each other's company in bed. She's entirely too much like my father—money hungry, success driven—for me to ever feel anything for her below the surface.

"Oh, air conditioner leaking again on the third floor, door handle broke and locked a guest in their room on the second, the toilet was clogged in the public bathroom down here, and she burnt an entire batch of cookies...or something like that. She was devastated. Mary sent her home to go to bed."

Fuck.

Right then, I decide to take care of the shit with my father and leave Carys out of it. She has enough on her plate. The last thing she needs is more stress or pressure from someone trying to buy the hotel out from under her.

"Jules?" I ask, lowering my voice and leaning in closer. "You wouldn't happen to have any idea if Carys is in any kind of financial... *distress*?" I decide to go with the word my father used and hope it conveys what I'm trying to find out.

Jules bites his lip and looks to his left and then to his right in almost a conspiratorial move. "I know she's not rolling in it. But from an employee standpoint, and I've only been here a short time, so I only have a brief experience to go from, I haven't seen any late notices or past due stamps on the envelopes that come in the mail. And I got a paycheck yesterday."

His response is way more straightforward than I expected, but it's much appreciated.

I nod and take a deep breath, pushing away from the counter. "That's good. I just worry about her, you know?" There's no need for Jules to know about my father's interest in the Blue Bayou either, so I play off my inquisition as pure concern, which isn't a lie...just a small omission.

"I know, and if I didn't think you had her best intentions in mind, I wouldn't tell you shit."

His well-groomed eyebrow goes up in a challenge and I smile.

I'm glad Jules is gay because if he wasn't, he might be competition, and I want Carys to myself.

Soon.

Carys

TAKING A SLOW SIP OF COFFEE, I BREATHE DEEPLY, letting the aroma soothe my soul. The last couple days have been a shit show of epic proportions. First, I got all weird with Maverick and pushed him away. That really set everything else into motion. I firmly believe if I could've gotten over myself and my sudden self-preservation, we would've ended up in bed and I wouldn't have been so wound up for everything else that followed.

Frustrated is more like it.

Sexually frustrated.

So, when the toilet overflowed downstairs and Mr. and Mrs. Townsend got locked in their hotel room and the a/c started leaking again on the third floor, it was more than I could handle. On top of everything else, I burnt a batch of macarons. It was like I couldn't do anything right. To make matters worse, I hadn't had much sleep. After George used a crowbar to break open the jammed door, I called Pete to take care of the rest. Mary sent me home, which is kind of funny, seeing I'm the boss, but that's how we roll around here.

Thankfully, I feel better this morning. I took over for Jules at five, checked out a handful of guests just before eight, and I've been holed up in the office ever since trying to make heads or tails of the stack of papers covering the desk.

We have five reservations for today, everyone checking in around three. Since it's only Thursday, that leaves me hopeful for the weekend. We should start seeing an increase in traffic as summer approaches. Although, I don't know why. People should really get a clue and visit New Orleans when they can walk around without melting.

It's hotter than two squirrels fucking in a wool sock today.

Speaking of hot, I haven't seen Maverick today, and that's bothering me. I even went as far as checking the guest log, just to make sure he didn't check-out yesterday without me knowing. Not that I think he'd leave without saying goodbye, but after how weird I got the other day, I wouldn't blame him. However, I do know he now has a job to do while he's here, and I have to admit, I'm kind of happy about that. No, *really* happy about that. I like that he has a reason to stay. Well, *more* of a reason. I'd like to hope that I haven't fucked things up too badly and part of the reason he wants to stay is me, but that might be giving this attraction I feel a bit too much credit.

Maybe it's not like that for him?

Maybe he's more of an adult than I am and he sees this for what it is: two people who find each other attractive and have needs?

I'm trying to be mature about this.

I can be.

The bell on the counter ringing practically makes me jump out of my chair and piss my pants. I was so far into my thoughts I kind of forgot where I was. Tidying the papers in front of me, I stand up and walk to the front.

"Hey." My greeting sounds dreamy and girly and swoony, so I clear my throat and try again. "Hey."

"Hey." Maverick nods his chin in my direction and takes the shades he's wearing and places them on top of his head.

Shit.

The action makes my mouth water—the sight of him is an oasis in the desert—but maybe he should've left the sunglasses on because he's now unleashing the full force of his gaze on me, and I don't think I was ready for that level of sex appeal. I thought I was, but now, not so much.

It's like the first day all over again—butterflies, nerves, and feeling flustered.

"How...how are you today?" I stutter, but quickly recover, trying not to fidget.

This is fine.

He's Maverick.

I'm Carys.

We're fine.

"Good," he replies, slow and steady. Deep. His tone is deep, like his gaze. Unapologetically, he lets his eyes roam my body, at least what he can see from where I'm standing behind the counter. "You?"

"Good." I nod my head several times, trying to decide where to take this conversation. "Enjoying your day?"

"Uh, yeah." He looks back toward the door and then back at me. "Are we okay?"

My eyes freeze on his as I try to determine what he's thinking... feeling. "Yeah."

"After the other day, I wasn't sure if I said or did—"

"No," I say fervently. "That was me. I just..." I pause, searching for the right thing to say that won't make me sound like an immature idiot. *I think I like you—like* really *like you—and that freaked me out. Sorry, can we kiss again and make up?*

"It's cool," Maverick says, saving me from myself. "I just wanted to make sure I didn't do anything to piss you off." Honest, open. I think it might be one of the things I love the most about him.

Like.

Like the most about him.

Feeling my cheeks heat up, I avert my gaze. Thankful he can't read my thoughts, I try again for comfortable, safe conversation. "What have you been up to? I didn't see you yesterday."

"I had some work to do, so I went over to Neutral Grounds. CeCe has great coffee and Wi-Fi." He smiles and it's innocent and unapologetic, but his admission makes the jealousy I felt the other night spike.

"Oh, so you and CeCe—"

"Met," he says, cutting me off abruptly. "She speaks highly of you."

I'm able to give him a genuine smile in return. CeCe is probably my closest friend, outside of the hotel. She understands where I come from and she just gets me.

"You mentioned her the other night."

"Thanks for that, by the way...helping me upstairs and taking care of me. I don't think anyone has put water on my bedside table since I was ten."

The scruff on his chin is perfect, accentuating his sharp jawline, and I'm mesmerized by the way his mouth moves when he speaks. It's weird, but I actually missed him yesterday. How is that possible? I just met him. He's a temporary fixture. I can't miss him.

"You said she's pretty." The words are out of my mouth before I can stop them. My cheeks flame as his smile grows.

"Why, Carys Matthews..." He pauses, cocking his head to one side. "Are you...jealous?" It's nothing more than a whisper as he leans into the counter, bringing himself closer to me, close enough I can smell him. The same thing I picked up on the first night we met—oak, spice, sweet. It's a lethal combination when paired with those sapphire eyes and perfect mouth.

Snapping out of it, I cough. It's fake, but it works as a nice cover while I process what he's just accused me of and clear my head of the seduction that is Maverick Kensington.

"What?"

"Jealous."

"Me?" I ask, going for denial, but landing somewhere between liar and guilty-as-charged. "CeCe is my good friend. If you like her...and think she's pretty, that's cool."

When he lowers his lids, I swear he rolls his eyes at me, but quickly covers it with a smirk...and then swipes his tongue along his bottom lip before taking it between his teeth. Those damn perfect white teeth. "You think I like CeCe?" There's that tone again—honey rolled in gravel—rendering me useless...a complete waste of space.

"Uh...I just," I start to reply and fail. Swallowing hard, I try again, "You said she was pretty and then you've been over there a few times." When he turns the full force of his gaze on me again, I feel like it's burning through my skin. I wouldn't be shocked if I looked down and my clothes were singed off my body.

"Well, I think you're pretty and I come here every day."

"You stay here."

"Because I want to."

"So, you like me?" The question tumbles out of my mouth and hangs between us for a second. I struggle to hide my smile, not knowing where the heck that came from. Normally, I wouldn't be so forward, but Maverick definitely brings out things in me I didn't know existed.

His honesty evokes honesty.

He doesn't reply, just nods—evil, sexy smile still in place.

"Wanna make out later?" I ask, forgetting myself as I remember the feel of his lips on mine and immediately turning into a hot mess. Shifting on my feet, I squeeze my legs together to relieve the heat and ache, fueled by the look Maverick is still giving me.

Now he's the one fighting a smile. Shaking his head, he steps away from the counter, walks around, looks both ways and pushes me into the office. His large hands come up to cup my face and his lips are on mine before I hear the door shut behind him. Breathless, intoxicated, out of my mind, out of my body—those are things I feel when Maverick is in my space.

When we're kissing, it takes me to another dimension, somewhere else entirely. The way his lips devour mine—fast and furious and then slow and intentional—it makes my head spin.

Eventually, my shock subsides and I'm kissing him back.

My hands are fisted in the front of his shirt, pulling him to me, trying to get as close as possible.

My leg hitches around his waist, causing him to chuckle, but he doesn't let me go.

I want him.

I want more of him to touch more of me.

"Sorry," Maverick mutters, removing his lips from mine but staying close enough our noses are touching as he breathes deeply. It's rough and desperate, exactly how I'm feeling.

"Don't apologize." There's no going back this time. No chickening out. No head getting the better of my heart. I'm all in.

"I'm only sorry because I can't finish what I started."

"Why not?"

"Oh, maybe because it's the middle of the day and you're technically at work." His tone is sexy and delicious, making his excuse sound a lot more provocative than it should.

Why an excuse? Why can't we have sex right here, right now?

"Nobody's here...they won't know."

Maverick takes this opportunity to pull back far enough to see my face. "Oh, mess, they'll know. I already told you, when I finally get you...under me...on top of me...I'm going to need to take my time and everyone within earshot will know."

My eyes grow wide at his promise, and it only spurs me on to want him...now.

The bell at the front desk scares the shit out of me for the second time today, and this time, I actually let out a small squeal. Covering my mouth, I hide my laugh.

"Fuck, you're cute." He kisses my nose, stepping back to straighten my shirt, even giving my hair a once-over, brushing a stray strand behind my ear, before opening the door. He hides behind it and smiles sinfully, motioning for me to leave the office.

I do. And I put on the best acting performance of my life as I check in two new guests.

Maverick

WAKING UP AFTER THE BEST NIGHT'S SLEEP I'VE HAD in a while, I feel refreshed. The night didn't go exactly as planned. Carys isn't lying next to me. But talking with her and making out in the office did relieve some tension and helped ease the tightness that had resided in my chest since my phone call with my father.

My grandfather's words of *everything will look better in the morning* filter through my mind. Followed by: *when in doubt, sleep on it.*

I've decided as far as my father will know, I'm investigating the properties he listed out for me, meeting with owners, and negotiating deals. What he won't know is that I plan to scout out new properties, as well. I realize this could potentially get me fired. He was very straightforward regarding his intentions if I don't follow through with his plan, but since I don't really care anymore, I'm doing what I want and I'm going to protect the Blue Bayou. Since I've been here, I've seen a lot of boarded up buildings, just sitting empty waiting for new life to be breathed into them. I feel like there's an equal or better opportunity out there, and if I can find it and perhaps save my father's client some money in the process, I don't know how he could refuse it.

Before I leave to meet with a property owner and walk through a few buildings, I check a couple things off my to-do list. Picking up the small tool box George lent me, I walk down the hall and pause at the fourth banister. I take a wrench and tighten the bolts at the bottom, putting some elbow grease behind it until the wrought iron no longer squeaks.

Next, with George's help and disapproval, I set about replacing the light bulbs in the stairway chandelier. "Mr...Maverick," George starts. "I'll get to this. There is no need for you to..." His comments trail off as I ascend the ladder.

I have no doubt he would replace the bulbs, but to reach the fixture, the ladder has to be precariously balanced on the edge of the landing leading to the second floor. There was no way I was going to let him climb it.

"No worries, George. It'll only take me a second." Reaching the top, I look down at him and give him a reassuring smile. So much about him reminds me of my grandpa—salt of the earth, hard worker, stubborn as a mule.

"Miss Carys won't..." he begins but stops when the ladder wiggles.

I laugh, partly due to nerves and partly due to his mention of Carys.

"Miss Carys won't what, George? Like that I'm fixing her light fixture?" I ask, breathing heavy for such a menial task. "I think she'll get over it when the foyer is once again bright and shiny. Toss me a rag and I'll give it a good dusting while I'm up here."

George huffs and mutters under his breath, but he retrieves a rag and tosses it to me, all while holding onto the ladder with one hand, refusing to let it go.

George and I make a pretty good team.

Once we've stored the ladder back in the maintenance closet, I grab my bag and phone. "I'll see you this afternoon," I tell him, stopping for a glass of water and pausing. "Where did these come from?"

On the small cart where the ice cold, fruit infused water always sits, there is a plate of bright blue macarons. My mouth immediately starts to drool. I'm not sure if it's the memory of how good the small cookies are, or the vision of Carys covered in flour and sugar, looking more delicious than I can even put in words. Regardless, I instinctively grab one and pop it in my mouth. The entire cookie. I don't have time for bites and nibbles. I need the whole thing.

"Miss Carys. Apparently, she couldn't sleep last night."

I smirk at the wall in front of me, thankful my back is turned to George, because I couldn't look him in the eye while having sinful thoughts about someone he considers a granddaughter.

Snagging two more for the road, I mumble around the cookie in my mouth. "Can you tell her thank you and that I'll be back later? Oh, and give her this."

Quickly, I slip the note out of my pocket and turn back around to hand it to George, who is giving me a sly smile.

"Will do," he says with a nod.

Waving over my shoulder, I head out the door and into the early New Orleans morning.

After mine and Carys' little tryst in the office yesterday, I spent the rest of the afternoon working in the lobby, while she worked the front desk and got some office work done. I just wanted to be close to her, hear her laugh when talking to guests, and catch her glances when she threw them my way. When I couldn't stop fidgeting from wanting to touch her so badly, I went for a run. I needed it. I've neglected my workouts the past week and I can tell.

When I got back, Carys was talking with Jules and they were going over the schedule for next week, so I left them to it. Went back to my room, showered, jerked off, and fell asleep early. I didn't mean for that to happen. My intentions were to find Carys and spend the night with her, but my plans were foiled. Again. I'm starting to feel like the universe is against us being together, but then I remind myself that it allowed me to find this place. So, I'm banking on fate just taking its slow, easy time.

But I'm also a guy who takes fate into his own hands, so I left her a note.

Mess,

I'm tired of eating alone. Please accompany me to dinner tonight. I'll be in your lobby at 7:00 sharp. Also, the beds at the Blue Bayou are spectacular. Would you like to sleep in mine?

Mav

In reality, I've only known Carys for a little over a week, but it feels like so much more. I don't know why, can't really put my finger on it, but I've felt connected to her since our first conversation. When we're together, I feel like I'm talking with an old friend. She's a favorite song, or that new song you hear on the radio, but swear you've heard before. This odd combination of fresh and familiar is something I can't get enough of.

I've heard of people falling in love after a few days together, and I still call bullshit on that, but there's definitely some instant attraction happening. In a short amount of time, she's worked her way under my skin and I haven't even had her in my bed yet.

Yet is the key word there.

Huffing a laugh at my fucking poetic waxing, I turn the corner and step into the full view of the cathedral. This scene is one that never gets old. I could walk these streets every day and never get tired of it. The thought actually makes me a little jealous of people who get to live here full time.

Except for the heat.

Fuck this heat.

And fuck this humidity.

My balls are already sweating at ten in the morning.

Instead of heading to Neutral Grounds, I walk to a bench in the shade and begin making phone calls. I don't want CeCe overhearing my conversations. They could easily be misconstrued.

"Hello, Mr. Grainger. This is Maverick Kensington from Kensington Properties. I'm calling about your property at..."

This same phone call is repeated half a dozen times until I've made it through every location on the list my father gave me. Some of them, I had to acquire myself, which is what I did yesterday morning, footwork. I walked around the block, peeking in abandoned windows and writing down any number or identifying information. It wasn't too hard to track down the few missing contacts.

I'm able to talk to three of the six. The others didn't answer, so I've left messages for them. Two of the three I spoke with agreed to walk-throughs tomorrow and are very interested in selling. It feels like wasted work, because ultimately, I'm not giving in on the Blue Bayou... and Carys won't be selling. But I feel like I have to do this part of things to keep my dad from flying his ass down here and ruining everything. So, I just look at this as buying time.

After stopping in Neutral Grounds for an iced coffee, I start hoofing it to the vacant properties I've seen around. The ones that are in larger clusters are on the outskirts of the Quarter. If I had to guess, it's the Blue Bayou's proximity to Jackson Square and Bourbon Street that makes it so appealing. So, I walk in the other direction, eventually running across a few potential locations. Jotting down the addresses and any information I see, I turn to make my way back to the Bayou.

It's almost two o'clock and I haven't eaten anything since Carys' macarons, so I stop by a small bistro down the street for a late lunch to hold me over until dinner, using the time to call my father.

"Maverick." That's always my father's greeting. No, "Hey son, how are you?" Just, "Maverick."

"Father," I reply, equally terse.

There's a rustling on the other end as he shuffles papers and talks to his assistant. "I'm hoping you're calling with good news."

"I have a meeting tomorrow morning with two of the owners. I've made contact with three of the six, but I'm having trouble reaching the others." One of those miscommunications is entirely intentional on my part.

"And the Blue Bayou?"

"That's a negative. The owner has been unavailable." That's not entirely a lie. Carys has been busy and extremely preoccupied.

"You know it's the granddaughter of the original owner. So, convincing her to sell—giving her an out—should be a piece of cake. Child's play. She's young, inexperienced, and from what I hear is doing a shit poor job of running a hotel."

His tone is demeaning, not only toward me, but Carys as well.

My jaw clenches and I twist my neck in an effort to relieve some of the pent-up frustration and tension. "I'll call you tomorrow after my meetings."

"The Blue Bayou, Maverick. Nail that or I will."

Over my dead fucking body.

Carys

"ARE YOU HUMMING?"

I look up from the filing cabinet and see Jules standing in the doorway of the office with his arms crossed over his chest.

"I don't know. Am I?"

He huffs out a breath and narrows his eyes at me. "Yes, you are. I've never noticed you humming before, and I'm trying to figure out why you'd be humming now."

"What's the big deal?" I ask, rolling my eyes at him.

"Listen, there are only two good reasons for humming: either you have a cock in your mouth, which you clearly do not, or you've recently had a cock in your mouth or somewhere else in your body, which is entirely possible, so that means you got laid!"

Where Jules was all serious and inquisitive two minutes ago, he's now all heart-eyes and big smiles while he claps his hands and jumps around the office. I, on the other hand, am craning my neck, making sure no one in the lobby heard him.

"Jules!" I whisper-yell, getting his attention. "For goodness' sake, calm down. Sorry to burst your bubble, but I did not get laid. No one got laid." I admit, there's disappointment laced in those words. Because I'd like to get laid.

His face completely falls and I don't know who's more upset with my declaration, me or him.

It's me, though. Definitely me.

"But, didn't you have a date with our resident dreamboat?"

"I did and it was wonderful, but there was no sexing going on, I can assure you."

Not for a lack of wanting, though.

The date really was great. I met Maverick in the lobby and he took me to a restaurant that was, again, new for both of us. We took our time eating and talking and ended up spending a good three hours at the place. I think we both needed some down time. Me, I'm always stressed with the hotel, but I could tell something was bothering Maverick. He eventually opened up to me and told me a little about the job he started doing for his dad while he's here. I got the feeling there was more to his story but I'm not going to force him to tell me anything he doesn't want to. The bottom line is, the poor guy was wiped out. He was so tired by the time we got back to the hotel, he didn't even put the moves on me. I was disappointed, of course, but I understood.

"Where's he from, anyway?" Jules asks with genuine curiosity.

"Dallas." Any mention of the fact that Maverick isn't from here and that he has a home, that is not the Blue Bayou, makes my chest ache.

"So, is it true what they say about those *long*horns?" Jules' tone is conspiratorial as he emphasizes the word *long* with a raise of his eyebrows.

I crack a smile, shaking my head with a laugh.

He huffs when he realizes I'm not answering that question and continues, "So, what's the hold-up, sister?"

"What do you mean? He's only been here a little over a week. What kind of girl do you think I am?"

"A girl that needs some dick, that's what. He has, what, another week left of his stay? That's just enough time to have some fun and then send him packing. You don't have to worry about falling in love or anything crazy like that, just use the man for his amazing body and be done with it."

If only it were that easy.

"But, Carys, if he breaks your heart, I don't want to know about it. He's just too pretty for me to hate."

I laugh at the man who's only been working here a short time but is quickly becoming a great friend.

"Scratch that," he amends. "Tell me so I can kick his ass. I won't like it, but I'll do it for you. Even though, I'm a lover, not a fighter, you know." Jules kisses my cheek, then heads back out to the lobby.

Turning back to my work, I try to get focused again. Even though I was *hoping* to wake up this morning in Maverick's bed, I woke up in mine, but unlike most mornings these days, I woke up well-rested and clear-headed. I was so happy about it, I decided to clean out the office while I felt motivated. Maybe that's why I've been humming. My mama used to say if a person is absentmindedly humming, that means they're truly happy.

Am I?

I guess I am, at least on some level. I love this hotel and I love the people I get to be around on a daily basis. I'm just ready for things to stop breaking and business to pick back up.

More money means less problems, right? Biggie Smalls may not agree, but it's what I'm hoping for.

An hour or so later, I've made some good progress. I have a substantial pile of papers to shred and my filing cabinet is cleaned out and organized. Now, I just need to finish cleaning off my desk and I'll be ready for a lunch break. Before I attack the stack of papers in front of me, though, I'm hit with inspiration regarding some plans I've been mulling over for the hotel, thanks to Maverick. So, I grab a notepad and pen and start making a list.

One of the things he suggested is that I use my connections in the city to help improve business here at the hotel, so I start writing down who I should contact and what services they provide. It won't be one-sided, of course. I'm willing to offer whatever it takes to make these possible joint ventures beneficial for all parties involved.

The first person that comes to mind is my friend CeCe. I've always thought it'd be cool to have a coffee bar in the lobby and I wonder if she'd be willing to set something like that up, or at least provide us with the coffee. Thinking about her now, I have to admit, I'm kind of embarrassed I got jealous over the idea of Maverick spending time at her coffee shop. The thought of them hooking up made me a little crazy. Admitting that, even to myself, makes me blush a little. I might need to wait a few more days before showing my face around there, maybe until Maverick is gone and out of the picture.

And that thought makes my chest ache, like always.

Frowning, I rub at the spot over my heart and take a deep breath before continuing with my list.

Next is Micah Landry from Lagniappe. I definitely want him on my short list for catering prospects. The food there is incredible, and he just seemed like a genuinely nice guy, definitely someone I'd like to do business with.

There's also a bar around the corner called Come Again that I've seen when I'm walking to and from the store I go to at the corner of Decatur. I've heard great things about it. Maybe I can hire a bartender or two from there if I ever have an event.

The idea of hosting events at the hotel has me spinning off into a whole new direction. I remember when my grandparents used to host parties here when I was growing up and I remember how magical they were. I loved watching the grown-ups dance and laugh under the twinkling lights. It was all so very romantic. I wouldn't even know where to begin on something like that, but my mind is racing with thoughts about the logistics, in a fun way. Nervous, but fun.

This train of thought causes me to start another list—things that need to be fixed or cleaned, as well as supplies to be bought. Once I'm done with that, I'm too pumped up to finish clearing my desk. It's not going anywhere, so I decide to take my lunch break early and find Maverick. I have a feeling he'll be just as excited about all of this as I am, if not more.

Stepping into the lobby, I walk to the side table and grab a glass of water. "Jules, have you seen Maverick today?"

"Yes, ma'am. He came in about an hour ago, mentioning phone calls that needed to be made and a shower that was calling his name." He pauses to look at me suggestively. "You thinkin' about crashing that shower?"

"No," I say, fighting a smile. "But," I pause, taking a healthy drink of water, partly to quench my thirst and partly to cool off since I'm now picturing Maverick naked and wet. "I do want to talk to him about some ideas I have to spruce this place up and I'm too excited to wait."

"Well, then, get up there, woman. I have everything under control down here."

"Thanks, Jules. I shouldn't be too long."

As I walk up the first flight of stairs, Jules yells, "Take as long as you need!" I ignore him and once I've cleared the second landing, I jog the rest of the stairs until I'm on Maverick's floor. Self-doubt starts to flood my body and mind as I approach his room. Maybe he doesn't want to be disturbed or maybe he's too busy to chat...or too tired from all the work he's been doing.

The closer I get to his door, the more convinced I become I'm overstepping boundaries and need to turn around and leave. I start to do just that when his door opens and Maverick steps out, startling us both.

"Hey." He pauses, looking me up and down. "Were you coming to see me?"

Damn, he looks good. His eyes seem tired and his beard seems fuller today than it was last night, but it works for him.

"I, um, yeah, I was, but now that I'm up here, I realize you're probably busy. We can, uh, chat later." I begin turning around when I feel his hand grip my arm, electricity flooding my body.

"No, this is perfect. I was just stepping out to get some ice for the room." He holds up the bucket to prove his point. "Why don't you go inside and wait for me. I'll be back in a sec."

"Oh, okay," is all I can manage to get out as I watch him walk away. Maverick's backside is a thing of beauty. His worn jeans hug his ass and it makes me want to take a bite.

Stepping into the room, it feels strange being in here without him. Even though I know these rooms like the back of my hand, it feels different—more intimate—like Maverick has made it his own. I take small steps and look around, noticing little things about Mr. Kensington. One, he's a pretty neat guy. I'm sure Mary made his bed this morning, but there's very little clutter in the room. Outside of a laptop and leather notebook on the desk, everything else is pretty much tucked away. And then, I spot something interesting.

On the bedside table is a stack of comic books, as well as a bag of candy. All kinds of candy, including some of New Orleans' famous pralines. Looks like my friend Maverick is a bit of a nerd with a sweet tooth, and learning these little tidbits only makes me fonder of him.

"Hey, I got you a Coke in case you're thirsty," Maverick announces as he walks inside. His eyes glance at where I'm standing and he gives me a nervous smile. "You found my stash, huh?"

"I did. That's quite a collection you have here."

"You don't offer porn here. I have to blow off steam somehow." He's no longer nervous or embarrassed as he stalks toward me, like a predator to his prey. When he reaches me, he wraps his arms around my waist and pulls me flush against him. He kisses me softly before whispering against my lips, "I'm glad you're here. I've missed you."

I can't help the smile that spreads across my face at his words. "I've missed you, too. Did you get a lot of work done?"

He lets out a deep sigh. "Yes and no. I have a couple of meetings later this afternoon, but I'm free now."

All thoughts of what brought me up here go flying out the window as he nips my collar bone.

Maverick slides his hands down and grabs my ass before kissing me again. This kiss, though, is nothing like the one before. This kiss is firm and confident and when his tongue pushes into my mouth, I gladly accept it. Kissing Maverick has quickly become one of my very favorite things. I love how he takes control but is also very intuitive to what I need or want. He always seems to know just when to change our position or the intensity of the kiss and he most definitely leaves me breathless and wanting more.

Like right now. I know it's not really the right time and it's not how he expressed how he wants our first time together to be, but I want him. Badly.

Maybe we don't have to go all the way this time. I mean, he pleasured me without benefitting the other day. Why can't I do the same for him?

His hands are all over me, caressing, squeezing, exploring. It's as if he's learning my body even though my clothes are still on, but I want them off. I want his off even more. I want to explore his body and learn what he likes and dislikes, what turns him on and what really drives him wild.

I want him.

I tug his shirt out from the waist of his jeans and push it up until he breaks our kiss and takes it off the rest of the way. Stepping away— already panting—I appraise him, and holy Jesus, his body is better than I'd imagined. His muscles aren't big and bulky but they're lean and well-defined, evidence of his love for working with his hands and going for runs. Maverick watches me as I study his torso, running my fingernails through the light smattering of hair on his chest, all the way down and over his abs. A hiss escapes his mouth and it's empowering, encouraging me to continue my exploration.

His belt is quickly undone, followed by the button and zipper of his jeans, but when I start to pull them down his legs, Maverick stops me.

"Do I get to undress you, too?"

I shrug and give him a small smile. "If you want."

"Oh, I want. I want very much. I have to admit, I'm a little surprised we're doing this now. Not complaining in any way, mind you, just surprised."

I reach my hand into where his jeans are open and palm his dick.

"I want to do what you did for me the other day. I can tell you've been tired and a little stressed, and I want to make you feel good."

"You always make me feel good, Carys. Don't feel like you have to pay me back."

"It's not payback. If anything, it's selfish on my part, because I've been fantasizing about this pretty much since we met."

The "fuck" that comes out of his mouth is barely a whisper and his eyelids are heavy, full of lust, as I finish taking his pants off, followed by his boxer briefs. It's now my turn to curse as I finally get to see him completely naked. Strong and lean, his body is simply perfect, but then there's his cock. I had no idea one could be so...I don't even know how to describe it. Pretty doesn't seem right or manly enough, but the only other word that comes to mind is delicious. It's fully erect with a gleaming head and I can't wait to get it into my mouth.

I swear, I've never been so anxious to give someone a blowjob in all my twenty-five years. Or more determined. I feel like a woman on a mission.

"Lay down," I tell him, pointing toward the bed.

"I will," he says with a slight chuckle, obviously getting a kick out of my tenacity. "But you're wearing way too many clothes. I wouldn't want you to be uncomfortable while you do whatever it is you plan on doing to me."

Laughing, partly at myself and partly at him, I pull my top off and slide out of my jeans.

"Hey, now, not so fast. I'm not going anywhere. Let me do the rest." Maverick's words calm me down but only briefly, because when he slips the bra strap off my shoulder and kisses the bare skin beneath, my heart starts racing again. Who knew that would be such a turn-on?

He does the same thing on the other shoulder before unhooking my bra and tossing it to the floor. I know, technically, his mouth has been on my boobs before and his fingers have been inside me, but standing here in front of him like this—naked, vulnerable, transparent—feels a million times more intimate. And intense.

"You're perfect," he murmurs before kissing my mouth. His hands are warm against my breasts, kneading them, pinching my nipples. His touch feels amazing, but it's distracting me from my mission, so I gently—or maybe not so gently—push him onto the bed.

His chuckles die down as soon as I position myself between his legs. Grasping his shaft, I waste no time circling my tongue around the tip before taking him fully into my mouth. My hair falls like curtains around me, but he's quick to move the strands away from my face so he can watch, gripping a handful of it at the nape of my neck.

I moan, which elicits one from him and his grip on my hair gets tighter, spurring me on.

So fucking hot.

I've never claimed to be an expert on going down on a guy but I'm not getting any complaints from Maverick. The few tricks I do know—swirling, sucking, licking—he seems to really like and when I improvise and try something new, he's equally vocal in his appreciation. Speaking of being vocal, I think I could orgasm just listening to his grunts and moans. Seriously, I'm so turned on right now, it's taking everything in my power not to straddle his leg and rub myself off.

No sooner do I think it, I feel Maverick lean up and grip my waist, lifting and twisting my body until I'm on top of him with his face right where I need it. He slaps my ass, not too hard, just enough to let me know he means business.

Well, this is new.

If I wasn't so aroused, I might be embarrassed with all my belongings out on full display, but I'm entirely too horny to care.

Maverick squeezes my ass where his hand had landed, rubbing and then biting, before he rips off my panties. Like, gone. The fabric pulls roughly against my skin, stinging before it gives way, but it's quickly forgotten as cool air hits the heat between my legs.

"Ah, yeah, that's much better," he says before pulling my pussy to his hot mouth. Even though I knew what was coming, I wasn't ready for how it'd actually feel to have Maverick's mouth on me like this. A loud gasp escapes me and all I can do is stroke his cock while I adjust to the sensations flooding my body.

Taking him back inside my mouth, I increase the suction while holding him firmly at his base. I'm able to distract myself from my looming orgasm by focusing on how Maverick's hips are rocking, pushing himself farther down my throat. I don't even think he's meaning to do it; it's instinctual and I love it. Just like Maverick seems to love it when I grind against him, or as he just so eloquently put it, "fuck his face".

His tongue flicks my clit over and over, like it's his job, and I know I won't be able to hold off much longer. I cup his balls, gently squeezing and pulling, causing his mouth to pull away from my center. He curses and calls out my name as he comes, his hot breath making my pussy ache for its own release. I continue to pump him until his body relaxes and his breathing returns to normal.

"Turn around." His voice is deep and raspy and I want to wrap myself in it forever.

I sit up and look over my shoulder at him, a bit confused by what he commanded.

"I need you on my face again, but I want you to turn around so I can watch you come."

Well, okay, then.

And, yes, sir.

Once I'm situated the way Maverick wants me, he wastes no time pulling my body back down to his greedy mouth.

"Holy shit," I yell, grabbing onto the headboard for dear life. It's even more intense, more amazing like this, and I am not prepared.

"Grab your tits. I want to see you touch yourself."

I do as he says and every time I pull my nipples, he sucks my clit into his mouth. I'm grinding so hard against him, he can't speak, but I can tell by his moans he's enjoying this as much as I am.

Well, almost as much.

"Fuck, Maverick, I'm coming!" He manages to nod his head in approval while tightening his grip on my hips and holding me against his mouth. His tongue works its magic and soon I'm seeing stars as my orgasm hits like a tsunami, releasing wave after wave of pleasure.

I'm barely coherent as Maverick gently shifts me to my back before getting a warm washcloth from the bathroom and cleaning us both up. When my orgasmic haze clears, I see him looking down at me, his face close, with the sweetest smile I think I've ever seen.

"So, uh, when can we do that again?" he asks.

I laugh loudly, thankful that he's able to look at me like that and set me at ease, because for a split second, I was scared it was going to be awkward. Then, I pull him to me, kissing him with as much passion as I can muster right now.

Eventually, we get dressed and he shares his candies, as we exchange knowing looks of *that just happened* and passing kisses. I can't help wondering, if what we just did was this amazing, how will I survive having actual sex with Maverick?

I'm not sure.

And there's a good chance I won't make it.

But I'm dying to find out.

"What did you come up here to talk to me about?" Maverick asks as we're sitting on the bed.

"Oh." I laugh, feeling my cheeks heat up a little with the reminder of what I actually came here for, because trust me when I say I did not know *that* was going to happen. Do you ever truly plan for a life-changing orgasm? "I just wanted to tell you about some ideas I have for the hotel...you know, cross-promo kind of things."

"Hit me with it," Maverick says with enthusiasm.

"So, first of all, I was thinking I'd have our old brochures redone and take them to Lagniappe, Neutral Grounds, Come Again...that bar around the corner," I tell him, pointing over my shoulder in the direction of the bar.

Maverick's eyes light up in approval. "What else?"

"Well, I remember Micah mentioned that his sister-in-law was opening an art gallery down the street," I begin, nervously fidgeting with the bed sheets we recently messed up, until Maverick's hand lands on top of mine and he forces me to look at him.

"Whatever you're thinking, it's not stupid."

"How'd you know I was thinking that?"

He shrugs. "You only fidget when you're nervous or anxious. I figured that out the first day I met you."

I smile and roll my eyes at him. The fact that he pays attention and notices those sort of things makes my stomach do this weird flip. "Anyway, I remember when I was young and my grandparents would host these parties. I was thinking I could get in touch with his sister-in-law and see if she'd like to do an art show in the courtyard. I could include other businesses, like coffee from CeCe's, and maybe have it catered from Lagniappe. And I'd need a bartender."

"That sounds like a great idea," he encourages. "I'm serious. It would be fun for any guests staying here, but it would also give the hotel some much-needed exposure. Plus, you could take some pictures and update your website and social media accounts."

"That's what I was thinking." I smile even wider, happy that he's here for me to talk about stuff like this. Then my smile falls, because he won't be here forever. "Maybe you could come back...sometime...for..."

"You're not getting rid of me."

"Okay," I tell him, feeling relieved at his words. They're not a promise or anything written in stone, but I trust Maverick. He's never been anything but honest with me. So, if he says he'll be back, I have to believe he will be.

When it's time for us both to get back to work, we don't make promises or plans. We both know whatever is happening between us is unexpected and unrehearsed, and for me, at least, it's something I've never experienced before. So, we have to tread carefully.

As I'm making my way down the steps and into the lobby, I realize what I must look like. My clothes are all put on correctly—except my panties, of course—but I didn't really put any effort into taming my hair. Passing the large mirror in the foyer, I see myself—pink cheeks, bright eyes, and wild blonde locks.

Yeah, I totally have sex hair.

When I reach the front desk, Jules looks up, and without saying a word sticks his hand in the air in front of me. I slap it, giving him the high five he's requesting.

"It's about damn time," he says, going back to the glossy magazine in front of him.

Feeling completely smug and satisfied, I walk back into the office and plop into the chair at the desk. I can't help the smile that takes over my face and the quiet laugh that escapes. Humming to myself, I go back to the large stack of papers.

Maverick

WHEN I WOKE UP THIS MORNING, I REGRETTED NOT going to Carys last night. I thought about it, about her, until I fell asleep looking over some final numbers for an offer I made this morning on one of the alternative properties. So, after I made my phone calls and shot off a few emails, one being to my father to keep him off my back today, I showered and now I'm walking down the stairs to the lobby.

No regrets. That's my motto for the day—for this week. I know my time in New Orleans is short and I know I've only known Carys for a couple of weeks, less really, but I feel like there's potential and I'm going to pursue the shit out of it—*her*—until I'm forced to leave.

"Carys Matthews," I say, waltzing up to the front desk and catching her off guard.

Her eyes go wide and her smile follows suit when she sees me. I love evoking this kind of response from her. I love that she's always happy to see me. I love how easy she is to be around and how good she makes me feel. Not just sexually. Carys Matthews feels like new beginnings and possibilities, and she makes me believe I can have those things too.

"Maverick Kensington," she replies in a faux-professional tone. "How was your evening?"

"It was great, but my afternoon was exponentially better. I have to say the amenities here at the Blue Bayou are exceptional."

"You know, speaking of updating our website, you should really consider leaving that in a review..." she trails off as she fights another smile, her cheeks turning a lovely shade of pink.

"I'd also like to commend your ability to, uh, unclog the...pipes... in my room."

She laughs. And, oh, God, Carys' laugh. It's not tinkling or like angels singing, like some girls' laughs are described. It's real and intentional, just like her. Not to mention, contagious.

"Ahem." She clears her throat and forces herself to rein it in. "Yes, and I hope that's all working properly this morning?"

Contemplating, I bite my lip. "Well, I might need you to take a look later."

"I am at your service." Her voice dips and her teeth scrape against her bottom lip. I'm not sure if it's on purpose, but it goes straight to my dick and all I can think about is that pretty mouth wrapped around my cock. Those teeth grazing my sensitive skin. Her tongue wrapping around...

Now, I'm clearing my throat, and discreetly reaching down to adjust my hard-on. Fuck.

"I was going to ask you if you'd like to show me around the Quarter today," I tell her, subconsciously running pictures of dead puppies and saggy granny titties in my mind on replay. "If you're not busy."

I'm rewarded with a soft, sweet smile for this offer, one that I hope means she's going to take me up on it. Because I need to be near her, hold her hand, smell her delectable scent, and listen to her laugh. I don't know what any of this means. I'm not trying to label it or put it in a box. I'm just letting myself feel.

"I'd love that," she finally says. "Let me see if Mary's finished with the rooms yet. She probably won't mind manning the desk until George gets here in an hour."

"Sounds great," I tell her, smiling across the desk at her in relief and...happiness. That's the only way to describe it. Carys makes me happy.

While I wait on her to track down Mary, I check my phone for any return responses. The property owner I sent the proposal to replied back that he'll think about it and give me a call later tonight. My father sent back his typical three-word response: get it done. Sighing heavily, I slide the phone back in my pocket and try to forget about all of that, focusing on the beautiful girl bouncing down the steps and into the lobby.

"Let's go." She grabs my hand and practically pulls me out the front doors where we're greeted by the dog that frequents the Bayou. "Oh, no, Rusty, not today. You march yourself home." Carys talks to the dog like he's a human, and it's the most adorable thing I've witnessed in a long time. "Go on home."

When she points in the direction he came from, Rusty obeys, albeit reluctantly, and tucks tail as he walks home, or where I'm assuming home is.

"Rusty a friend of yours?" I ask as I slide my sunglasses down over my eyes and we begin to walk.

"Ha," she laughs, looking over her shoulder to make sure he's doing as she told him. "We're friends until he ransacks my lobby. Ornery doesn't even begin to describe him, but he definitely takes after his owner. Have you met Floyd? He drives a horse and carriage around the square. Watch out for that one." Her warning falls flat due to the sentimental smile on her face, telling me she really cares about him.

She cares about a lot of people.

And as she takes me around the Quarter, I start to see more of who she is and how she became this wonderful person. And people really care about her too.

"Have you met Betty?" she asks as we walk up the east side of Jackson Square. Pointing to the lady sitting at the small table with the pink umbrella, I realize she means the palm reader I've spoken to on a couple of occasions.

"Uh..."

"Let me introduce you. She's fantastic. I used to hang with her all the time when I was younger."

Before I can protest or clarify, she's pulled me over to the table and Betty is smiling up at us. "Hey, Betty!" Carys says enthusiastically. "I wanted to introduce you to my friend...Maverick."

"We've met," Betty informs. "Well, not properly, but we've met." She gives me a wicked smile before patting the table. "Sit."

Carys urges me toward the table. "Come on, this is fun."

"Uh," I go to make an excuse, but Betty cuts me off.

"Sit, I don't bite...not hard, anyway."

"Oh, God. You're so bad." Carys swats a hand toward Betty and they both laugh.

"Don't tell me you don't wanna take a nibble out of this one?" she asks Carys, like I'm not sitting right in front of her. Her eyes are focused on my palm, but she cuts them up at me. "You're picky when it comes to love." I feel her finger move gently across a line on my palm. "But you have had lovers, none of them serious."

I swallow, because that's true. I'm not celibate, but I've never felt like I've been in love before.

"This," she says, drawing a line down my palm. "This tells me you're logical and organized, but you also have a sense of adventure and enthusiasm for life."

Clearing my throat, I shift in my seat, because I've always felt that way, but having someone validate it makes me feel vulnerable. Even if that someone is Betty the Palm Reader.

"You have good health and stamina." On this note, she looks up at Carys and waggles her eyebrows. "Very good in bed."

"Betty," Carys chides, but I hear her chuckle under her breath.

"You've got a deep fate line," she says, pointing to a line that runs up the middle of my palm. "This means you'll be strongly controlled by fate, but see how it joins your life line here?"

I follow where she's pointing and nod.

"This tells me you're a self-made individual. Whatever dreams you have or feel like you were born with, follow those."

Staring at my hand, I swallow hard again. How can a three-minute chat with a palm reader feel so life altering? Can some lines on my palm really hold that kind of information?

"Your fame line is strong," she says nonchalantly after a few long seconds. "Any aspirations of being a model?"

Now, it's my turn to laugh and I'm grateful for the change in atmosphere. "Ha, no."

"One marriage line. That's good."

Something tells me Betty is now reading my palm more for her benefit than mine. Her musings become more introspective, like she's taking inventory.

When she's finished, she turns my palm over and pats the top, like a grandmother would. Smiling, she says, "This one is on the house." With a wink to Carys, she conveys something like approval and I can't help but smile.

And to think I was scared of Betty. Well, not scared, but leery. I wonder if there's anything she's not telling me because Carys is here. Maybe I'll stop back by on my own sometime and get the full report?

"Do you want to have yours read?" I ask Carys.

She shakes her head. "Nah, I've had mine read so many times. I think Betty and I both know the results like the back of our hand. No pun intended."

They both laugh and Betty reaches across and squeezes Carys' hand. "How've you been, sweetie?"

"Good," Carys says with a sigh. "Busy. Sorry I haven't been by lately." She offers her an apologetic smile. "Oh, but I did want to tell you I started making macarons for the lobby. You know, like my grandmother used to. So, you'll have to stop by sometime or I can bring you some."

"Sounds wonderful." Betty beams as Carys and I stand to leave. "I'll see you around, Maverick."

It's not a question, it's a statement, and it makes me think she can do more than read palms.

"Betty knows everything," Carys whispers as we walk away. "Like, it's kinda creepy, but cool. When I was younger, she'd know what I was thinking before I ever did. I think she told my mom ahead of time. Not like ratting me out, but just to keep me out of harm's way. I guess you could say she's a fairy godmother, of sorts."

"A palm-reading fairy godmother," I muse, using my body to block Carys from a group of people walking by on the sidewalk. "What other surprises do you have for me today?"

I feel her looking at me before I make eye contact. It's intense and full of unsaid words. Unable to stop myself, I direct her into an alcove and kiss her, good and hard and proper.

"What was that for?" she asks with hooded eyes and breathless words.

"For being you," I admit honestly. "I don't need another reason, but if you must know, sometimes I feel like kissing you because it's a Wednesday. I *want* to kiss you because the sun rose this morning...and because of this freckle." I brush my thumb across her cheek, right over my favorite one. "For any and every reason I can think of, and for no good reason at all."

Her eyes are always bright and blue, but I watch as they start to shine even brighter. "Stop," she mutters. "You can't say stuff like that and expect me to walk down the street like a normal human being."

"It's the truth," I shrug, lacing my fingers through hers as we continue walking.

"It's too much," she sighs. "You're too much."

I don't respond to that, because I kind of feel the same way about her—like she's too much, and also like I can't get enough. When thoughts like that enter my mind, I'm slapped with the reminder that my time here has an expiration date that's quickly approaching.

Could I do a long-distance relationship?

Would I want one with Carys?

Glancing over at her, I feel like I already know the answer to that. I think I'd be willing to take her any way I could get her. And I mean that in every sense of the word.

A ruckus comes from somewhere down the street and Carys' grip on my hand tightens.

"Ever joined a second line parade?" she asks. When she turns around to look at me, her smile is wicked and her eyes are wild with delight as she begins to jog down the sidewalk, pulling me along. She looks like an angel and a thought crosses my mind: I'd follow her anywhere.

Carys

"So, you and Mr. Maverick," Mary starts as we tackle the last of the rooms that need new linens. Due to an increase in guests, we've been so busy, meeting ourselves coming and going. For a while, things were slow enough that Mary could take her time cleaning rooms and preparing them for the next guest, but now, thankfully, business has picked up and she needs my help on a daily basis.

It's great, except I'm exhausted.

"Me and Mr. Maverick, what?" I ask, breathing heavily as we lift the mattress and tuck the sheets in nice and tight, just like my grandmother taught me.

I know one thing me and Maverick aren't: getting busy. Please see my previous comment about being exhausted. Also, Jules has been filling in for someone at Revelry, meaning he hasn't been able to fill in for me during the night shift. Meaning, I haven't had time for sex. I want it. I know Maverick would give it to me. He tells me all about it with his deliciously, filthy mouth. Sure, we've made the most of the last few days, but most of the time we've spent together has been in public places. I feel like every time we try to sneak off to his room or my apartment, a crisis arises or someone needs something.

"You're sweet on him." She smiles over at me with a wink. For someone old enough to be my grandmother, she's a shameless flirt and a hopeless romantic. She's also more boy crazy than someone half her age...or half mine, for that matter. Mary is always the first one to point out a fine specimen. However, I also know that she only window shops, because no one has Mary's attention quite like George.

"I am," I admit, because there's really no reason to lie. Besides, she'd see right through me if I tried.

I like Maverick.

I like him a lot.

"How much longer will he be staying with us?" This time, when she asks the question, she can't quite look me in the eyes.

"Another few days," I tell her, feeling the twinge of pain in my chest that accompanies my thoughts every time they turn to Maverick leaving. "He's already extended his stay twice. When he first showed up, he'd just planned on spending a few days. Then his father called and gave him a job to do while he's here, scoping out some properties or something like that. He called yesterday and asked for a few more days."

Our time is short; I've known that from the get-go. I also know I'll miss him. These last couple of weeks have been a whirlwind of unexpectedness—romance, happiness, him...none of it was planned. For the past week, Maverick and I have spent every free second together, both of us with an unspoken understanding that he'll be going back to his real world soon—Dallas, his job, his father. Five hundred miles away. That's how far it is from here to there. It doesn't seem like much until I think about not seeing him every day and the possibility that what we've had is fleeting.

"What about when he leaves?" Mary prompts.

"We haven't really discussed it." I blow a stray hair out of my face and walk to the cart for a dust rag and cleaner. "I'd like to stay in touch, at least."

"And him?"

"I think he'd like the same." I shrug, turning to wipe down the desk and side tables. "I hope. But I guess, there's a chance I'll never see him again."

I've been forcing myself to be a realist these past few days, preparing my heart for whatever's coming.

My chest really aches with that admission.

Mary sighs, walking across the room before asking, "And you'd be okay with that?"

"I guess I'll have to be." I try to make the words sound sure and strong, but my voice wavers. "I told myself going into this that I'd have to be alright with him walking away. I knew his time here was short and temporary. It might just be a...fling. People have those every day, right?"

Standing in the middle of the room, Mary looks at me with one hand on the vacuum and one on her hip. I'm staring back at her, begging her with my eyes to say yes...or no...or at least that everything is going to work out fine. Because I'd believe her, no matter what. Mary never lies to me.

"Yes, but not everyone is you, Carys. I know you, you wear your heart on your sleeve. You've been guarding it well the last few years, but this man has found a loophole. He's gotten in there. I can see it on your face when you talk about him and I can see it in your eyes when you look at him." She pauses, giving me a soft, wary smile. "Be careful. I know I'm the one who told you to go for it, and I meant everything I said. You should get out there, give your heart a chance, but don't fall for someone who won't be around to catch you."

There's something like regret in Mary's expression, like she feels responsible for me falling for Maverick.

Not that I've fallen for Maverick.

"I've only known him two weeks," I say absentmindedly.

"Your grandfather proposed to your grandmother after one month of knowing her. The only reason it took him that long—"

"Was because he had to wait until her father came to the States to ask his permission," I finish for her, knowing the story by heart.

"You are your grandfather's girl," Mary whispers with a tinge of pride, and also heartache. "There's so much of him in you."

"Except all the know-how to make this place run successfully," I reply, huffing out a laugh and biting the inside of my cheek to keep from crying. All this talk about Maverick and my grandparents has my emotions riding a tidal wave.

"You've got that too. You're already doing so much better. I saw what you did with the office, and George was telling me about your ideas on involving the community." Mary pauses for a second, walking toward me and taking my hands in hers. "That is a move straight out of Jenson Matthews' playbook. You're going to figure it all out. It just takes time."

"Thanks, Mary," I tell her, leaning into her and letting her warm arms surround me. Her hug and scent are so familiar. I feel like I'm wrapped in my favorite blanket. "Not just for saying you believe in me, but for always being here. I don't know what I'd do without you and George."

"Well, we're not going anywhere, honey." She sighs, pushing me back by my shoulders and forcing me to stand tall. "We're family. That's what families do."

After drying my eyes and finishing the room, I head downstairs on a mission. I'm going to finish getting the office in tip-top shape today. It's going to look so good, it would meet my grandfather's approval.

I want to make him proud.

"Hey, Jules," I say when I see his bright smiling face at the desk. "Thanks for working a double today."

"No probs, Care." He smiles offering me his cheek to kiss. And then the other. "I need the extra hours. Do you know how much textbooks cost these days? I'm trying to make it through law school without having to sell my first born to gypsies to pay for my student loans."

I laugh, shaking my head. "Good looks and brains. You're going to make some man very happy one of these days."

"Girl, I can cook too." The look of pure confidence on his face makes me laugh again.

"You're the total package."

"Mm hmm. That's what he said." Jules goes back to busying himself with something on the computer. "Well, something about my package...and the size of it."

"Okay, on that note, you can find me in my office."

"Yes, ma'am, boss ma'am."

"Don't call me ma'am."

"Boss bitch."

"Better."

I work for what feels like hours, opening old mail that should've been opened the day it came in the door, filing old bills, sorting receipts and papers. My grandfather and mother ran a tight ship. They would've never let things get like this, but I also remember how things were after my grandfather passed away. It took my mother a couple of months to pull herself together and get caught up. So, I try to give myself a bit of a break. Sure, my eighteen months is a bit longer than her two, but she had a lot more experience than me. Plus, she was already basically running the everyday business of the hotel by the time my grandfather died. I was a frivolous college student, staying up too late, eating too much junk food, drinking too much coffee... partying on the weekends and not thinking past the next paper or test.

My days were spent here at the hotel, but I wasn't responsible for anything. My mother would probably say she did me a disservice, but I'd say she was letting me live. And I did. I loved my life. I missed my grandmother, and especially my grandfather, but I had Mary and George and my mama. It was an easy life.

Looking at the semi-organized mess, I sigh.

Every time I'm in here, I feel like I'm missing something. Like there's a piece of the puzzle I'm forgetting. Fortunately, my mother had what I like to call a master list of important items. I found it the day after she died. Weirdly, it was sitting in the middle of the desk, like she knew she wasn't going to be here any longer and that I'd need some instruction.

George and Mary get paid every Friday.

Mr. Johnson picks up the rugs and linens on Tuesdays and drops them back off on Wednesday morning. Pay him at drop-off.

Sales tax reports are due quarterly. Never skip this.

Insurance is paid yearly. Mr. Collins will call you for payment.

Utilities are due on the 25th of every month.

Miss Lily has the best flowers. Buy them for the foyer.

And that's where it ends. It feels incomplete. Maybe it's because I miss her and I *know* there was so much more for her to teach me. Maybe it's because if you look closely, it looks like there's a mark where a next line would be...a small dot on the paper under the last line. Maybe that's my crazy, overactive imagination. Maybe it's because I've looked at this paper—touched this paper—at least once a day for the last five hundred and forty-eight days.

Sighing deeply, I put the piece of paper back in the drawer for safe keeping. As I push my chair back a little to stretch, I take inventory of the stacks and try to decide what to do next. I've got everything in piles of how important they look. If it's from the state or the IRS, it's in one pile. If it's from the city, it's in another pile. If it's a credit card offer or coupons, it's in the shred pile.

"Knock, knock."

My favorite voice draws my eyes to the door. Maverick is standing there looking like someone who just stepped out of a magazine, one catering to hard-working sex gods with perfect scruff and perfectly imperfect hair. Blue eyes blaze, taking me in, as a wicked smirk forms on his perfect lips.

Perfect.

Perfect timing.

Perfect distraction.

Perfect man.

"Hey," I finally reply. My voice sounding raspy from non-use.

"How long have you been in here?" he asks, stepping further into the office. I'm hoping he'll shut the door behind him, so we can have more of the office fun time he's gifted me with over the last few days, but he doesn't. He stops just short of the desk and crosses his strong arms over his chest, drawing my attention to the button-down shirt he's wearing. Lately, he's been living in t-shirts and worn jeans, which is perfectly okay with me. But I do love him like this.

"Going somewhere?" I counter, with my own question.

"You first."

"A while," I reply, fighting a yawn. "I think I need to stretch my legs."

Maverick quirks an eyebrow. "I can help with that."

I nod, slowly standing from my chair. "What did you have in mind?"

"Dinner. My place."

"Oh, really?" I ask, unable to keep the smile from my face. "You cook?"

"I order," he says in a husky tone, leaning over my desk, coming closer but not close enough. So, I do the same, making up the difference.

"Oh, really?" I ask again, but this time, my lips are practically touching his. "I think I might like that."

"I was hoping you'd say that."

Maverick

"WHY ARE WE TAKING THE ELEVATOR?" SHE ASKS
with a squeal as I back her against the wall before the door even has a
chance to shut.

"Because I've been thinking about having you in tight quarters
all fucking day," I confess, pressing my arousal against her as I lean
forward and kiss her neck.

I had every intention of walking Carys up the stairs, taking my
time, talking to her about what's been on my mind lately—her, us, and
some sort of long distance relationship. I knew right then why they say
the road to hell is paved with good intentions. Because my intentions
had been fucking honorable as hell, until the second I saw her.

Her hair a mess of blonde, piled on top of her head.

V-neck t-shirt that shows just the top swell of her breasts.

Then she stood up and I all I saw were her bare legs.

And a vision of them wrapped around me.

Carys' laugh fills the small elevator and it spurs me on even more.
A few more seconds in this thing and I'd have her naked, plunging

deep inside her.

Maybe we'll do that.

One of these days.

"What if someone—" she starts on a moan, but I cut off her what-ifs when I pull down her t-shirt and expose her bra, dipping my tongue under the lace and then sucking the edge of one of her nipples into my mouth.

"Maverick." My name is part invocation, part admonition.

"I've been thinking about you all day," I groan around her soft skin. "Fuck...I've been thinking about nothing but you since the night I walked through those front doors." The confession is easy.

Looking up, I watch as her hooded eyes slowly go wide and a lazy smile caresses her lips. "You have?"

"Yeah," I swallow, ready to tell her exactly how I feel about her, but she's the culprit this time. She launches herself at me, pushing me back against the opposite wall and making the small elevator shake. I have no choice but to catch her as she wraps her long legs around my waist.

Fuck talking.

Talking is overrated.

I'll show her exactly how I feel.

Stumbling out into the hallway, I make it to my room on rote memory. As I fish the key out of my pocket, I'm thankful for the piece of antiquity. It's easy to find and easy to slip into the lock. Carys' lips are devouring mine, her hands laced into my hair, as I push the door open and then kick it closed behind me.

Once we're inside the room, she pauses, pulling back to look at me. "You got shrimp and grits," she moans, like it's part of the foreplay.

"How'd you know?" I ask, loving the way she's looking at me with hooded eyes and swollen lips, knowing I did that to her. I own this look of ecstasy and it's delectable; *she's* delectable. As good as the food smells, Carys is better. I could have her for breakfast, lunch, and dinner. And I plan on starting right now.

Leaning forward, she places her lips near my ear, whispering, "It's my second favorite smell in the world." When she sucks the sensitive skin into her mouth, grazing it with her teeth, it sends shivers down my body, straight to my cock.

"What's your first?" I manage to ask, loving the way she feels, needing more everything.

More of her sweet words.

More or her sweet skin.

More of her sweet mouth.

More Carys.

She stops, meeting my gaze—deep and unguarded. Swiping her tongue along her bottom lip before answering, "You...Maverick." Her tone is vulnerable, yet confident. "I want you. Now. Please."

"We can take our time," I offer, wanting her to know we don't have to rush, not this time.

Normally, when we sneak off to make out, we never know how long we'll have, so we're used to going fast. But I talked to Jules and he told me he'd cover for Carys tonight. And even though my mind knows that, I'm having to convince my dick to slow its roll, because it has one objective—sinking into Carys' warm, wet heat.

But I want to savor this. I want to savor her.

"You're leaving soon," she adds, a hint of sadness dulling her bright blue eyes.

"Not tonight." I wish I could say never, but I can't. "And Jules is covering for you, so we've got time."

When her smile returns, it's slow and assuming. "All night?"

"All night."

She loosens her legs on my waist and slides down my body, reigniting the fire I felt in the elevator. Without another word, she steps back and quickly untucks her t-shirt, pulling it over her head. She then shimmies her shorts down her legs. Her bra and panties follow close behind, and the next thing I know, she's standing in front of me with nothing on, making my mouth water and my heart practically beat out of my chest.

With her eyes glued to mine, she reaches up and unties her hair, letting her blonde waves cascade over her shoulders.

I take a minute to appreciate and memorize the perfection that is Carys. I want to take this vision, her memory, with me. She's carved out a place in my heart I'll never get back, but I wouldn't want it, even if I could.

"You need to get naked," she says with an even tone, her mouth curving up with a hint of mischief and confidence. It's fucking sexy as hell.

She's fucking sexy as hell.

Without preamble, I discard my shirt and step out of my jeans and boxers. Her eyes blaze as she greedily takes in my body, not even trying to hide the fact she's gawking. We've been semi-naked before, half-clothed, but not like this. So, I give her a moment, letting her gaze own me.

Turnabout is fair play.

But I can't stand the small distance between us. I need her. I need to touch her and feel her...hear her.

When my hands are literally itching to touch her, I stalk forward, backing her up until her knees hit the bed and she falls back. Placing my hands on either side of her, I stare down, taking her in—blonde hair everywhere, cheeks flushed, freckles peppered on her nose and cheeks...those eyes. I remember the first day I saw her, I couldn't quite tell if they were green or blue or some crazy combination, but now I know they're blue, just a unique shade...and they change depending on her mood and what she's wearing. Right now, they're a bright blue—needy and excited.

"You're so fucking gorgeous," I tell her, leaning forward to sweep my mouth over hers, letting our lips touch but not lingering.

Teasing.

Tasting.

Tempting.

"Maverick," Carys moans as I do the same with the lower half of our bodies, letting my cock graze her slit. "I need..."

"Don't worry," I whisper. "I'm gonna take care of you."

Moving back down her body, I place soft open-mouthed kisses to her skin. Kneeling on the bed and towering above her, I lift her and toss her playfully where I want her, eliciting a squeal. "Stop manhandling me," she demands with a laugh.

"I'm getting ready to manhandle the shit out of you," I warn, crawling back up the bed like a predator. Stopping at my favorite place, her pussy, I dip my head and dart my tongue out, loving the way she bucks at the contact. The more I lap and suck, the more she whimpers and grinds herself into my face.

I fucking love it.

Sliding two fingers inside her sweet, wet heat, I pump them in tandem with the strokes of my tongue on her clit. It doesn't take long until she's gripping the sheet and writhing beneath me.

"Oh, God. Ahh," she moans, letting out a soft scream as her hands go to my hair and she pulls, driving me wild.

I want to hear her pleasure.

I want everything she has to offer.

"Come for me, Carys," I coax. "I want to hear it."

Her hips lift off the bed and then her legs tense as her orgasm crashes through her. I can feel her walls squeezing as I continue to massage her slowly, making sure she gets every last fucking drop of bliss.

When she's panting and pulling on my shoulders, silently begging me for more, I kneel on the bed and reach over to the nightstand, grabbing a condom from the box I procured a few days ago in anticipation of this moment.

Ripping the package with my teeth, I look down to see Carys watching me intently, her bottom lip trapped by her teeth. Expectation, longing, need, want...so many emotions are etched all over her beautiful face and I want to give her everything.

"You're gorgeous. Have I told you that lately?" I ask, pinching the tip of the condom and rolling the latex down my shaft, stroking myself lightly. I don't need any help getting hard. Carys makes me hard by breathing...by fucking existing.

"Uh, you might've mentioned it right before that mind-blowing orgasm," she says with a hint of shyness to her voice. I watch as she swallows hard, glancing down between us, eyes on my cock.

"I just don't want you to forget it...ever," I tell her softly, decidedly, as I lean down and use my knees to spread her legs wider, giving me room to settle between them.

"You're gorgeous too," Carys says in a rush. "Beautiful." One of her hands comes up to brush a piece of hair from my forehead; such a tender gesture for a moment like this. But her other hand is firmly on my ass, squeezing.

I kiss her. Once. Twice. Then, I pull back just in time to see her face as I push inside her.

Carys and I have been intimate with each other before and it's always fucking fantastic, but this—finally being inside her, feeling her warmth surround me, pulsing and pulling me deeper—it's even more than I was expecting or hoping for. It's better than any fantasy I've had about Carys or anyone, for that matter.

Looking into her eyes, hooded but alight with passion, I'm certain she feels the same way.

Her lips are parted, so I take advantage and slip my tongue inside her mouth, kissing her deeply and matching the rhythm of my thrusts.

"Ahhh," Carys cries out in pleasure, pulling her knees back, allowing me to bury myself deep inside her. The room is filled with her moans and the sound of our bodies coming together.

Deeper.

Harder.

More.

"It's so good...so fucking good, Mav."

"I know, baby, I know," I tell her, gritting my teeth in an effort to pace myself, wanting this to last forever, but already feeling the coiling in the pit of my stomach. "You feel incredible, like your sweet pussy was made for me, so tight and perfect. I can't get enough of you."

"I love your dirty talk," she pants. "Now, fuck me faster."

"Your wish, my command," is all I can grunt out as I speed up my movements. Straightening my arms, I lean back, causing my pelvic bone to hit Carys' clit with every push. When she cries out, I feel her walls tighten around my dick.

Beads of sweat drip from my forehead onto her beautiful breasts, mingling with her own, and I immediately lean forward to lick the moisture off her nipples.

"Yes...uhh...do that again," she demands and I'm more than happy to oblige. I absolutely love that Carys isn't shy or afraid to tell me what she wants. In fact, it turns me on even more, and I didn't think that was possible.

Pleasure begins to build at the base of my spine and I know I can't hold off much longer. Carys moves her hands back to my ass and pulls me closer to her. I slip my hand between us and rub her clit, giving her the friction she's so desperately searching for. We're both close, toeing the line between the growing tension in our bodies and the ecstasy that awaits us once we fall.

Finally, the tautness snaps and we come. It's fast, it's loud, and it's everything we've been working toward for the past two weeks. Pure bliss rushes through my body as I spill inside the condom, leaving me feeling completely spent.

Carys is still shuddering and holding onto me tightly, making the most delicious noises in my ear. The sights and sounds of her orgasm are my new favorite things, and I want to experience them over and over.

"I knew it," Carys says in a voice that is deep and scratchy and sexy as hell.

"What's that?"

"I knew sex with you would kill me dead." Her laugh is otherworldly, blissed out, and pure sex goddess. "In all the best ways, of course."

"But, what a way to go, am I right?" I pepper her neck with hot kisses as she continues to laugh this lazy, sedated, amazing laugh. I've always loved Carys' laugh, but this is a new one and I want to own it. No one gets this one but me.

A deep sigh is her only response as she tangles her fingers in my hair. She's relaxed and content, without an ounce of stress, and she's absolutely breathtaking. I wrap my arms around her, turning so she's laying on my chest. With deep breaths, I inhale her scent, marking this moment in my mind.

How am I going to leave her in a few days?

It hurts too much to think about, so instead, I distract myself by kissing her until we're both panting and ready for round two.

Carys

WAKING DUE TO THE URGENCY OF MY BLADDER, IT takes me a second to realize where I am.

Maverick's room.

In Maverick's arms.

And deliciously sore in all the right places, thanks to our multiple rounds of sex throughout the night.

Craning my neck while trying not to wake him, I see that it's only five in the morning. A tiny bit of early morning light is coming through the sheer curtains, just enough to let me make out Maverick's features. He's beautiful, always, but especially when he's sleeping. The night he fell asleep in the lobby while I was working, I indulged myself, watching him—his long eyelashes that should be illegal for a guy, his chiseled jaw that could cut glass, his high cheekbones.

Softly, I reach up and run a featherlight touch across his cheek and then follow that with a kiss to his jaw. He doesn't budge. I don't blame him. There's no good reason to be awake right now, except for the fact that if I don't get to the bathroom, I'm going to have a situation on my hands and some explaining to do.

As I slip out of bed and tiptoe my way across the room, I bump into the desk. A folder, that must've been precariously positioned, falls to the floor and papers scatter.

"Shit," I whisper, glancing over to make sure Maverick is still out. Sighing in relief when I see he's completely unaware of my clumsiness, I continue to the bathroom to take care of business.

When I'm done, I leave the door cracked and the light on, so I can see to clean up my mess.

Kneeling on the floor, I begin to collect the papers, shuffling them into a stack, until something catches my eye.

Blue Bayou — 123 St. Ann, New Orleans, LA
Owner — Carys Matthews
5200 SF
12 rooms
Approx. Value — 1.2m
Proposed Purchase Price — 899,999

My heart starts beating fast as my eyes scan the document in my hand, and then I scan it again, trying to make sense of what I'm reading. All of this is information on the Blue Bayou. I begin to flip through the rest of the papers, searching for anything that would tell me what this is all about. I know I shouldn't. These are Maverick's papers, but this is about me and I have a right to know.

There's information on every property surrounding the hotel—printed papers from Kensington Properties, along with notes made by someone. I recognize the handwriting as Maverick's from the note he left me. Going back to the papers regarding the Blue Bayou, I see where he's written figures and numbers down...nothing more than chicken scratch to my uninformed eyes, but I'm guessing they mean something.

Another line catches my eye: *ask Carys about taxes.*

Taxes? What about them? What would he care about my taxes?

When I look over to the bed, where Maverick is still sleeping, my heart drops.

Was all of this a ruse?

Was it all orchestrated?

My throat tightens at the thought. All this time, I've felt like I've been gifted this man. Like he fell out of the bright blue sky, right into my hotel, just for me...just when I needed him. But now, I'm putting the pieces of the puzzle together. He was so interested in the Blue Bayou... and me...because it was his job. He was here to make an offer on my hotel? Buy it?

For what?

My thoughts go to a conversation we had at Lagniappe, when he was telling me about what he does for a living...*buyer, seller, and disposer of dreams.* What did he say? *By proxy*, but by proxy doesn't equal innocent.

I trusted him.

Believed him.

Fell for him.

A fool.

I'm a naive, stupid fool.

Sucking up the building emotions, my eyes stinging with unshed tears, I stuff the papers back into the folder, climb to my feet, and search for my clothes. I have to get out of here. I need to leave before he wakes up and I'm forced to face him with the new knowledge of who he truly is.

I can't.

I don't want to.

I want him to leave.

I'll pretend this was a fling and that I got what I came for...but he won't. He won't get the Bayou. That's not happening. Not now. Not ever.

Throwing my t-shirt on and scrambling into my shorts, I grab my shoes and bolt for the door, allowing myself one look back. One look back at what I thought could potentially be my future, someone I could lean on and be with...grow with. Maverick felt like someone who could make me a better version of myself. But standing in the half-open door,

I realize I let myself believe those things because I wanted them. So badly.

When the door is closed, I take off down the stairs and stop. I can't look Jules in the face like this. I can't let him see the devastation that I know is painted all over me, because the second the latch on the door clicked, my tears let loose. I stand there for a moment, frozen with indecision—take the stairs and face Jules or take the elevator and be reminded how happy I was a mere ten hours ago. How quickly things can change.

How quickly I allowed myself to fall for someone I barely knew.

I didn't know him.

I only knew the Maverick I made up in my head—caring, considerate, strong, dependable, amazing. But now, armed with the truth, I know he's none of those things. He's just like his father—selfish, out for himself, manipulative...a liar...who was trying to steal my hotel right out from under me.

The sadness and hurt starts to morph into anger as I stomp down the stairs, ignoring the concerned look I receive when I reach the bottom.

George. Of course.

Jules probably went home an hour ago.

"Carys?" George asks in a gentle, caring tone, making the lump in my throat grow. My throat constricts as I force down a sob. I can't, not here, not in front of George.

I can't respond with words, only a shake of my head, as I walk past him, straight out the back door, and run across the courtyard to the safety of my apartment. Opening the blue door, I walk in and look around my space...a space I once shared with my mother and grandparents... home. When the lock slides into place, I finally feel free to let go. As I slide down into a puddle on my kitchen floor, hot frustrated tears, accompanied by loud, therapeutic sobs fill the otherwise quiet space.

Sometimes, you have no choice but to cry. My grandfather once told me that tears are not a sign of weakness, only a sign that we care.

I do care.

I care a whole fucking lot.

After a while, I feel all cried out so I peel myself off the floor and drag myself to my bedroom. I feel drained, exhausted. Standing in the middle of my room, I feel lost. Even though I'm home and in my own space, everything feels off. My world feels out of balance and I can't think of what to do next. Logically, I should shower and get to work, but I know I can't do that. I can't face George or Mary, or God forbid, Maverick.

He's leaving soon, I already knew that. He has to go back to Dallas. But now, I also realize what the holdup was—why he kept asking for more time. Foolishly, I thought it was me. I thought he wanted to spend more time with me, allow us a few more days to solidify our relationship before we plunged into the unknown territory of a possible long-distance relationship.

"So fucking stupid, Carys," I cry to no one but myself. "So incredibly, fucking stupid." Falling onto my bed, I stare at the ceiling for a long time, letting the words I read on the document play in my head—trying to make sense of them, trying to think of a good reason Maverick would have that information, other than wanting to buy the Blue Bayou.

I can't think of anything.

A knock on my front door makes me jump. Practically falling off my bed, I crouch down beside it, like it's going to hide me from the outside world, protect me from whatever is on the other side of my front door. I'm in the back of my apartment, no one can see me, but I still feel exposed.

I'm not ready to face anyone. I need a while longer to wrap my mind and heart around this.

Seconds later, there are three more knocks.

Eventually, the knocking stops, whoever was at the door giving up, and my heartbeat gradually goes back to normal. Thankfully, the rush of adrenaline cleared my head a little.

A shower.

I need one.

I need to wash and get rid of the sex—me, Maverick, us. I need to wash it away, flush it down the drain, along with my feelings and hopes and dreams. Because right now, I'm surrounded by a cacophony of smells, reminding me of last night and killing me softly each time I take a breath.

My thoughts are overly dramatic for a relationship that is barely two weeks old. I know this.

I shouldn't feel this strongly.

I shouldn't want him this badly.

I shouldn't hate him this much.

Shedding my clothes and stepping into the steamy shower, I let it all out once more until my chest physically aches, my throat hurts and my eyes burn. I feel like punching the wall, but think twice, thankfully.

If I've learned anything over the last year and a half, it's that we can't change circumstances. We can't make the world treat us kindly. We take what we're dealt with and we move on with life.

After dressing and putting my wet hair into a ponytail, I take inventory. My eyes look dull, nothing like they looked when I caught a glimpse of myself in the bathroom mirror in Maverick's room. But that's also how life is too, right? Everything can change on a dime.

One second, I was a carefree college student, and in the next breath, I was without a mother and had a hotel dropped in my lap. I didn't know what I was doing. Those first few months, it was all I could do to pay the utilities on time and make sure George and Mary had a paycheck. I couldn't remember what day it was or when I'd eaten last. It took a while for me to pull myself out of the dark hole I fell in the day of the car crash. But I did it. And I know I'm not winning any awards for hotel management, but I'm learning and working to make this place better.

Bracing myself on the kitchen counter, I take deep breaths, working hard to suppress the urge to scream. Because I feel like I'm back to that day, the day my whole world shifted and I felt like I was floating in the universe, alone.

"Carys."

Maverick's voice on the other side of the door makes me swallow my breath.

Walking toward the door, I place my hand on the wood, wishing I could open it and pretend like I don't know. I wish I could go back to being ignorant, when I thought he was here for me.

"Carys," he says again, my name sounding rushed. He knocks. Once. Twice.

Then, my phone rings from the kitchen counter.

I know he hears it too, because when it stops, he knocks again. "Carys." This time, my name sounds like a plea. He's worried. Something has triggered him. Maybe I left the papers in the wrong order? Maybe he already knows that I know?

Slowly, I unlock the deadbolt and then the bottom lock. Leaning against the door, I rest my head on wood as I look down at my hand on the brass knob and feel the weight of the moment.

I want to go back.

I want to go back to Maverick's room.

Back to bed.

Back to being with him.

I want to go back to yesterday when everything felt possible.

"Carys," he whispers. "Open the door, please."

When I'm standing face to face with him, the door no longer a barrier, I see the confusion on his beautiful face. His forehead furrows and his eyes look concerned. "Hey."

I swallow, searching for words that fail me.

"What's wrong?" The look of concern begins to morph into something I can't quite name—fear, uncertainty.

"I know why you're here."

Maverick cocks his head and runs a hand over his scruff and then through his hair. It's then when I take in his appearance—button up shirt from yesterday, jeans, bare feet. "Could you enlighten me? Did something happen?"

"I found your papers. The ones about the Blue B—" He goes to interrupt me, but I stop him, raising my hand into the air.

"Please let me—" He starts again, but this time I raise my voice, talking over him, "I know you're here for *him*! Your father sent you here to scope out the Blue Bayou." I don't want excuses. I know what I saw. "*You* want to buy my hotel."

I huff out a laugh as Maverick pretends to look confused again, but I know that's a front too. He's not confused. He knows exactly what I'm talking about.

"Don't do that!" I roar, pushing him out of the doorway and back out into the courtyard. I don't want him in my apartment. I don't want him in my space. I don't want him in my hotel. "Don't pretend like you don't know what I'm talking about. I might be naive, but I'm not stupid. Fool me once, shame on you. Fool me twice, shame on me. You won't fool me twice."

I breathe heavily, my chest rising and falling as try to get control of my emotions.

"Carys," Maverick starts, walking toward me with his hands up in surrender.

"Don't! Don't touch me." Now the tears decide to make a return. "I trusted you. I thought you..." I stop, searching his face, but then I turn away, looking for an escape. I can't look at him. I'll cave. I'll listen to him and let him convince me his lies are the truth. "I thought you were someone you're not."

"I am, Carys. I'm exactly who you think I am...I'm here for *you*," Maverick pleads. "I'm not sure exactly what you saw or read, but you have to believe me."

"No! I don't have to believe you. I did that and look at us...look at me. I was doing just fine before you came. I'll be even better after you leave! Go! Go back to your father and tell him that I'm *never* selling this hotel, not to him or anyone else!"

Maverick's face falls and his hands fall limp at his sides.

I feel my features harden, something resembling hate rolling off me in waves.

"Carys."

"Leave."

My jaw is set tight, so tight it physically hurts. My shoulders squared. I want him to know I'm not weak. I'm not going to let him or anyone else push me over. I may be young and inexperienced, but I have a backbone...actually, I might have just found it, but now that I have, I'm using it. If I can't stand up for myself, who will?

Definitely not Maverick.

He reaches for me again and begins to explain himself and his motives, but I turn my back to him, tuning him out. I don't want to hear anything else. Nothing he can say will make this better.

I walk back into my apartment and slam the door, but I don't leave from the spot until I'm sure he's gone. Maybe it's the last piece of me that longs for him. Maybe it's the part of me that still wants him even though my heart feels broken. Maybe it's the part of me that wants to believe him...

No.

Some part of me knew from the beginning that Maverick was too good to be true. It's ridiculous to think a dreamboat of a man can walk into my hotel at just the perfect time with blue eyes and a smile that rivals the New Orleans sunshine...and that he would fill in all the cracks of my heart, making me believe in fate and destiny. He made me feel like I was always meant to meet him, like my heart and his had waited their whole lives to be in the same place at the same time.

When Mary mentioned my grandparents' whirlwind romance, it made me think maybe history was repeating itself. I'd never been a girl who sat around planning her future or her wedding. I didn't think about the guy I was going to marry. I didn't dream about babies.

That's not me.

But Maverick made me want all of that—marriage, babies, a family.

The tightness in my chest is back and it's radiating up into my throat, causing me to press my lips together to keep the deep ache from spilling over.

Pushing off the door, I walk back to my bedroom, pull the curtains, turn off the lights, and crawl under the blankets, hiding from the world. From the protection of my cave, I pull my phone inside and send Jules a text message.

Me: I'm sick. Can you cover for me?

A few minutes go by before my phone dings with a response.

Jules: Did you catch the herpes from Dreamboat?

That should be funny. I should laugh. So, I fake it and send him a laughing face emoji.

Me: No, worse. I can't leave the bathroom.

Two seconds later, the emoji with the medical mask followed by the green puke face shows up on my screen.

Jules: Say no more. Do you need soup? Is Dreamboat sick?

I pause with my thumb hovering over the screen before I finally reply.

Me: He's leaving.

Clicking out of our message, I call Mary. A text message will never work with her, but with my voice as hoarse as it is from crying, she'll believe a phone call.

Maverick

STUNNED.

Stunned and confused.

Hurt, dejected, and a little pissed off.

But, mostly, I'm stunned and confused.

I'm still not sure what the hell happened in the short time between waking up and now. I really wish this was just some fucked-up dream, but it's not. The look on Carys' face was real.

The anguish on her face.

The anger in her voice.

The door that slammed in my face.

The fact that she wants me to leave, for good.

All real.

And yet, I'm still standing here in the middle of the courtyard, surrounded by the echoes of her cries, too stunned to move.

Eventually, I manage to make my feet move and somehow end up back in my room. Thankfully, no one saw me or tried to talk to me on my way up. I honestly don't know how I would've responded.

Once inside the room, I toss the key onto the dresser and head straight for the table where the stack of papers resides. I don't allow myself to look at the bed because I know I'll be flooded with memories from last night. Memories of Carys' body, her sounds, the feel and taste of her that easily make up the best night of my life.

I grab the papers and look through them, trying to see what Carys saw and what set her off. There, in black and white, are details about the hotel that I shouldn't know. Details I wouldn't know or even care about if my dad hadn't guilted me into another job.

I get it. I understand why she reacted the way she did. What I don't understand is why she didn't let me explain. Why didn't she just ask what the papers meant instead of storming out and shutting down? I would've told her everything and apologized for keeping my actions a secret from her.

Maybe I should go back to her apartment and try again. Maybe she's calmed down enough to listen to what I have to say. Without another thought, I grab my key and rush out the door. I can't just sit in this room and do nothing. I had every intention of telling Carys how I felt—how I *feel*—about her last night, but there wasn't much conversation once things turned physical and I'll be damned if I let her push me away without telling her now.

Rushing down the stairs, I come face to face with George. Normally, he greets me with a big smile but not today. Instead, his eyes are narrowed and his forehead is creased. He, obviously, knows something has happened between Carys and me and he's none too pleased about it.

"George, I—," I start.

"No." He holds his hand up to emphasize his command. "Carys doesn't want to see you and I'm not gonna let you bother her." His words are calm as he levels me with a stare. "Not now, not ever."

This definitely isn't the warm and welcoming man I've come to know and respect over the past two weeks, but I can't help but be glad Carys has him in her life. She deserves someone like George in her corner—wise, caring, and loyal.

"I just need five minutes with her," I plead. "I swear, I can explain everything. Can't you just give me that?"

"No, Mr. Kensington, I cannot."

Not "Maverick", but "Mr. Kensington". So, it appears George is done with me too.

"I believe it's time for you to leave, sir. You're all checked out. All I need from you is a signature and you'll be free to go."

I run my hands through my hair and look around the lobby, trying to think of something...anything that might make George ease up, but when he crosses his arms and clears his throat to get my attention, I know there's nothing I can do.

"Fine," I say with a sigh, exhaling sharply through my nose. "Let me go get my things and I'll be out of your hair."

This time, I take the elevator up to stop George's evil eye from following me, but it's a hundred times worse being assaulted by memories of Carys and me inside this metal box last night.

Will every elevator ride remind me of her? Probably.

It doesn't take long for me to gather my things. Because I was already planning to leave for Dallas tomorrow, my bag was mostly packed. I don't like the idea of leaving now and feeling like I didn't fight hard enough, but I'm at a loss at what else I should do. Carys refuses to talk to me and George has made his thoughts on the matter loud and clear. The only thing left for me to do is go home and give Carys the space she wants right now. I don't have to be happy about it, but I'll respect her wishes with the hopes this isn't really the end for us.

I head back down to the lobby, but before I reach the front desk, I spot Mary refilling the pitcher of water and walk up to her. She doesn't seem surprised to see me, especially after spying the bag in my hand, but she does seem somber.

"Hey, Mary. Can I ask a favor of you?"

She graces me with a small, but sad, smile. "I can't let you see her, Maverick, I'm sorry."

"No, I know. George made that very clear a few minutes ago." I pull out my journal, the one my grandfather gave me, with all his words of wisdom and advice, and look at it while a lump forms in my throat. "Can you please give this to Carys? It's very special to me and has helped me a lot throughout my life, but I think it's time to pass it on. I hope she can listen to my grandfather, even if she doesn't want to listen to me." I rub my thumb across the worn leather one last time before handing it to Mary.

She gingerly takes it from me and holds it to her chest. "I will, Maverick. Just give her some time, okay? She's been through a lot and is still trying to find her way."

I nod my head and hoist my bag over my shoulder. "Take care, Mary."

The sky is dark and cloudy, matching my mood, as my cab drives me to the airport. Once there, I'm able to get a flight back to Dallas, which was quiet and uneventful, thanks to what I assume are mostly hungover passengers. Whatever the cause, I'm appreciative of it and manage to sleep for most of the trip, trying not to think about the girl I'm leaving behind and wondering how it all went so wrong.

Carys

"You're No Good" by Linda Ronstadt blares through my speakers as I take in the mess around me. Macaron ingredients cover every surface in my small kitchen, including me, and I can't be bothered enough to care. When I'm sad or lonely or depressed, I bake, but I also listen to Linda Ronstadt. She was my grandmother's favorite. She's the reason the Blue Bayou is the Blue Bayou. So, listening to this album makes me feel connected and gives me a soundtrack to escape to.

I've done a lot of that the last few days.

Escaping.

Forgetting.

Stewing.

I've tried pouring myself into work by implementing my new marketing plans, but I just can't.

I'm trying to get over it and I'm failing. Miserably.

I've tried to convince my heart to fix itself. It's not that bad. I'm not this sad. It didn't cut that deep. But it doesn't listen. It keeps hurting and I keep remembering. The odd thing is that I can't find it in myself to regret it. Maverick served a purpose. He helped me see what I was missing. He helped light a fire and make me want to do better...be better, work smarter.

Maverick.

I growl out my frustration to no one, except this fresh sheet of macarons. He left his mark here, in this kitchen. It's in these cookies I'm glaring at. It's in the courtyard outside my window. It's in my lobby... my office...room 201, and especially room 304. I haven't been to either of them since he left. Actually, the furthest I've been inside the hotel is the lobby to man the desk, and my office to stare at the piles of papers I made the night Maverick and I had sex.

Made love.

That's what it felt like.

To me, anyway.

Angrily, I pick up my bag of frosting and forcefully fill the macarons. These cookies require care, but I can't find it in myself to give them any. It's like I'm punishing them for being made, for being delicious, and for giving me visions of Maverick sitting at my table and closing his eyes as he tasted one for the first time.

Now, I know that face he made—one of utter and complete ecstasy—is nearly identical to the one he makes when he's coming. And I can't get it out of my head.

That pisses me off too.

A knock on the door makes me jump. I've been super jumpy lately, probably due to my lack of sleep. Even though I've spent an exceptional amount of time in my bed under the covers, my time there hasn't been productive.

Mindlessly, I continue to pipe white filling onto half the cookies, blocking out the knocking behind me.

"Carys June Matthews," Jules bellows. "Open the damn door right this second." Since when does Jules sound like an angry southern mama?

I don't open the door. I roll my eyes and continue my task at hand instead, hoping he'll get the message—I don't want to talk—and leave.

"Carys," he warns. "If you don't open this door, me and this sledgehammer are coming through."

I pause, lifting my head and staring at the cabinet in front of me. There's a chip in the wood I've never noticed before and I focus on it, hoping if I don't make any movements, Jules will think I'm gone.

"One..." The southern mama is back.

Huffing in frustration, I slam the bag onto the table, causing icing to squirt out, but it doesn't matter. It blends in with the rest of the mess.

"What do you want, Jules?" I ask to the closed door.

"I've been sent here to get a visual. Mary says I can't come back inside until I've physically laid eyes on you. She hasn't seen you since your shift yesterday and she said you looked like death warmed over, her analysis not mine." He pauses for a second, probably waiting for me to give in. "Carys, I am not made for the New Orleans humidity. I'm fucking melting out here. If you love me at all, you'll open this goddamn door."

My shoulders slump and my chest falls as I exhale loudly. Feeling frustrated and defeated, losing my battle in solidarity, I unlock the deadbolt and then the bottom lock and slowly open the door.

Jules eyes go wide when I come into view and I glance down at myself. Powdered sugar. Everywhere. I try to brush it off, but that shit sticks to yoga pants bad. Blowing a loose strand of hair out of my face, I wipe my brow and then smooth down my shirt.

"Hot fucking mess," he mutters, shaking his head.

Leaning in, he takes a whiff. "And, oh my God...have you showered? Like, ever?"

"Yesterday," I reply defensively, wrapping my arms protectively around my torso. Also, trying to hide whatever stench might be radiating off my body.

Jules raises an eyebrow and his eyes bore into mine.

"Fine, the day before yesterday."

He breathes deeply, looking up at the sky, like he's searching for inner strength. "Listen, here's what's going to happen..." Pausing as he takes a step forward, his eyes go wide again when he notices my kitchen. "What the fuck is going on in here? Because it looks like World War III and flour is the weapon of choice."

"It's actually powdered sugar," I say distractedly.

He rolls his eyes as his hands go to my shoulders. "Listen, I'm being a good friend. Okay?" he asks, waiting for me to respond, but when I don't he continues. "This is coming from a place of love, but..." He takes another deep breath and another look around before continuing in a flat, no-nonsense tone. "You stink. You look like shit. Your hair..." He cringes, doing a full body shiver. "It looks like squirrels are living in it. You're covered in flour...powdered sugar, whatever the fuck. Your kitchen is a disaster zone. And I know...you're...well, you're..."

"Pissed," I offer.

"Right," Jules says, nodding as he scans my face.

"And..." My throat tightens as I try to form the words without tears accompanying them, but I feel my nose start to burn as I try to hold them back. "I...I think I was falling for him," I admit on a whisper.

"I know, honey," he says, pulling me into a hug, albeit an odd one, because he's also trying to keep me at arm's length as he pats my back. "Me too."

I chuckle, for the first time in days. Jules makes me feel something besides sad.

"Can we turn this fucking depressing music off?" he asks, letting me put my head on his shoulder as we start to sway. "It's making me want to eat a pint of ice cream, and I can't afford that right now. I have a show this weekend. My fans expect svelte, not svat."

We continue to pseudo-slow dance in my kitchen until the vinyl screeches, signifying the end of the song. "This is the problem with records," I murmur into his shoulder. "You have to physically flip them over. But it's also awesome...because you have to physically flip them over."

"I really love that you're a seventy-five-year-old trapped inside a smoking hot twenty-five-year-old's body, but you really should consider catching up with the twenty-first century."

I laugh, again, and it feels good. It feels like maybe this elephant that's been sitting on my chest since I found those papers in Maverick's room might vacate the premises at some point.

"Mary told me to bring you this," Jules says, putting some space between us and pulling a brown leather journal from his back pocket.

I know that journal.

Trying to ignore the spike in my heart rate and the jolt in the pit of my stomach, I ask, "Where did you get that?"

"He left it," Jules says without emotion, like he's hiding his reaction while he's waiting on mine. "He told Mary he wants you to have it. Something about his grandfather...and he hopes you'll find it useful." He shrugs, holding it out and letting it hang in the balance between us.

Looking at it, I can't decide what to do. Part of me wants to take it and run away with it. The other part wants to take it and light it on fire. And then, there's a small part that wants to sit down, right here in the middle of this mess and devour every word...searching the pages for a glimpse of the Maverick I thought I knew.

"He left it for me?" I ask, just needing to hear that again. I don't know why. I just do.

"Yep."

I nod, still looking at the worn cover and pages...the leather strap that keeps it closed...remembering seeing Maverick carry it around with him.

"I'll leave it...here," Jules says, finding the one clean spot on my kitchen table to set it down. Patting it, he looks at me and shrugs. "Maybe see what's so important. Couldn't hurt anything, right?"

I nod again. "Right."

"Okay." Jules' tone changes to one of determination. "But first. Shower." He points to the hallway that leads to my bedroom. "I'm not bathing you, but..."

I give him a small, reluctant smile and shake my head. "You can lead a horse to water, but you can't make them drink."

He rolls his eyes and clicks his tongue. "Bitch, I'll throw your stinky ass in the Mississippi River if that's what it takes. Now, get in there."

"Fine," I acquiesce. "I'll shower."

"And then, you'll get dressed in something besides yoga pants and you'll brush that nappy hair...and those teeth, because, damn girl." Shaking his head, he covers his nose, giving me a look of disgust. "And then, you'll get your ass to work. We can't fill in for you forever. You gotta be a big girl...suck it up, pull yourself up by your bootstraps, and get a fucking grip."

My eyes go wide at his candor, but it's what I need. He's right. I can't neglect my life. It's selfish of me. I can do this. I've done it before. Losing Maverick, or the hope of what I thought could be with him, isn't the worst thing I've lived through.

"I'm sorry," I tell Jules, taking his hand in mine and giving it a squeeze. "I'm fine." I take a deep cleansing breath and shake my head, trying to clear my mind and rid it of the black cloud that's been following me around. "You're right. I have responsibilities and you all depend on me. What kind of boss abandons their employees?"

Jules smiles softly at me. "Don't go getting overly dramatic. The place is running just fine without you, but..."

"Thanks, Jules," I tell him, leaning in to kiss his cheek. "I'll shower and then I'll be over to take the front desk for the rest of the day...and night. I know you've filled in for me a lot lately, so thank you and I owe you one."

"You don't owe me. That's what friends do."

Hearing those words and feeling them ring true deep down in my soul, I still believe in fate and destiny. Even through everything that's happened. Finding a friend in Jules makes me believe. Sometimes, people come into your life for a season, but sometimes, they come to stay.

"You can't ever leave me, okay?" I tell him in all seriousness. "Even when you're a big, powerful attorney one of these days, you're still going to be stuck with me."

"If we're both not married in five years, you can be my beard."

With that, I throw my head back and laugh, for real, feeling some lightness seep back into my bones.

After I'm in the shower, Jules yells that he's heading back, giving me some privacy to get ready, but also warning if I'm not there in thirty minutes, he'll be back banging my door down.

Twenty minutes later, I'm feeling more human than I have in the last three days. Showered, dressed in jeans and a yellow top to help with my mood, and my hair still damp, but braided out of my face—I feel like I look human too.

The smile on Jules' face when he sees me come through the back door is confirmation.

"There's my girl." He offers me his cheek, which I kiss, and then the other. "And, by golly, you don't smell like a trash dumpster. What a difference some basic essentials make."

"Stop."

"Oh, girl. You'll be hearing about this for a while. I can't let you forget where you came from."

I shake my head, but before I can say anything, Mary is wrapping her warm arms around me from behind. I don't know where she came from, but I'm happy to see her. "Sorry, Mar," I whisper, knowing she'll forgive me, but feeling horrible about worrying her.

"It's okay, baby." She walks around, taking in my full appearance as she gives me a once-over. "Better." Her and Jules share a conspiratorial smile and it makes my heart swell.

These people are my family. They're the ones I can count on and trust to always be there. I just need to focus on the positives and keep my chin up, because they're counting on me just as much as I'm counting on them.

"I'll take over the front desk. Y'all go and get some rest."

Mary pats my cheek, her eyes lingering on mine as she searches for the truth. Happy with whatever she finds there, she smiles and nods. "I've got a few things to take care of. Call if you need anything. George said he'll be back by later."

"Thanks, Mary," I tell her, squeezing her hand as she walks away.

Walking to the desk, I look over the guest book, seeing that we have four rooms booked for the night. "Everything been going okay?" I ask as Jules stands beside me and punches a few things into the computer.

"Yeah, but this did come for you yesterday," he says, pulling a very official looking envelope out of the drawer. "I wasn't sure what it was so I put it in here for safe keeping."

"Thanks, Jules," I tell him, glancing over the envelope and then back up at him.

"I've got to go get ready for my shift at Revelry tonight, but if you need me, I'm just a phone call away. I can always get a bitch to fill in for me," he says, collecting his keys and a magazine from under the counter. "You should eat something."

"Any other instructions for me?" I tease.

His eyes scan from my head to my toes. "I wish I was as flawless as you with such little effort." He shakes his head, like I've seriously disappointed him, but I smile at his compliment.

"You are," I assure.

Two seconds later, Jules is out the door, offering a wave over his shoulder as he struts his stuff out onto the sidewalk.

When I'm alone and the lobby is quiet, I flip the envelope over in my hand, looking at the address and then the certified mail label. The only things I've ever received through certified mail had to do with money—owed or earned, but usually owed.

City of New Orleans

What could be so important that the city is sending me something certified? Have I won the lottery? Maybe it's bad and I've broken some kind of code or inspection?

Do they do those for hotels?

Feelings of frustration and dread come creeping back. All I need is one more thing I don't know about or know how to handle. Just when I feel like I've crossed the last hurdle, something else pops up. I roll my shoulders, trying to keep my calm demeanor.

Open the letter, Carys. It can't be that bad.

Right. Running my finger under the loose flap of the envelope, I wiggle it until it's open. As I take out the letter inside, I see the stamp from the city at the top and my stomach does a weird thing. There's a small inkling in the back of my brain, like my mind trying to play connect the dots.

Notice of Tax Sale

Confusion muddles my mind as I read through the rest of the letter.

A tax sale? What does that even mean?

Setting the letter down on the desk, I look around the lobby, like the answer or explanation will be written on the walls.

Ask Carys about taxes

Maverick's note on one of the papers regarding the Blue Bayou floods my memory and my stomach drops. What did he know? What did he know that he didn't tell me? Why didn't he just tell me?

Even if he was here to find out information about the hotel, he could've just told me. I'm not saying I would've understood or been nice about my response, but at least he would've been honest. Honesty I can work with. Deceit and lies I cannot.

Firing up the computer in the office, I wait what feels like an eternity for it to boot up. In the meantime, I start searching through the pile of papers I had deemed important the other day, going to the bottom of the stack for another envelope I remember seeing from the city. I had assumed it was some kind of reminder or notice. I thought it was important, but not *tax sale* important. Whatever that means.

"Come on, you slow-ass machine," I mutter, tapping my fingers harshly on the keyboard, like that will help it come to life quicker.

Eventually, the log-in screen appears and I enter my information, heading straight for my good friend Google.

What is a tax sale?

Still trying to wrap my brain around all of this, I scan back over the notice again. It says *due to delinquent taxes*, but I know I've paid taxes. That's one thing I used to help my mother with. She did them by the quarter, which is what I've continued to do. So, this is probably a mistake, but I need to know what it is before I can dismiss it or fix it.

Glancing back up at the screen, I see my answer.

In some states, the government will seize properties with unpaid property taxes and then sell the properties at a tax deed sale, which is a public auction.

Property taxes?

I owe those?

And public auction?

My stomach drops a little and my mouth goes dry as I read over the explanation from Google once more, and then I do a further search, typing in things like: *tax sales in New Orleans, what happens when you don't pay property taxes, how much are property taxes.* The questions go on and on, and by the time I've exhausted everything I can think of to ask the Internet, I'm panicked, to say the least.

Could that happen?

After opening the rest of the mail and seeing the other letters, I hate myself. I hate that I let all of this pile up and I hate that I wasn't being more proactive, taking care of business. *My* business. The realization that they could put a lien on my property and sell my hotel, at least that's what I gathered from my Google search, scares the shit out of me.

Is that what Maverick was trying to do?

Or is that what Mr. Kensington sent him here to do?

Immediately, I walk back out to the lobby, and for once, I'm thankful it's a slow day as I pick up the phone and dial Mary's number. I don't know who else to call. I can't bother Jules at work and I don't want to worry George. He never takes bad news well. He's a worry wart. So, Mary is my only option.

"Carys?"

"Mary," I say, trying to keep the panic out of my voice, but not succeeding. "What do you know about a tax sale?"

"I'll be right there," is all she says before hanging up the phone.

Shit, this can't be good.

By the time Mary steps into the office, I'm a huge ball of nerves. I've started pacing the floor since I've already chewed my fingernails down to the quick. I guess my next step will be pulling my hair out.

Mary wraps her hands around the tops of my arms to stop my movements. "Tell me what's going on."

With shaky hands, I show her the papers Jules gave me earlier. I watch as she reads over them, studying her face for a sign of what she's feeling. Relief, confusion, worry, anger, horror...she's giving me nothing.

Eventually, she looks up at me and states matter-of-factly, "According to this, you're behind on your property taxes for the hotel."

I nod my head, ashamed, and hand her another paper. "I just found the original tax bill under all these papers. Mary, what am I going to do? How could I have let this happen?"

Feeling as though my legs are going to give out on me any second now, I make myself sit on the couch in the corner of the office. Mary joins me, still not offering any advice.

"I accidentally found some papers while I was in Maverick's room," I start. "It was information on a few different places, including the Blue Bayou, and they contained things like what the properties are worth and what they could sell for. I don't know if you know this but Maverick works for his father, the owner of Kensington Properties in Dallas, and he works deals so that his dad can buy out businesses. I assumed the reason he was here this whole time was to get close to me and get information that would help his dad buy me out. There was a note on one page that mentioned asking me about the taxes, but he never did ask. Is this what he was talking about? Did he know I could potentially lose the hotel but decided to keep it from me?"

When I finish spilling my guts I'm breathless and nearing hysterics. To think and to say out loud my suspicions about Maverick hurt as much, if not more, than when I originally found the papers.

"Calm down, honey," Mary says in her usual calm, firm manner. "You're going on so fast I'm having trouble keeping up. Now, let's try to figure all this out together, okay? Can I get you something? Some water, tea, maybe? A shot of bourbon, perhaps?"

I manage to chuckle and agree to a glass of water. Once I've calmed down and related the details more calmly and rationally, I ask, "What's going to happen to this place if I can't pay these taxes? Will I lose the Bayou?"

"It's a possibility, yes. At a tax sale, the property is put up for sale for the taxes owed. Since this property is paid off, someone could come in, pay the taxes, and then own this hotel."

Mary has just voiced my worst fear and I feel my nose burn as I try to suppress tears. The thought of losing this hotel, the only home I've known, makes me sick to my stomach. I don't have time to wallow, though. I have to stay focused and figure out my next step.

"I feel so stupid and immature. I've worked my ass off since my mom died to keep this hotel afloat and it may have been all for nothing. I know this is my fault and could've been avoided if I had a better handle on the business side of things, but I can't help and wonder why my mom didn't teach me more—more about how to run this place? I was twenty-three when she died. I could've had more responsibilities than occasionally working the front desk, but she just let me come and go as I pleased."

Mary clears her voice and straightens, grabbing my hands and forcing me to look at her. "Your mama wanted you to live your life and have choices...choices she never had when she was your age. She never forced you to work or to go to college and settle on a major; she wanted you to have fun. Vivienne always knew running the Bayou was her future and she didn't want to force that upon you. Don't get me wrong, she loved this place and she loved working here and she even hoped you'd feel the same, but she wanted you to come to that decision on your own. She thought you had time; we all did."

"You're right, but look at me now. I'm so lost and I'm about to lose everything. I'm an idiot."

"Now, you hush," she says firmly, causing me to come to attention. "You're not an idiot and you're not stupid. It's true you're young and you lived a carefree life up until your mama passed. Nobody planned for any of this, so don't go putting unnecessary blame on yourself."

"But, it's my fault I'm behind on the taxes."

"Then, let's focus on that and figure out a way to get them paid, *if* that's what you want to do."

This gets my attention, so I ask Mary directly, "What do you mean *if it's what I want to do*? I don't have a choice."

"You always have a choice. If you want to keep the hotel open, then we'll figure a way to pay the taxes, but if you want to do something else, then we'll do that. No one would blame you if you decided to sell. If you don't want to run the business and are tired of the stress it brings, then now's the time to get out."

"I can't do that, Mary. I have people depending on me, on this place. I can't hurt you, George, and Jules like that!"

"You can't base your decision on us, but know this: we'll be fine and we'll understand whatever you decide. That goes for your mama and grandparents, too."

"How do you know that? This place is all I have left of them; it's all I've ever known."

"No, Carys, *you* are what's left of them. The hotel is a great place, but you are how your mama and grandparents live on."

Maverick

"So, let me get this straight," **Shep says, taking** another sip of his drink and then setting it back down on the table between us. "Your girl kicked you out of her hotel and your father fired you? What's next? Are you planning on getting evicted from your house? Do you need to sleep on my couch?"

"Fuck you," I groan, scrubbing my face with my hands.

"Dude, how did everything go to shit so fast?"

"I've been asking myself the same damn thing. I mean, a week ago, I was trying to figure out how I was going to make a long-distance relationship work," I pause, leaning onto the table. "A relationship, man. *Me.*"

Shep nods, his eyes going wide. "I know. I thought I might never see you again."

"I'm being serious."

"Me, too. I don't even know Carys, but I could tell you were balls deep."

"She's..." I start, but stop, not knowing what to say. "I don't know, man. I wish you could meet her."

Shep sighs, leaning back in his chair. "What about your job? Do you think Spencer will change his mind after he cools down?"

"No," I answer without having to think about it. "I knew it was coming. If he hadn't fired me, I would've quit. I'd already made up my mind about that."

"What are you going to do?"

I shrug, thinking about it for a second. "I'll scrub toilets for the next two years if I have to, but one thing's for sure, I'm done with Kensington Properties. My only regret is that I couldn't sell him on my alternative plan with the other properties. I wish there was a way for me to deter him from the Blue Bayou."

"Do you think he'll still pursue it even though you told him she's not selling?" Shep asks.

I look at him, wondering if we're still talking about my father.

"Never mind," Shep groans. "This is Spencer Kensington we're talking about. He'll attack until he gets the kill."

"That's what I'm worried about."

"But you said she's not selling," Shep says.

"She's not," I tell him, confidently. "I just wish there was a way I could protect her from him. I know him. He'll be on her front step within the week, if he hasn't shown up already."

"Did you find out what information he has on her or the hotel?" Shep asks, thoughtfully.

Letting out a deep, frustrated sigh, I shake my head. "No, I just hope it's something she's aware of. If I'd had a couple more days, I could've maybe gotten to the bottom of it, but there's nothing I can do now."

"You can call her, warn her about your father and give her a heads up about what he said about biding his time."

"She won't talk to me. I called yesterday and George answered the phone. He said he'd give her the message that I called, but I know him, he was just being polite. I was still Mr. Kensington, which means he's still pissed at me and protecting Carys."

"Well, maybe call again and if she doesn't answer, just leave a message about your father. That should get their attention."

"Maybe," I tell him, willing to give it a try.

Later that evening, with Carys weighing heavily on my mind, as she often does, I decide to call the hotel again.

"Blue Bayou, this is Jules. How may I help you?"

"Hey, Jules. This is Maverick," I start, hoping for a warmer reception from him than George.

"Well, if it isn't the *Big D* and I don't mean Dallas."

Fuck. So much for that warm reception.

"Um, yeah, so is Carys around?"

"No."

I take a deep breath and start over. "Look, Jules, I'm sorry for the way things turned out with me and Carys...sorrier than you'll ever know, but it's extremely important that I speak with her. It's about the hotel."

"I wish I could help you, but she's not taking phone calls at the moment. She has more pressing things to attend to."

"Like what? She hasn't been approached by my dad, has she? Spencer Kensington? That's why I'm calling, to warn her."

"That name doesn't ring a bell."

I let out a frustrated groan and bang my fist down on my kitchen counter. I can tell I'm getting nowhere with Jules. With no other option than to fly my ass back there, which from the way things ended and the fact it's only been a week, doesn't sound like a very smart option, Jules is my only chance to make things right.

"I appreciate your loyalty to Carys and contrary to popular belief, I'm loyal to her, too. I don't even work for my father anymore; I was fired my first day back. I only want what's best for Carys and the hotel, so please tell her my dad has some kind of information on her that makes the hotel extremely vulnerable for a buyout. Because I don't have all the facts, I'm not exactly sure how to help her, other than to warn her. Can you do that for me, at least?" I plead, my tone sounding as desperate as I feel.

I don't hear anything from Jules for a couple of moments and I wonder if the call was disconnected during my little tirade.

"Okay, fine, I'll tell her what you said," he finally answers. "This better not be some kind of ploy to hurt her even more than she already is. I'd hate to bust that beautiful face of yours with my fist, but I'll do it."

My lips twitch with a mental image of an angry Jules popping into my mind. Actually, he probably could kick my ass if he wanted to. He's tenacious as fuck.

"I'd never do anything to hurt her," I reply, quieter. I mean it, and I hope to put the sincerity I feel in my heart into my words to Jules. "You have to believe me. I'm the Maverick she thought she knew...the same one you knew. I swear. But, if I do somehow fuck up and hurt her, I'd be happy to let you bust my face."

When I hang up, I sit in my dark living room. Nothing feels the same since I got back and it has nothing to do with losing my job and everything to do with losing Carys. Not that I feel like I've lost her for good. My stupid heart is holding out hope that she'll change her mind, but I don't know when or how that's going to happen. My grandfather's words come back to haunt me anytime I think about flying back to New Orleans: *everything good comes to those who wait.*

I've never been good at waiting. When I turned fifteen and a half, I wanted a car. My father told me to call my grandfather and my grandfather told me *don't get the cart before the horse.* At the time, I rolled my eyes, thinking he was old and didn't know what he was talking about, always trying to sneak his bits of "wisdom" into every conversation we had. So, instead, I took matters into my own hands. I sold some baseball cards my grandfather gave me and bought a piece of shit truck from a guy on my football team.

I wrecked it two weeks later.

Not only did I have a broken wrist and was unable to play football that season, but I also had to wait to get my license.

Everything good comes to those who wait.

Don't put the cart before the horse.

And my favorite: *Don't expect everything to go right the first time.*

Letting out a deep breath, I stand from the chair and walk to my office. The lights in here are dim too, but I don't turn any more on. Instead, I open up my laptop and bring up Facebook. It's not the first time I've done this since I've been back. Actually, it's my nightly ritual. There's one old photo of Carys on here, a photo she probably took back when she was in college and opened up her page, but she's gorgeous. The way the sun is behind her, haloing her face, reminds me of the days we spent walking around the French Quarter.

I want to go back.

To the Blue Bayou.

To Carys.

But I know I have to be patient. Carys needs this time. She needs to figure out what she wants. I want her to trust me and believe me, but I also want her to come to those feelings on her own. I'm hoping the journal I left behind will help, if she gives it a chance...if she didn't use it for kindling to make s'mores. That thought makes my entire body tense. Leaving that journal behind—a piece of myself, tangible memories of my grandfather...a piece of him—was one of the hardest, yet easiest decisions of my life. Thankfully, I've read it so many times, it's ingrained on my heart...in my mind, woven into my soul. Even if it didn't exist any longer, I'd still take it with me everywhere I go.

Kind of like Carys.

She's in there too.

Carys

"Miss Matthews, Mr. Wallace will see you now."

"Oh, okay. Thank you."

I try to discreetly wipe my sweaty palms onto the chair before grabbing my file folder and standing. This folder is filled with every paper I thought I'd possibly need for meeting with Mr. Wallace, and then some. I'm determined to be as professional as I can and show that I mean business. I'm even wearing a dress, for crying out loud.

The secretary leads me into a large office and motions for me to sit in a large chair before quietly stepping back into the main lobby of First National Bank. The man I'm here to see, Mr. Buford Wallace, is sitting across the desk from me and speaking on the phone. He's not a very intimidating looking man like I'd imagined. In fact, he kind of looks familiar, which helps me relax a little. When he looks up and sees me sitting across from him, he smiles as he continues talking on the phone.

"All right, Ethel, I have to go now. I have someone special here to see me, but I'll see you when I get home." Pausing for a second, he gives me a nod of his head before replying, "Yes, I believe, red beans and rice will be perfect this evening. Bye, now." Hanging up the phone, he stands to greet me.

"Carys Matthews, it is so good to see you. How have you been?" He reaches over for my hand and when I extend it out to him, he takes it in both of his, squeezing tightly. "You probably don't remember me, but I handled all your granddaddy's and your mama's banking when they ran the Blue Bayou. I don't think I've seen you since Vivienne's funeral, though. You holdin' up okay?"

I can't help but be charmed by his kindness but I'm afraid to answer too honestly, because if I was okay, I wouldn't be here. I'm not a fan of airing dirty laundry, but if my family trusted Mr. Wallace, I should be able to as well.

"Well, to be honest, sir, I'm not."

"Please call me Buford or, at the very least, Mr. Wallace. None of this *sir* business. I've known you all your life, so that practically makes us family." His warm smile eases me and my nerves. "Now, tell me how I can help you."

Not sure where to begin, I place my folder on his desk. "Well, I'm sorry to say that I'm in a real mess. I thought I was keeping up with things but, apparently, I'm behind on my property taxes."

The expression on his face is sympathetic but not condescending in any way. He opens the folder and reads the first document, which is the notice about the tax sale. After a brief moment, he hangs his head and lets out a deep sigh. When he looks back up at me, his eyes are sorrowful.

"Miss Carys, it appears I owe you an apology."

"What do you mean?" I ask, trying hard not to get my hopes up about this all being a mistake.

"It seems as though I've failed you. I always promised your granddaddy I'd look out for you and your mama, making sure your finances were in order. Vivienne never seemed to need my help in that area. So, I took you not coming to see me or asking for any kind of help as a sign you had everything under control, as well. But I should've reached out to make sure. I'm so sorry, my dear."

"Mr. Wallace, there is no need to apologize. I know this is my fault. *I* misplaced the tax bill and *I'm* the one who let it go unpaid."

"And that is where my fault lies. I should've come to you. Please forgive me for my negligence. Your mother had a savings account she had money deposited into on a monthly basis, so that when the property taxes were due, she didn't have to worry about coming up with such a large sum of money. I should've spoken with you, asked if you'd like to continue using the account."

"We'll call it good if you can help me," I plead. "I was thinking that perhaps I could get a loan." My tone is hesitant, because I have no idea what the protocol is here; I just know I'm desperate for help. "I mean, if that's even possible. I don't know what I'm doing here, Mr. Wallace. I've never had a loan. I just know that Mary told me you used to help my grandfather and my mother with financial issues, so I'm hoping you can help me too."

Mr. Wallace clears his throat and scoots his chair up closer to his desk, leaning his elbows on the dark wood and tenting his fingers, as he gives me an inquisitive stare. "You do realize that the Blue Bayou is paid for, right?"

I nod, swallowing. Actually, until Mary mentioned it the other day, I hadn't really thought of the Bayou as property, in the sense that I could sell it. It's always seemed like so much more than just a building to me. It's family. And I would never sell family. So, why would I sell the Blue Bayou? Sure, the less stress part wouldn't be bad, but I would miss it too much. It's a part of me, a part of who I am, and I'm willing to do anything I can to keep it.

"Miss Carys, you have enough collateral to borrow as much money as you need and then some."

I feel like I should probably be upset by the fact that I didn't know any of this, but it wouldn't do any good at this point. So, it's relief that washes over me with this knowledge, and I feel my shoulders relax a little. "Is that something I could get today, or at least, in the next few days? The tax sale notice was dated a week ago and it states that I only have twenty days from the time it was written," I tell him, feeling the familiar panic start creeping back up as I point to the date typed on the top of the letter.

"Yes, yes," Mr. Wallace says, picking up his pair of glasses and setting them back on his nose as he skims over the letter once more. "We should be able to type up the papers today. I can give you a list of the items we'll need to secure the loan." He clears his throat and sets the letter back on the desk between us.

"I have some money saved, but most of that I planned on putting back into the hotel. It seems like since my mom..." I pause, because even after a year and a half, I still have trouble saying died. *She's gone.* "Well, since she's been gone, everything has seemed to go wrong."

Mr. Wallace reaches across the desk and places his hand over mine, causing me to look up at him and see the kindness and genuine care in his eyes. "I know things have been hard, but I have faith in you. You're gonna get your head above water and then...well, sky's the limit."

I huff out a laugh, wiping at the dampness under my eyes. "Now you sound like Mary."

"Oh, Miss Mary," he says with a nostalgic smile. "How is she these days?"

"Good," I tell him with a smile and a nod. "She's good. I don't know what I'd do without her and George."

"Your grandfather thought the world of them. Your mama, too, for that matter."

"They did, and I do too. They're part of the reason I must fix this. I can't let them down, Mr. Wallace, and I can't let myself down. It's been a rough year, but I want this more than I ever dreamed. And it's not just because it belongs to my family. I want it because it makes me happy." I stop, thinking about the change I've felt inside regarding the Blue Bayou and my heart expands. "Recently, I met someone, and he really opened my eyes, made me see it in a new light. I have plans for the hotel, things I think are really going to bring it back to its glory days, even better."

"Thatta girl," Mr. Wallace praises, giving the desk a good slap.

"I'm going to have the remaining balance of your mother's savings account transferred over into your name. That should give you some wiggle room on operating expenses. And my secretary will draw up the necessary papers for the loan. They should be ready for you to sign tomorrow morning and we'll cut you a check shortly after. Once you make the deposit, you'll be good to go pay the delinquent taxes at the courthouse."

"Thank you, Mr. Wallace." Smiling, I feel like jumping over the desk and kissing him, but I decide to refrain.

When I get back to the hotel, George, Mary, and Jules are all waiting for me in the lobby. I stop just inside the door when I see them, wondering if something happened while I was gone. I'm learning to not think that way and just roll with whatever happens. The statement I made to Maverick the day he walked into the hotel still rings true: we should rename this place Murphy's Law.

But I like Blue Bayou too much.

So, it stays.

"What?" I look around for signs of catastrophe.

"So?" Mary asks, and I see her grab George's hand.

"So, what?" I counter, glancing over at Jules who is chewing on his bright blue fingernails. That's totally unlike him. He never messes with a fresh manicure.

"Miss Carys, please don't keep us in suspense," George implores.

I fight to hold back my smile but fail. "You all still have a job. I mean, if you want it," I tease. "And Mr. Wallace is writing the loan for a little more than the taxes to give us some cash flow to fix this place up," I add. "I was thinking, once everything is taken care of, maybe we'll have a grand re-opening, something to kick off this new era of the Blue Bayou. What do y'all think?"

The smile on Mary's face says it all, but when Jules takes a few steps forward and wraps me in a hug, twirling me around, I let out my first real sigh of relief.

We're gonna make it.

I should be happy, and I am, but I'm also sad because there is one other person I wish I could share this news with, someone I thought would always be on my side, but he's not here. I miss him. Even though he ended up not being who I thought he was. I miss the idea of him. I miss the comfort and strength he brought to my life. I miss the way my body felt when I was near him. I miss the way he looked at me.

Can you force yourself to look at someone like they hung the moon and painted the stars?

Because that's what it felt like every time I caught him watching me.

If that was an act, Maverick deserves an Oscar.

Carys

WALKING UP TO THE BACK ENTRANCE OF THE HOTEL, carrying a basket full of individually wrapped macarons, I smile at Jules when he gets the door for me.

"Thanks, Jules," I tell him, offering him a kiss to his cheek.

"You can pay me in cookies," he demands, closing the door behind me. "Also, the new computers are the shit and have you seen our website?"

I smile, setting the basket down on the front desk and handing him a cookie. One. If I don't ration them to him, he'll eat the whole damn batch, and I need enough to put in the rooms before check-in.

Glancing over at the guestbook, I see we only have three vacancies, one being the room we're currently remodeling due to excess water leakage in the bathroom. The infamous room 201.

"I know, right? It's so fancy and pretty," I agree, placing the extra macarons, all bright blue and happy looking, on the table by the water.

"Fancy is right."

"Thanks for that hook-up, by the way. Your friend saved me

hundreds of dollars." Jules' friend from Club Rev just so happens to be getting his degree in graphic design and has an incredible talent for building websites. He helped me renew the domain name, thankfully acquiring thebluebayou.com. The wooden doors and hanging baskets, a perfect portrayal of our street here in the French Quarter, is everything I had dreamed and more. If someone searching for a hotel sees that and doesn't want to stay here, then they were never our kind of guests to begin with. I've decided that I'm okay with the antiquities. I'm going to monopolize on what we do have to offer and not worry about keeping up with the Joneses, or the Hotel Monteleones.

Jules shrugs. "No biggie. I owe him. He owes me. We all get paid."

The last line comes out dripping with insinuation and I laugh.

"Well, be sure to pass along my gratitude. Also, tell him I'll email him as soon as I'm ready to add the link for reservations. I just want to make sure our new computers and software are up to the task."

We both go about doing things around the lobby. Jules checks on our guests. His hospitality skills are one of his best qualities. I refill the water and put the rest of the macarons in my office. Out of sight, out of mind. CeCe recently started selling them in Neutral Grounds, so I've been staying up late a few nights a week, making extras to sell. My little side hustle has turned out to be quite profitable. A little exhausting, but profitable.

But, I can't complain. Business is picking up as the summer rolls on. Our remodeling is going well and we're close to having everything complete. The website is updated. Facebook is now being maintained and managed by Jules. I'm not sure I completely trust him on that front, but I'm happy to delegate. He's also started an Instagram account for the hotel.

For once, I feel like I truly have a grip on the business side of the Bayou. After the scare with the taxes, I stayed up for almost twenty-four hours straight, going through every stitch of paper and balancing every ledger. I didn't want to leave room for any more surprises.

"If you don't need me for anything else, I gotta run," Jules says, peeking into the office where I'm currently going through the daily mail and filing it away in its appropriate file.

I smile up at him. "Nope, I've got it covered. I'll see you tomorrow."

Jules blows me a kiss and then disappears. I hear the bell on the door chime with his departure and then a few minutes later, it chimes again.

"Welcome to the Blue Bayou," I call out, finishing up my filing and then stepping into the lobby to greet my guest.

A man in a three-piece suit is standing just inside the door, gazing around the large open lobby, taking it all in with a whistle. "Quite the place you've got here." His words come out in what seems to be surprise, but also approval.

"Can I help you?" I ask, walking up to the computer on the front desk and wiggling the mouse to wake up the check-in screen. "Are you looking for a room? We've got—"

"No," he says, cutting me off mid-sentence. "I'm not here for a room."

It's then I realize that his eyes are familiar, something I've seen before.

Up close.

And personal.

My mouth goes dry as I wait for him to say something else, hoping my intuition is wrong...hoping those blue eyes are a coincidence. Swallowing, I wait.

He walks closer to the desk, his eyes on me, and he cocks his head. "Miss Matthews?"

"Yes," I confirm, forcing my tone to be firm and steady, despite the nerves building in my stomach. Where are George and Mary? I need back-up. I want someone else here who's on my side, because even though there is just the two of us, I feel outnumbered.

"I'm Spencer Kensington," he says, cutting straight to the chase. "I believe you met my son, Maverick."

"I did." I nod my head once, my heart squeezing at the mention of Maverick's name, especially coming from his father. I had hoped my suspicions about Maverick were false. I hoped I had jumped to conclusions, and that at some point, I'd be able to forgive him for not telling me the truth. However, standing here now, face-to-face with his father, I feel completely...well, sad. Disappointed. Heartbroken all over again, but I don't let him see that.

Mr. Kensington barks out a sharp laugh as he smooths down his tie. "I sent him here to do business, not..." Pausing, he waves his hand in my direction, a mixture of what I can only assume are disgust and annoyance on his face. "Not fall in love or whatever he was doing."

Love?

Did he say...

"Mr. Kensington," I begin, not knowing what his purpose is for coming here, but wanting to make one thing clear. "I'm not selling the Blue Bayou. If that's what you sent Maverick here to do, it was a failed mission from the start. That will never happen. No offer would ever be good enough. This is my home, my business...my family. I'm not going anywhere, and neither is this hotel."

My chest is heaving when I finish my spiel, but I feel ten feet tall. It feels good to say those things out loud and to take charge. This is mine. I own this place. No one can take that away from me.

I'm Carys Matthews, hear me roar.

"Huh," he says, his demeanor placid as he unbuttons his jacket and adjusts the waistband of his pants. Smoothing his tie once more, which must be what he does when he's trying to stay calm, he continues. "I must say, you're a lot tougher than I thought you'd be. I can see where Maverick would've been swayed. He's weak...always giving in too soon, never sticking around long enough for the kill."

Those words make my blood instantly boil. Even though I'm not *exactly* sure who Maverick is, I know one thing for sure: he is not weak. Not once in our time together did I ever associate that description with Maverick, not even when I thought he'd lied to me. I'm starting to think I made a mistake. I don't know how, but I feel it in my bones.

"He's not weak," I counter, gripping the edge of the counter for support. "He's actually one of the strongest people I know. Strength is not measured by how many kills you make, it's measured in how many lives you save." That last statement is something I just read last night in the journal Maverick left behind, his grandfather's journal. I haven't taken the time to read much of it, partly because I still miss Maverick so bad it hurts and when I open the journal I'm reminded of him, but also because I just haven't had the time. Since we started remodeling the hotel and getting ready for the grand re-opening, I've met myself coming and going, only stopping to lay my head down on my pillow for a few hours.

"You sound like someone else I know," Spencer mutters under his breath, rolling his eyes as he places his hands on the desk in front of me. "Listen, I'm going to cut to the chase. I know you're behind on taxes. I also know you were left this hotel due to a death in the family, which I'm sure was a huge inconvenience to someone your age. You should be going to college and having fun, not running some outdated hotel."

I bristle with those words. "It's not outdated," I growl. "It's antique and it has character. And if you don't like it, leave." My words are menacing and stern. I don't even know where that came from, some deep hidden, badass part of myself. I like it. I also like the look of shock on Spencer Kensington's face. "And as for my taxes, they're none of your concern, but I'll have you know, they're current. I'm current."

He stands there for a moment, looking me over, searching for a crack, but I don't give him a chance to find one. "Please leave, Mr. Kensington, and please pass on to whoever is interested in *my* hotel, I'm not selling."

Without another word, I give him my best smile and turn around, walking back into my office and leaving him standing at the counter. He can see himself out, letting the door hit him where the good Lord split him.

Eventually, the bell chimes and the door shuts, albeit a smidge forcefully, but I can't help the smile on my face, feeling like David who just defeated Goliath. I'm not toting around a severed head, but I do feel like I earned a badge of some sort, because damn, that felt good.

Something inside me shifts as I try to reconcile that vile man being the father of Maverick. The morning he left, I told him he was just like his father, but I lied. Now that I've met them both, I know for a fact they're nothing alike. I still don't know what to make of the notes I found in Maverick's room or everything that happened, but one thing I know for sure: Maverick is not his father.

Later that evening, when the hotel is quiet and all of our guests are checked-in and turned-down for the night, I pull out the old, worn journal and flip through a few more of the pages, finding the one I stopped on the last time I opened it.

At the top of the page, in handwriting that conveys age and wisdom, come the following words:

There's a lid for every pot. My mama told me that when I was dating your grandmother. She said "sometimes, we think we've found the right lid, and it's a close fit, but it won't keep the steam in or the cold out, and it won't produce the best end result." *She also said that sometimes we lose the lid, but it'll turn up again in the most unexpected place.*

I thought Maverick might be mine.

I smile as I read the words and notice my hand is covering my chest, right over my heart, like I'm trying to hold something in there. His words ring true, because I believe that too. I believe we all have a lid out there somewhere and it's our perfect fit.

There's so much wisdom in this book, I wonder, not for the first time, why he left it for me. I know it means a lot to him, so why would he part with it? Thumbing through it, I go to the back. I'm guilty of often reading the end of a book first. I can't help it. Sometimes, I just need to know how it ends. What was Maverick's grandfather's last entry? What were his parting words?

As the pages are turning, I stop when I notice a change in the handwriting.

I know this handwriting.

For a moment, I'm fixated on the letters and the freshness of the ink. Whereas the earlier words were worn and the pages often smudged from excessive use, these are relatively clean. I close the journal for a minute, taking a deep breath as I close my eyes and try to get my heart and mind under control, before opening it back up and continuing to read:

May 21

I found the most interesting place today...stumbled right into the door and into the most beautiful, hot mess.

I'm gonna stay here...for as long as I can get by with. After that, we'll see.

Lesson learned today: do something out of the ordinary.

My heart beats faster seeing Maverick's words on the paper and knowing they're about me. Checking the date, I know it's the first day he stayed at the Bayou.

I'll remember that day for the rest of my life.

It changed me.

He changed me.

Unable to stop, I continue to read, devouring the pages line by line. They're unlike the rest of the journal. These pages are filled with daily observations and Maverick's notes on how he was applying his grandfather's wisdom to his life. Almost like an answer to a question. The older Maverick giving the younger Maverick a challenge and the younger saying: challenge accepted.

May 23

I kissed Carys tonight, or rather, she kissed me. And I'd be happy if she was the last girl I ever kiss.

Lesson learned today: let her lead, because you'll be pleasantly surprised with the outcome.

May 25

I've been asked to do something today that goes against everything in me. My father wants me to pursue the Blue Bayou for a client who is interested in purchasing the block of buildings the Bayou sits on. I won't do it. I don't care what happens to me, but I know I'll do everything to protect her.

Lesson learned today: if you know who you are, you'll know what to do.

I'm holding my breath. I started a few entries up and I've been unable to release it the further I read, the further I delve into Maverick's thoughts and mind, memories of what he's describing flooding my mind. My body responds to the reminder of our first kiss. I feel the warmth spread from my heart to my stomach to lower regions as I read about his recollection of our time together.

Can this be real?

Can I allow myself to believe the words on the page?

I don't know. I don't know if I can. I've felt the invisible wall raise around my heart over the last few weeks, like armor, protecting myself from memories and desires. I want Maverick. I want to believe him. I want to call him and tell him that I forgive him, but I don't know if I can. I don't know if it's too late or if he still wants me.

June 1

Is love at first sight real? I don't know the answer to that, but I know Carys Matthews is real and she was meant for me...she was meant for me to find...she was meant to be in my life. I know this because I feel it every time I'm with her. My body literally sparks to life when she's near. My heart feels fuller. My steps lighter. The uncertainty I felt when I got here still lingers, but it also feels inconsequential, because she's here.

Lesson learned today: be open to possibilities, even the far-stretched ones.

Maverick

PLACING MY BOOK ON THE SIDE TABLE, I GLANCE OUT the window. I've been doing a lot of this the past few weeks—reading, sitting, thinking, reflecting. Being unemployed allows you the time to do such things. I don't have my grandfather's journal to mull over, so I've moved onto books he recommended. This week's reading material: *What We Talk About When We Talk About Love.*

I thought it might be good fodder, something that would help me work through the storm of emotions I've felt ever since I left New Orleans—left Carys—but it's really dark as shit. Some of it makes sense though. I see symbolism with the sun. At the beginning of the book, it's bright; and by the end, it's gone. As their friendly conversation turns into more, the sun in the kitchen fades, showing the way love complicates things.

Thoughts about the sun naturally leads me to thoughts about Carys. She's the sun incarnate. I miss her warmth. I thought about calling again today, to see if today would be the day she'd talk to me, but I didn't. I'm trying to give her space and allow her to come to me, but I'm feeling antsy and unsettled, much like I felt when I escaped this place and took refuge at the Bayou.

"Fuck," I moan, standing up and running a hand over my face and through my hair. I've got to get out of this funk. Shep will be here in a few minutes and he'll give me shit if he finds me sitting in my dark office again, with only the lamp on.

He warned me last week he was considering an intervention that included pussy and beer, but I'm pretty sure my precise punch to his shoulder made him think differently.

I don't need pussy.

And I don't need beer.

Now, this whiskey, I think, taking a sip, it seems to be doing the trick. Also, reminding me of Carys and my night at Revelry with Jules. I really miss them all—Carys, George, Mary, and Jules. In the couple of weeks I was there, they felt more like family than my own. I chalk them right up there beside Shep, except for Carys, of course, she has her own place.

Deciding to stretch my legs, I open the front door and jog down the sidewalk to the mailbox. I need some fresh air, anyway, and it's been a while since I remembered to check it.

Reaching inside, I'm surprised when it's full. Usually, all I have are a few random envelopes, mostly advertisements or political propaganda. My bills are paperless and on auto-draft. And let's face it, people just don't send correspondence through the United States Postal Service like they used to.

I bet Carys hates that. I bet letters through the mail have a special place in her heart, right along with antique room keys. That thought makes me smile. I wish I could call her up and ask her where she stands on the topic.

Shuffling through the mail, I quickly discard most of it, tossing the envelopes in the nearby trash can on my way back up to the house, but a package wrapped in brown paper makes me pause in the middle of the sidewalk. The return address catching my attention.

123 St. Ann, New Orleans, LA

Blue Bayou.

Quickly, I rip open the end of the paper and shake out the contents.

My grandfather's journal slips into my hand and I flip it over, staring at it. Instinctively, and without thought, I bring it to my nose and inhale. It smells like her—sweet and good. Running my hand reverently down the wrinkled leather cover, I just stare at it for a moment. A pang of jealousy hits me square in the chest. This book has been held by Carys. She wrapped her hands around it and touched the pages.

Just as I'm getting ready to bring it back to my nose for another hit, a car horn startles me, making me nearly piss my pants.

"What the fuck, Shep," I growl, glancing up to see him pulling in my drive, smiling at his antics. I'd like to punch that cocky grin right off his face.

"Hey, douchebag, still sulking?" he asks, climbing out of his Porsche. Unlike me, Shep doesn't shy away from public displays of wealth. He might not like his father, but he appreciates the money the man provides.

"Who's the fucking douchebag?" I mutter, tucking the journal back into the brown paper before he can give me shit about that too.

"I brought takeout and beer," he announces, holding up the preferred offerings. "Let the business meeting commence."

Walking back inside the house, Shep follows and continues past me, setting the food on my kitchen table.

"Let's eat first," he calls out, banging cabinets like he lives here. "I'm starving."

"Okay." I slip back into my office for a second and deposit the journal into the top drawer of my desk. I want to hide away with it, open it and see if she left anything—a word, a response, a smudge... anything. Instead, I close the drawer and walk to the kitchen, placing what I hope is a look of indifference on my face, because I don't want to talk about it—about her. Not yet.

"So," Shep says around a bite of food, once we've opened every container and popped the top on some beers. I said I didn't want beer, but I lied. It's good. Between this and the two fingers of whiskey I had earlier, at least I don't feel as wound up as I've been lately.

"So," I return, taking a heaping chopstick full of Moo Goo Gai Pan and shoving it into my mouth.

"I talked to Ros today," he starts, quirking an eyebrow.

"So," I reply again, only this time with distaste. I don't give two shits about Ros.

"Just thought you might be interested in some information she passed on."

I wait, chopsticks midair and motion for him to continue.

"Apparently, your father took a trip to New Orleans last week."

My heart drops into the pit of my stomach as I immediately imagine him walking into the Blue Bayou, harassing Carys...forcing her hand on something she doesn't want...acquiring the hotel. My mind goes to the worst-case scenario before I squeeze my eyes together and take a long drink of beer in an effort to clear my head. "What else did she say?"

"Well, I guess it didn't quite go as planned. She said before he left he was talking about what a pussy you were and how you never can close a deal." Shep pauses to roll his eyes and mutter expletives under his breath. He hates my father almost as much as I do. "Anyway, I guess he felt confident he'd walk in, lay it on the line, and Miss Matthews would roll over and give him what he wanted."

Talking about Carys and my father...and her rolling over and giving him anything has me seeing red. I tighten my jaw so hard it hurts, grinding out, "And?" He needs to keep talking before I flip this fucking table and ruin our dinner.

"Didn't happen," Shep says smugly. "He got back a few days ago and was royally fucking pissed. She said he canceled his meetings for the day, one being with her, and wouldn't return her calls. His assistant, some guy he brought in from Peterson's, who Ros has been fucking, gave up the deets. He told her when Mr. Kensington got back he said the deal was off. He called a meeting with the prospective buyer later that day and has been in a shit mood ever since."

My heart is back up in my chest where it belongs, beating soundly, full of pride.

I don't know what happened, but I can take a guess, and I wish I'd been there to see it. The new vision of Carys handing my father his ass on a silver platter has me grinning from ear to fucking ear.

"That's my girl."

Shep gives me a wink and continues stuffing his face.

Best news I've had in a long time.

"Let's talk about this new venture," I tell him, feeling rejuvenated and ready to kick some ass.

After we discuss our ideas and go over the properties I collected information on when I was in New Orleans, Shep sits back and nods, quiet for longer than usual. "I like it. I think this is going to be a good investment."

"You sure?" I ask, knowing I'm asking a lot of him, needing his financial support to follow through with what I want to accomplish. Most of the cash flow will come from our clients. We plan on orchestrating deals—a matchmaking for property owners of sorts.

"It might take a while for us to see a return on investment. We might need to acquire a few of these properties on our own and do some upgrades, just basic improvements, to make them more attractive to possible buyers," Shep says thoughtfully. "But I'm on board. One hundred percent."

"It might require going to New Orleans occasionally," I warn. "Seeing that the properties we're considering are all within the city limits."

"I'm okay with that." Shep sighs, taking a swig of his beer. "I've been wanting out of this damn city for a while. You know that."

I nod. "Okay."

So, we're doing this.

Shepherd Rhys-Jones and I are going into business together. I mean, we should've seen this coming ten years ago when we started swindling our classmates out of money, selling everything our parents sent us, but up charging due to delivery fees. I always wanted to give them a break and sell stuff cheap, but Shep was the one who wanted to monopolize on the supply and demand.

We balance each other out.

I'll keep us on the straight and narrow and he'll make sure we don't get fucked over.

It's a match made in heaven.

After Shep is gone and the kitchen is cleaned back up, I stand at the counter, looking out into the great room. I love this house, but since I've been back, it hasn't felt like home. Since I found the Blue Bayou, nothing else feels quite right.

At that thought, I walk into my office and take the journal out of the drawer. Leaning against the desk, I pull it back out of the brown paper package and run my hand along the leather. Bringing it to my nose, I inhale again, wondering if it was just my wishful imagination that thought I smelled Carys on the pages.

No.

It's definitely her.

And it makes my throat tighten with the visions her scent brings.

Carys smiling.

Carys laughing.

Carys' blue eyes.

Carys' long blonde hair.

Carys moaning beneath me, on top of me. Her soft pale skin under my hands.

Heaven.

That's what it was. My two weeks at the Blue Bayou with her was like a slice of heaven or maybe a taste, just enough to let me know I want to go there. I want to live there.

Flipping it open, I go straight to the back, where I know there are blank pages to be filled, and my heart stops. Beautiful, swooping handwriting fills half a page.

July 2nd

I miss the way you tell me things without saying a word. I miss the feeling of complete contentment when I'm with you. I miss the way my skin zips with electricity when you walk into the room. I miss the way you felt like an old friend. I miss the way you tease me and challenge me to be a better version of myself. I miss feeling like I can take on the world when you're by my side.

But I've been doing it.

I've been slaying dragons and taking charge of my life.

You helped me do that.

A wise man once said that love is a risk and trust doesn't come cheap.

So, I'm sitting here, asking myself:

Is this relationship worth that risk?

Is it worth feeling vulnerable?

Is it worth forgiving?

Reading Carys' words is like having a piece of her here and I immediately feel elated and sad all at the same time. So fucking sad, because I miss her. And I'm sorry I didn't tell her the truth from the beginning. The day I got the papers, I should've told her about them and we could've worked on a solution together, or she could've at least known what she was facing. I did her a disservice by not telling her, and for that, I'm sorry.

I wish I knew what her answers are to those questions. I wish I could hug her and tell her how much I feel for her. I wish I had another fucking number besides the hotel.

We never had a reason to exchange phone numbers. I thought I'd get it before I left. I pictured a tearful goodbye, filled with kisses and promises of seeing each other again in a few weeks. I didn't picture everything going so terribly wrong, and now, I'm terribly unequipped.

Walking over to my desk, I sit down and fire up my computer. Immediately, I open Facebook and search out Carys' old profile. But when I get there, the photo I've come to love is gone.

I pause, my mouse hovering over the new image and I swallow down a lump in my throat.

It's Carys and Jules.

She's mid-laugh and it looks like Jules is the one who took the picture.

My eyes take in every aspect of the photo—the way the light is hitting her hair, the shape of her lips, the crinkle in her nose. Rubbing my chest, I try to ease the longing I feel seeing her beautiful face. It feels like a lot longer than a month since I've seen her and there's something different about her. The thought that she's changed and that I missed it kills me.

I can't quit staring at her and it might be a bit stalkerish, but I hover my mouse over the photo and right click, saving it to my computer.

Scrolling down the page a little further, hungry for any information about her, I notice where she's changed her profile and it now says she's the owner of the Blue Bayou with a hyperlink, which I immediately click.

There's a new cover photo and albums. It's completely revamped and it looks great—inviting, cozy, eclectic—everything the Blue Bayou is.

As I follow the website, I'm pleasantly surprised when I see the new design, so open and fresh, with a button for reservations. Instinctively, I click it and go to two days from now.

Booked.

Just for kicks, I plug in a bunch more dates and every one of them shows *no vacancy.*

Picking the journal back up, I flip through it again, wanting to re-read Carys' entry before I try to call the hotel, and that's when I see it. On the very last page is another note in Carys' handwriting.

Grand Re-Opening
Blue Bayou Hotel
123 St. Ann, New Orleans, LA
July 6th
Come for a taste of the French Quarter.
Come back to the Blue Bayou

Without a second thought, I pick up my phone and hit redial.

"What's up man? You already reconsidering?" Shep asks, obviously half asleep.

"Sorry if I woke your ass up, but I need you to pack a bag."

"Where are we going?"

"Blue Bayou."

Carys

STEPPING INSIDE THE BAR, I IMMEDIATELY NOTICE
it's unlike most of the bars in this area. Most bars in or around the
French Quarter have their doors and windows wide open with music
blaring in order to catch the attention of those walking by. But this
place, interestingly called Come Again, only has one door propped
open and it's not until I'm completely inside and seated on a stool that
I notice the hard rock music coming through the speakers. There's also
not a strand of Mardi Gras beads to be seen.

Very interesting.

"How can I help you?" I turn to see a man with dark hair and
equally dark eyes watching me closely from behind the counter, using
a white bar towel to dry a stack of freshly washed glasses. He doesn't
have the typical welcoming demeanor one expects in a bartender, but
there is something about him that's just...intriguing.

"Hi, I'm Carys Matthews. I run the Blue Bayou hotel around the
corner," I say, pointing over my shoulder but having no idea if it's the
right direction or not. "I called earlier about hiring a bartender from

here for a party I'm hosting and was told to come speak with a Mr. O'Sullivan." My voice goes up like I'm answering a question and I'm probably coming off sounding like a stupid kid, but I can't help it. This guy is intense and it's intimidating.

"You can call me Shaw." His tone is gruff as he thrusts his hand in my direction, offering a business-like handshake. I immediately accept it, giving him a smile.

"Nice to meet you, Shaw. I've heard great things about your place."

He nods his head once, but his facial expression doesn't change. For a second, I think that's all the conversation I'm going to get out of him until he finally asks, "What kind of party are you hosting?"

"It's a grand re-opening party for the hotel. I've recently done a few upgrades, spruced the place up a bit, while keeping its original charm." I throw that last part in there because it's important to me. "Anyway, I thought it'd be fun to re-introduce it to the community. I'm also all about supporting other local businesses so, if you have any brochures or business cards you'd like me to display in the hotel lobby, I'd be happy to."

He seems to be mulling over my words while he continues to watch me. Approaching him like this is so out of my comfort zone, but I made myself pull up my big girl panties and just do it. If he says no, I'll find someone else. It's as simple as that.

But, why doesn't it feel as simple as that?

"How fancy are we talking?"

Shaw's question catches me off guard and I have to think about it for a second.

"It's not anything super fancy, but it'll be nice. Casual but charming," I say with a slightly nervous laugh. "The party will take place in the late afternoon in the hotel's courtyard, so the drinks should be refreshing, as well as tasty."

"Will food be served?" He grabs a pen and notepad from his side of the bar and starts writing, like he's taking notes.

"Lagniappe will be serving finger foods and I'll be providing macarons."

Shaw looks up at me with his eyebrows raised. "You make macarons?"

"I do. My grandmother taught me," I reply with pride.

My answer must impress him because he nods his head, thoughtfully. "Those aren't easy to master. I own the cooking school next door with my sister and we reserve that particular class for those we know are serious about learning."

"A cooking school? How fun! I had no idea, but then again, I haven't been out much lately."

"Yeah," he replies gruffly, almost like he regrets mentioning it and then continues hastily, "It was closed for a while, but we recently reopened it."

"I bet that's going over well. I'd love to have some info. I could pass it along to my guests, if you'd like," I offer.

"I'd appreciate that, thanks." He gives what could almost be considered a smile and a nod. I'm guessing he's normally a man of few words, so I find myself appreciating the gesture. "If Lagniappe is doing the food," he continues, "why not have them do the drinks as well?"

"Well, like I mentioned earlier, I really love supporting local businesses and I thought the party would be a great way to showcase some that are close by. If I have Lagniappe do the food and the drinks, that's kind of like letting them bogart the party, you know?"

Shaw lets out a quick laugh, but stops, almost like he caught himself and thought better of it. It's deep and scratchy, perhaps from lack of use, and very attractive, if I'm being honest.

When he brings his hand up to scratch his beard thoughtfully, I also notice a wedding band on his left hand. At that, I smile, feeling a bit of a blush creep up on my cheeks. I've always thought monogamy is sexy.

Not in a "I'm gonna steal her man" sort of way, but rather a "good for her".

"I guess that'll work," he finally says. "Just let me know what time to be there."

"That's great!" I slide him one of my new fancy business cards and tell him I'll be in touch to firm up the details tomorrow. I still need to check back with Micah on the exact menu.

I'm almost to the door when I remember to ask the question that's been nagging at me since I got here. "Hey, Shaw, why is this place called Come Again? Besides the obvious, of course."

"The obvious?"

"Well, you want your customers to *come again*, right? To come back to the bar?"

"Yes, that's true, but the bar is actually named for my signature cocktail...something so good, you'll be asking to *come* again and again," he deadpans, and I expect him to follow it up with a smile or laugh, but he doesn't. There's no wink, no smirk... nothing. He just drops that bomb and goes back to business as usual.

Holy shit.

I'm now blushing from my head to my toes, and on that note, I hightail it out of the bar before he gets a chance to see my flustered state. If I was getting some on the regular, a statement like that might not have affected me in such a way, but since Maverick left, my whole body has been out of sorts.

Thankfully, I have a couple blocks to walk to my next stop and I use the time to cool my jets and clear my mind. The last thing I need is to be thinking about Maverick. Every time that happens, I tend to lose hours of productivity to daydreaming and feeling sexually frustrated.

After stopping by Lagniappe and finalizing the menu with Micah, I head back to the hotel. I hired a crew to clean up the courtyard and decorate it with fresh plants and flowers, as well as those cute, little fairy lights and I'm anxious to see how everything is coming together.

It was an expense I wouldn't normally opt for, choosing to take the time and do it myself, but I haven't had time and I still have some money left from the loan that I set aside for this specific task. Also, it's not just for the grand re-opening. Afterwards, I plan on starting a new tradition on the weekends, treating our guests to hors d'oeuvres and drinks at sunset.

When I step inside, I hear Mary's happy voice say, "Oh, here she is", and my heart does a flip. For a fleeting, hopeful moment, I wonder if Maverick is back. I can't help it. Ever since I sent him the journal, I've let myself start to hope he'll walk through the doors at any moment.

There's so much I want—*need*—to say to him and it should be done face-to-face. Even if he never forgives me for what I said to him, I must apologize. Then, I need to thank him for encouraging me to make all these necessary changes to the hotel. And lastly, I'd like to tell him how much I've missed him and that I was—*am*—falling for him.

In short, this grand re-opening is nothing without him showing up. Sure, I'll put on a happy face and pretend like everything is fine, like I've been doing, but deep down, it won't be a success in my book if he's not here.

My excitement is tampered down, just a little, when I see that it is in fact not Maverick standing in my lobby, but CeCe. She turns to face me and I notice she has something flat, but huge, wrapped in brown paper next to her, leaning against the front desk.

"Hey, whatcha got there?"

"A little surprise for you. Well, for the hotel, that is." She smiles as I walk over and give her a quick hug. I just saw her yesterday, when I dropped off some macarons and new brochures, and she didn't say anything then about a surprise.

"Can I open it now or do I have to wait?" I ask, sounding like a kid on Christmas morning. I can't for the life of me guess what it is but I love surprises, so I'm excited.

CeCe laughs. "You can open it now." She steps to the side but keeps her hand on the top to keep it from falling over. Now that I'm closer to it, I can tell it's something framed and I can't wait to see it. Even though I want to rip the brown paper to shreds to get to it, I force myself to peel the paper back carefully, so I don't mess anything up.

When I'm finally able to see what's inside, I'm too shocked to do anything but stare at the gorgeous painting in front of me. I'm even more shocked when I glance down at the bottom, right corner and see the artist's signature.

Peeling my eyes away, I look at my friend. "Camille Benoit-Landry painted this?"

"Yep! It's an original, painted just for you. I think it'd look great right up there behind the desk, don't you?"

I'm utterly speechless, nothing but stuttering sounds coming out of my mouth, as I look over the painting again. The swirls of colors on the canvas are breathtaking and I can't believe CeCe did this for me. It's absolutely beautiful and I get to look at it every day.

Finally finding my voice, I say, "Thank you so much. This means the world to me. I just can't believe it's mine!" I hug CeCe tightly while she giggles.

"Well, it's kind of becoming a tradition here in the Quarter—a Cami Benoit-Landry original is like a lucky rabbit's foot for businesses. I figured the Bayou could use all the luck it can get, and since you're having your grand re-opening...I just wanted to say congratulations and I'm proud of you." She sighs, looking down at the painting with a pleased expression. "Oh, and you can thank Cami yourself. She'll be here for the party."

"Shut your face! Oh my God, I'm just..." I hug her again. "Thank you. And I'm so excited to meet her. Please don't let me do anything to embarrass myself in front of her," I beg.

"The woman can only do so much, Carys," Jules announces as he strolls in. "And, I like to think we're all doing the Lord's work when it comes to you. Can I get an amen?"

CeCe and Mary both say "amen" while laughing with Jules. I tell them to hush but they don't listen. And really, I'm not at all insulted by Jules' words because I know he's right. I know I can be a hot mess and these people keep me in check. They're my tribe and I'm so thankful for them.

The grand re-opening party is here and so are my nerves.

My brain is telling me to relax, that there's nothing to worry about.

It reminds me that this is just an opportunity for people within the community to come and see our renovations and what we have to offer. It's also a chance for everyone to network and mingle.

So, no pressure, right?

Wrong.

My heart is arguing that today is extremely important and that the hotel's future—*my future*—depends on the success of *this* party. Even though I know that's not entirely true, it still feels that way.

A text brings my attention away from my inner turmoil.

Jules: Get out of that pretty, little head of yours and get your ass out here. You're missing all the fun!

I sigh, knowing he's right, and give myself one last look in the mirror before deciding nothing more can be done to my hair and face. I kept my makeup light and fresh because I'm just going to sweat it off anyway, and my hair is long and flowy, with the sides pulled back, because it has a mind of its own and, also, humidity.

I still haven't heard from Maverick, but I don't allow myself to dwell on that... too much. Last night as I read over the pages I copied out of the journal before sending it back to him, the ones he wrote while he was here at the Bayou, I tried to convince myself that if he doesn't show up tonight, it won't be the end of the world. I'm trying to be happy that he happened and not regret any of it, because all of it got me to this point. Who knows, maybe one of these days, I can take a little trip to Dallas and see what his world is like?

Stepping into the courtyard, I feel completely in awe. This is *my* courtyard, but it's not. The flowers are bright and colorful, just like this city. They're also fragrant and perfect for the space, along with the twinkling lights, faint jazz playing in the background, and the brush of sunlight still left in the sky, I feel transported to another world. Everything is simple and beautiful.

And hot as hell. Who on God's green earth decided it would be a good idea to host an outside party in New Orleans during the summer?

Oh, yeah, that would be me.

Thank goodness I also had enough sense to rent some of those cool air machines that are basically like air conditioning for the outdoors. God bless technology.

When I see Jules standing on the other side of the courtyard, I walk quickly to him.

"So, what's all this fun I'm missing?" I ask, picking my hair up off my neck and draping it over my shoulder, allowing some of that air I was talking about cool me off.

"Hello, you look *gorge*, by the way," Jules says, air kissing my cheeks. "And the fun I was referring to is this." He swoops his hands out in front of him before ending the movement with jazz hands. He's quite annoyed when he realizes I still have no idea what he means.

"This," he repeats with a hint of annoyance, his eyes going wider to emphasize his words. "Watching all this man meat work up a sweat while they set everything up." Biting his lip, he fans his face and continues devouring the scene before us.

I can't help but laugh at my friend. "Don't ever change, Jules," I say, patting him on the shoulder as I turn to see if there's anything I can do to get things ready.

"Listen, sis, just because you're still pining for Dreamboat's *longhorn*, doesn't mean you can't appreciate the scenery."

"You're absolutely right and these guys all look like nice, respectable, hard-working men. Thank you for the distraction."

"Oh, my God. Just get out of here and leave the drooling to me. You don't even know how to gawk correctly." He rolls his eyes, then walks off toward where Micah and his crew are setting up the food table, presumably to get a closer look.

I take that as my cue to leave and walk inside, admiring the changes that were made this past month as I go. We didn't do anything drastic, just enough to make everything shiny and pretty again, while keeping its original charm.

Mary and George are the smart ones. They're still enjoying our bought air indoors, manning the front desk. They smile as I walk up and I see the pride all over their faces. It makes my heart feel so full.

"Everything looks just great," Mary says, walking from behind the desk to give me a hug. I fold into her embrace, soaking her in and smiling at George over her shoulder.

"I want y'all to get out there and enjoy the evening. Jules and I will take turns working the desk. Besides, most of the guests will be out there, anyway."

"Oh, we will," George says with a wink. "We might even cut a rug if you turn that good music up just a little."

I laugh, a memory of him and Mary dancing from many years ago filling my mind. "Definitely. Just for you." *And me*, I think, as I lean over and kiss his cheek.

I've been waiting for this feeling since my mom died—contentment, happiness...feeling like my grandparents and my mama are looking down on me and smiling, proud of who I am and how I'm living my life. And it feels good.

An hour later, the music is turned up, people are mingling and I couldn't be happier.

Okay, I could be. But I'm making the best of it and telling myself this is good enough. Maverick is the only thing missing, and him showing up tonight was a wild card. So, I'm trying not to dwell on it as I make my way around, greeting guests and thanking everyone for coming.

"The drinks are great," I tell Shaw, actually a little surprised to see him. I thought he might send one of his bartenders, but I didn't think he'd actually come himself. "I really love this one." I hold up the reddish orange drink before taking another sip.

"That's the Come Again." He gives me the same wink from the other night and I laugh, shaking my head when I feel the blush.

Shit.

He has an effect on me, what can I say. I want to tell him that his wife is a lucky lady, but I refrain, since I don't know him that well. Besides, I wouldn't want him to think I'm flirting, because I'm not. I'm just appreciative of his...appearance...and those tattoos.

He's so interesting.

A hand touches my shoulder lightly, getting my attention, and I turn to see a tall guy with blue eyes—not Maverick's blues, lighter. He also has deep dimples and a wide, kind smile that immediately endears me to him.

"Hello."

"Hey," he replies. "I'm Deacon, Micah's brother. My wife Cami is—"

"The artist," I finish for him, excitement building. "I'm Carys."

When I offer him my hand to shake, he takes it and places a chaste kiss on the top.

Oh, he's a schmoozer. I can't help the girly giggle that escapes as I shake my head at the gesture, earning me another wide smile from him as he laughs at his own antics. "Just wanted to say that this place is so great. Thanks for inviting us."

"Thanks so much for coming," I reply, glancing around him. "Is Cami here?"

"Oh, yeah, she and Dani, Micah's wife, went on a tour of the hotel." He grins, his blue eyes twinkling with a bit of mischief. "You better get used to seeing our faces, because I have a feeling we're going to be taking up residence. They were gushing before they even stepped inside."

"I'd be honored, and please, let me know anytime you'd like to stay. It'll be on the house. I'd love to be able to repay Cami for the amazing painting she did for me. It's hanging in the lobby," I tell him, pointing behind him toward the hotel. "Would you like to see it? Maybe we can catch up with Cami and Dani."

"Sounds great."

He shoots a wave over his shoulder at Micah as we walk by, getting his attention, and then points toward the hotel.

Maverick

STEPPING OUT OF THE AIRPORT IN KENNER, LOUISIANA,
I groan as the heat and humidity hit me like a Mack truck.

"Holy fuck." Shep lets out a disgusted huff. "This has got to be what hell feels like. Are you sure you want to come here?"

I slap his back and start walking toward the Uber by the curb. "Come on. You'll get used to it."

"And I thought Dallas was hot."

Laughing, I toss my bag into the trunk and then slip into the back seat. Shep does the same, and a few minutes later we're on our way. My heart starts beating faster with every mile and I start second-guessing my choices.

I should've called.

I should've come last night when I finished reading her note.

I should check my mail more often.

I should've never left.

"Dude, you've got to stop," Shep demands. "You've been worrying and fretting like some grandma for the last five hours. You either want to do this or you don't. I've never seen you like this before. Snap out of it."

I want to do this.

I want to see Carys.

I want to hold her and feel her skin.

I want to breathe her in.

"Okay," I tell him, too distracted to argue or offer a rebuttal. Also, he's right. "Thanks for coming with me."

"Don't thank me," he huffs, watching the scenery as we ride along. "I was ready to get the heck out of Dodge, so this was just a good excuse for a weekend getaway. Plus, I figure we can make this a business trip, so, tax deduction."

That's Shep. Always planning, always scheming. But he's a damn good businessman and I'm happy he's agreed to be my partner in this new venture. It'll be good to get him to New Orleans and help him loosen up a little.

"You know, I might need you to come here from time to time."

"Fine by me." He pauses, looking over at me thoughtfully. "You're not planning on coming back, are you?"

I give my head one firm shake. "Nope, not if she'll let me stay. I mean, no offense, but the only real thing I have keeping me in Dallas is my house and it's a seller's market right now. So, I'm following my gut on this one."

And my gut is telling me to listen to my heart. And my heart is saying Carys. New Orleans. Freedom. Do what makes you happy.

Shep sighs. "I don't blame you, man." Turning, he looks out his window. "If this thing works out and we can make some money. I might consider it myself."

"Yeah, right. You'd leave Dallas and your country club and your fancy gated community?" I laugh, shaking my head. "No fucking way."

He gives me his easy smile, but I see a smidge of sincerity there.

"I guess anything's possible," I tell him, realizing that if I can take a spur of the moment trip and end up in a hotel off the beaten path and find the woman of my dreams...dreams I hadn't even allowed myself to have yet, I guess Shepherd Rhys-Jones could move to New Orleans... one of these days.

Fifteen minutes later, our driver lets us out in front of the familiar building, but I stop in my tracks as I collect my bag from the trunk. Sure, it's the same hotel, but there's a fresh coat of blue paint on the front doors and a brand spanking new sign that hangs sideways, getting the attention of people coming from every direction.

Welcome to the Blue Bayou

And in smaller print: *where everyone always wants to come back*

Smiling, I immediately feel the stress and tension release from my shoulders. And the humidity doesn't feel oppressive any longer. It feels welcoming, as does the jazz music filling the night air.

"Come on," I say, slapping Shep on the shoulder. I don't miss the way he scrutinizes the place, taking in the exterior and the surrounding buildings, all different colors. When we walk inside, the place is vacant. Not one person, but there's a tented note on the desk.

Welcome. Come to the courtyard. The party is waiting.

"This is my kind of place," Shep muses, picking up a small glass of something pinky orange from a tray and downing it in one drink.

I take one for myself and sniff before doing the same.

We both shrug and take another, sipping on these.

"Let's leave our bags here," I tell him, motioning around the counter, feeling completely at home, even though I don't know if I'm welcome here anymore.

That thought brings back a small knot in my stomach and I pull up short, turning toward the door and then back to the front desk.

"Maybe this was a bad idea," I think out loud. "What if she didn't write that note thinking I'd show up? What if she just wanted me to know? Or—"

"Do you know what you sound like right now?" Shep asks, one hand on his hip while he holds his fruity drink in the other. "A fucking girl," he replies without waiting for my response. "And not a smart one, either. A stupid one. Who's overthinking everything, when you should just shut the fuck up and walk out there, find your woman, and tell her how you feel." He pauses his tirade for a moment, just long enough to take a drink and then continues. "And then you need to get laid."

"A-fucking-men," a familiar voice chimes in from somewhere behind Shep. I step around to see Jules walking up to us, taking in me and then going for Shep. "Speaking of getting laid."

I'm glad I wasn't taking a drink, because if I had, it would now be all over the now shiny floors of the lobby.

And the floors are super shiny.

Nicely done, Carys.

I take a second to look around the entire space, noticing each detail.

"Nice," I mutter to no one but myself.

"I know, right?" Jules adds, still a bit standoffish, but also more welcoming than I thought he might be. We've spoken a couple of times on the phone, so it's not like he's completely surprised to see me here. "Who'd you bring with you?"

"Oh," I say, trying not to laugh when I take in Shep's raised eyebrows as he keeps watch on Jules. "This is Shep. Shep, Jules."

Jules offers Shep his hand and Shep takes it, expecting a shake, but instead, Jules takes it to his lips and kisses it. "The pleasure is all mine."

This is fucking fantastic.

Seriously, I couldn't have planned our reception better if I tried.

"Okay," Jules says matter-of-factly, when he drops Shep's hand and turns back to me. "To get the full effect of the evening, in my personal opinion." His hand goes to his chest. "You really should enter from the side. It's much more dramatic."

Without another word, he whirls around us and motions for us to follow him back out the front door, so we do. Shep gives me a wide eye stare as if to ask, "What the fuck?" But I just laugh, shaking my head. I should've known he and Jules would hit it off. Shep is exactly his type.

Too bad Shep has a serious thing for busty brunettes.

If it weren't for that tiny little tidbit, this could be a match made in heaven.

I'm still chuckling to myself when Jules leads us into the side entrance of the courtyard and everything comes into view. And by *everything* I mean Carys.

Her blonde hair.

Her pale blue dress.

Her creamy skin.

Her.

I feel like my chest is going to explode.

She's standing next to a table, talking to a guy. His large frame leans in to say something and when his hand lands on her arm, everything inside me tenses—my jaw, my expression...my fist. I don't like it. I don't like the way he's making her laugh. I don't like the way her big blue eyes look as she talks to him animatedly. I don't like any of it. Because I want that.

Before I get to make my move, they're walking...heading into the Bayou and I pause, wondering if I'm too late.

Who is he?

What is he to her?

"Stop," Jules demands, and I turn to see him and Shep making the same expression of exasperation. "He's a guest...or...well, a friend of guest of a...oh, who the fuck cares. He's not with her. She's not with him. She's waiting for you, jackass."

Shep's now the one chuckling and I glare at him.

Wait.

"Yeah," he continues. "Don't look so surprised. And be glad you showed up because if you hadn't, I would've driven to Dallas and beat your ass."

My heartbeat picks up and then evens out as the tightness in my chest begins to fade with Jules' words of encouragement. Well, tough love, but let's face it, sometimes we all need a little.

She's waiting for me.

"Now, drink up and wipe that pained look off your face before she gets back. I'm gonna need you to bring your A-game and make this good."

Watching Jules walk off, I take a deep breath and let it out.

Make it good. I can do that.

Carys

"It's so great meeting you," I gush.

I think I have a girl crush. Cami is probably the nicest, prettiest person I've ever met. Well, the gorgeous redhead standing next to her is a close second. They're both so sweet and friendly. I can see why CeCe and Cami have been friends all these years.

"It's great meeting you," Cami replies. "And I'm glad you love your painting. I always get so nervous when I do a commission piece like this."

"Nervous?" I ask in surprise. "Are you kidding me? I think you could splat paint on a canvas and I'd still love it."

We laugh and Dani chimes in. "She's crazy. Don't listen to her."

"Thanks for coming," I tell them both. "And whenever y'all wanna come for an extended stay, let me know. I'll get your rooms ready." I wink.

Tilting her head up to the ceiling and then giving the lobby another look, Dani sighs. "Well, hopefully soon. Micah works late sometimes when he has to fill in for someone or they have a busy weekend. So, I'll have to come crash here. We can hang out and I can see him. That'd be a win-win."

"Dani is a photographer," Cami adds. "You should totally hit her up for some fresh shots for your website."

My eyes grow wide in delight. "That would be amazing."

"You should see her work," Cami says proudly. "She's so talented."

Pot meet kettle, I think, but I'm trying to play it cool. Artists and authors are my rock stars, so this is a very fangirl moment for me.

"We can barter—rooms for photos."

"Sounds like a deal," I tell her.

After we exchange a few more minutes of small talk, I glance behind me where the backdoor is open to the courtyard. "I should probably get back out there."

"Us too," Cami says. "I need to make sure Deacon didn't go back out there and eat all your macarons."

We laugh, but I reach around the counter and pull out a few wrapped macarons. "For the road," I tell her, pausing when I see a brown leather bag sitting beside a black leather bag.

It's the brown one that gets my attention and makes me pause.

MHK is etched into the leather.

That could be anyone I tell my stupid heart, trying to not get my hopes up. I've done so well tonight, not letting my mind stay on Maverick or the fact he's not here. I've mingled and smiled and visited. To anyone looking at me, I'm the perfect picture of the welcoming hostess—Carys Matthews, owner of the Blue Bayou.

But inside, my heart stutters a little every time someone new shows up, thinking maybe it's him.

"We'll see you soon," Cami sings, she and Dani heading back outside.

"Uh, okay," I call back, my voice shaking as my heart jumps to crazy conclusions. Clearing my throat, I turn to follow them, but stop, my breath catching. "Hey."

Giving me a crooked smile and devouring me with his eyes, he replies, "Hey." We both stand there for a second, frozen in place until he finally adds, "Love what you've done with the place."

I swallow hard, willing my heart to stay in my chest and not leap out and run for him.

Be cool, Carys.

"Thanks." I nod, looking around at the newly painted bookshelves and the new chairs I found at the flea market down the street for the reading area.

"This is a nice touch," he adds, following my gaze.

I knew he'd like it.

I think, subconsciously, I did it for him.

I smile. "Thought you'd like it."

"I'm sorry—" we both begin and stop, gesturing to the other to continue.

"Me first," I tell him, taking a few steps forward, closing the distance between us. Man, I missed him. I missed the way his eyes look when he's watching me. I missed how blue they are, such a contrast with his dark hair, which has grown a little since I saw him last. Pressing my lips together, I inhale through my nose, mentally rehearsing the speech I've been preparing in my mind.

"I'm sorry," I repeat, knowing I want to start there. I've never been afraid of saying I'm wrong. "I recently read that if you're wrong, you should own up to that shit." I smile when Maverick's eyes squint in recognition, his features relaxing as he patiently listens. "I'm sorry I jumped to conclusions," I admit. "When I found those papers in your room, it was an accident. I wasn't snooping around in your things. I got up to go to the bathroom and I was trying to be quiet, but ran into the table, knocking the file onto the floor."

Maverick's smile morphs into a cringe as he rakes a hand through his hair. I can tell he wants to say something, but he's biting his tongue and giving me my moment.

"I'm a mess, I know," I say, trying to lighten the moment.

"My mess," Maverick mutters and it makes my heart stutter.

Continuing before I forget what I want to say, I tell him, "I saw the information about the Bayou and couldn't think of any other reason you'd have it except for wanting to buy my hotel. I trusted you and your opinion so much, but seeing that made me feel like I didn't truly know you. I acted in haste and let my emotions get the best of me. I should've—"

"I'm sorry," Maverick interrupts. "I know I should let you finish, but I really need to say something." His features are pained, and I watch as his hands flex and release, like he's trying to reign in his own emotions. "I should've been truthful with you from the beginning."

My heart drops at that and I swallow again. "So, you did come here to buy my hotel?" The hurt is thick in my voice as I try to keep it steady. No tears, not today.

"No," he says forcefully, shaking his head. "No, I didn't come here to buy the Blue Bayou. I came here for exactly what I told you—to get away from work and my father and clear my head. All of that was true. I didn't have any of that information about the Bayou until the day my father sent me those files and asked me to stay and work." His face falls and he rubs a hand across his jaw, his eyes boring into mine. "I should've told you then, but I thought I could fix it without you ever knowing. I didn't want you to stress out over something like that."

"And the taxes? Did you know about that?" I ask, needing the complete truth. Because if he had known and didn't tell me, I'm not sure I can trust him.

"No." Maverick shakes his head, looking pissed and it's strangely turning me on. "I didn't know anything about the taxes. When I got back to Dallas, after my dad fired me—"

"He fired you?" I blurt. "Are you serious?"

"Yeah." He waves away my question and continues. "Anyway, Shep and I were talking, trying to rack our brains to think of what my father could have on the Bayou that would give him the upper hand he felt he had. Property taxes were the only thing we could think of. I tried to call and talk to you, but neither George nor Jules would let me." Frustration is written all over his face. "I tried."

"Thank you," I tell him, and he looks confused. "I know you tried. Jules didn't tell me until after the fact, but thank you."

"Don't thank me," he demands, sounding defeated. "I tried to protect you and I failed."

"I didn't need protecting."

Maverick's expression changes again and this time, he looks proud, and a hint of a smile starts to reappear, smoothing out his hard lines.

"No, I guess you didn't." He smirks and it's everything I can do to not launch myself at him, wrapping my arms and legs around him and showing him how much I missed him, but I have one more thing to say.

"Thank you."

He cocks his head and rolls his eyes with a huff.

"I mean it. The day you walked into my hotel, you found me at my worst. I was confused and frustrated, a bit lost. I didn't know how to pull myself out of the hole I was in, but you saw the big picture. You gave me the encouragement I needed and you shared your passion. A few weeks ago, I decided that even if I never got to see you again, if what we shared was just a fling," I pause, chuckling to myself and shaking my head as I try to curtail the lump in my throat. "I decided that it was worth it. Even if I had to miss you every day for the rest of my life, I'd be grateful I had you to miss."

"Stop it," Maverick demands, closing the space between us and finally, thankfully, wrapping an arm around my waist and pulling me to him. He smells so good, just like I remember and it's starting to smell a lot like home.

Gripping the front of his shirt to keep him here, with me, I ask, "Stop what?"

"Showing me up," he says, leaning forward until his nose is running along my jaw, up to my ear, where he whispers, in my favorite husky voice that goes straight to my core. "I was supposed to make this good."

"You did." My voice is just above a whisper as I'm already losing myself to his touch, tilting my head to the side, I give him permission to continue. "You came back."

His lips graze softly on my neck and I feel the electricity I've been missing—the want, the need, the...I want to say love, but that's so crazy.

It feels crazy, but it also feels right. But instead, I just say, "Thank you."

"Don't thank me," he murmurs, placing one final, searing kiss to my jaw before looking back up at me. "It's my turn." He smiles, putting a few inches between us, but not taking his hands off me, which I'm grateful for, because I need his touch. "I'm sorry I didn't tell you about the offer my father was trying to make on the Bayou. My intentions were honorable, but omitting the truth is as much lying as anything."

We both smile, knowing those words came from his grandfather—from the journal. I love that we share that. I love that he left it for me and took the leap of faith that I'd read it and come back around.

"I'll never do it again," he promises. "I'll never intentionally do anything to hurt you. I..." he pauses, giving a hard look like he's trying to figure out a complicated problem. "I'm..." He huffs and then finally settles on, "I'm here to stay, if you'll have me."

"What?" I gape at him, unsure I heard him correctly.

"Unless, you don't want me—"

"No," I protest. "I want you." I shake my head, my gaze bouncing from his lips to his eyes as I fight the battle inside to talk first and act last. I want to kiss him, so badly, but I also want to make sure I just heard him correctly. "If you're saying you want to...move here...live here?" What starts out as a statement morphs into a question as I try to process the words coming out of my own mouth. "You want to stay here? At the Blue Bayou?" I ask.

Maverick's smile grows and he gives me a sexy nod. "That's what I was thinking. I'm kind of unemployed and looking to relocate."

"I might need someone who's good with their hands...if you know someone—"

He cuts me off mid-sentence, his lips on mine as he pulls me flush to his rock-hard body. I melt, conforming to his embrace, letting him lift me until my feet are off the ground. Our mouths go slow and then fast, forgetting we're standing in the middle of the lobby until a throat clears behind us.

He stops first and I reluctantly remove my mouth from his. When he places me back on the ground, I look around him to see George standing a few feet away. Maverick turns.

"George," he greets with a dip of his head, his arms still around me.

"Maverick," George replies and I smile, knowing that it took a while for him to come around. I wasn't even sure how he would feel when, and *if*, Maverick showed up, but I'm happy to see he's found it in his heart to forgive him.

"Miss Carys," George continues. "I was just coming to find you and see if I could maybe have a dance." The twinkle in his eyes is something I can't refuse.

"Of course," I tell him, letting my hand slide down Maverick's arm until our fingers are laced together. He follows me as I walk with George back into the courtyard, with the rest of my family and friends—new and old—and the guests who are enjoying the festive evening.

As George and I dance to an old song, I place my head on his chest and relish in the goodness of the moment. When he turns me, leading my steps, I catch Maverick's eyes on me. He's watching with a soft smile and I don't look away until I'm forced to.

He's here.

He came.

"He's a good one," George says quietly, just loud enough for me to hear. "He'll do."

Inhaling deeply, I can't help the ridiculous smile on my face or the joy in my heart. George is the closest thing I have to a father or grandfather. His approval in my life is something I lean on and need. "I think so too," I tell him, closing my eyes for the last few notes of the song.

When it's over, Maverick walks up and takes my hand. "I'd like to introduce you to someone."

I glance over his shoulder to see a man, around Maverick's age, in a starched white shirt with the sleeves rolled to his elbows, making him look a little stuffy, but handsome nonetheless. He also has an expensive looking watch on his wrist and a look of importance about him. And somehow, just intuition maybe, I know who it is. "Shep."

Maverick chuckles, turning toward me and kissing the top of my head, before he says, "Shep, I'd like you to meet Carys Matthews."

Shep offers me his hand, which I take, allowing myself a few seconds to look him over. He is Maverick's best friend, after all. So, I need to know everything there is to know about him.

"Nice to meet you," I tell him with a smile.

"Likewise," Shep says. "This guy hasn't quit talking about you since he got back to Dallas."

That earns him a glare from Maverick, followed by an eyeroll.

"Don't try to deny it, man."

"I didn't," Maverick retorts, then turns to me. "I thought about you...every day."

"Me too."

There's an unspoken thing that passes between us, something along the lines of *never again*...and *I'm here to stay*.

Later, when everyone is gone and the mess is cleaned up, Maverick and I are the only two people in the courtyard. It's late, like so late it's early, but we just sent Shep upstairs to the one vacant room and Maverick went inside to grab his bag. He's staying with me.

Forever, if I have anything to do with it.

"You tired?" he asks, a hint of suggestion in his voice.

"I'll sleep when I'm dead, right?" Another little piece of wisdom from his grandfather which has us both chuckling. He might regret leaving that journal with me after all.

"You know," he says, taking his bottom lip between his teeth and giving me a look that should be illegal—his blue eyes piercing right through me. "He also said something about when you see something you can't live without, take it..."

"To bed," I tell him, making up my own words of wisdom and loving the wicked grin that takes over his face. Tugging on the front of his shirt, I lead him through the courtyard, under the twinkling lights, and into my apartment.

In reality, the words of his grandfather were much more romantic: *If you find something you can't live without, take it with both hands and hold on tightly.* I do want to hold on, tightly...with both hands, but in this moment, more than anything, I just want Maverick. I want to touch him, taste him, feel him...hear him—be as close to him as physically possible.

"We should definitely write that down," Maverick teases in a low, gravelly voice as he bends forward and kisses me deeply. His hands dipping low and caressing my backside before wrapping firmly around my thighs, lifting me up and carrying me to the bedroom.

ONE MONTH LATER

Maverick

I'M MAVERICK KENSINGTON, NEWEST EMPLOYEE OF the Blue Bayou.

Even though Shep and I have started our business matchmaking venture, it's still in the early stages and hasn't taken off yet so, my main job title is resident handyman for the hotel. Basically, I do whatever Carys needs me to do and I'm loving every minute of it.

I mean, I get to take care of her needs day and night...it's the best fucking job ever. She also pays well, if you catch my drift.

I've been here a month and we've fallen into a very comfortable way of life. Carys was concerned she wouldn't be able to be my boss and my girlfriend, but I think we've found a good balance. Things are going very well at the hotel, so we're keeping busy, but we manage to have fun, too.

Lots of fun, actually.

With me being here, George and Mary get to take a little extra time off. Carys manages the office and fills in where needed, as always, and Jules picks up the slack where anyone needs it. We're a well-oiled machine. Even when business picks up for me and Shep, I still plan on doing what I'm doing now, fixing shit and working beside Carys.

I'd like to do it every day for the rest of my life.

Marriage has been on my mind, but I'm trying to take things slow. Since the beginning of our relationship was a whirlwind, or maybe a hurricane, I'm making a conscious effort to make this middle part slow and easy, like New Orleans...like the Blue Bayou.

There's an entry in my grandfather's journal that has played over and over in my mind ever since I met Carys, especially when I realized my feelings for her. It talks about how love is passionate and often obsessive, but you know when it's real, because you won't be able to live without that person.

That's me and Carys...I feel nothing but passion for her and I'm obsessed with being near her. The month I spent apart from her was the longest month of my life, and I knew then I didn't want to live without her. I had to make her mine, permanently.

I feel like if my grandfather was here, he'd tell me to take Carys with both hands and hold on tightly. Because once you find that person you can't live without, why waste time? Sure, I could find my own place and find another job, but why? I know who I want, and I know where I want to be. It wouldn't matter if we knew each other three days, three months, or three years, I'd still know. And in thirty years, I'll feel the same.

If you haven't loved, you haven't lived.

Now that I've loved, I feel like Carys was what I was missing all along. She helps define me, who I am.

I'm Maverick Kensington and I'm in love with Carys Matthews.

And that's all that really matters.

THE END

Acknowledgements

As always, we have to take the time to thank everyone who joined us on this journey. And every book is just that, a journey. Especially books like Blue Bayou. Even though we've always had a clear picture of what this book would be, getting that down on paper was not the easiest job. We had a major case of writer's block with this one and were never so thankful as when the fog finally cleared. Thankfully, our team stuck with us through it all and were understanding and gracious enough to be patient and continue to encourage us, and for that we are so grateful.

To the people in our lives—family, friends, readers. Each of you make our world a little brighter and make it all worth it.

First, we'd like to thank Pamela Stephenson for being there from the get-go. She was in the hotel room with us during our brainstorming session to come up with the title and she never left our side. Thank you, Pamela, for always being there for us, whether it's to swoon over a scene or giving us constructive criticism. Your support is incomparable.

We'd also like to thank Nikki, our editor. Thank you for allowing us to push back our appointments and for not quitting us. LOL. You always push us for more and encourage us to bring more insight—dig deeper. Our books wouldn't be what they are without you.

Someone else we have to mention is our pre-reader and friend, Shannon Mc. Your keen eye and intelligent approach to reading is amazing. Thank you! We appreciate the time you spend on our books!

Our proofreader, friend, and drinking buddy, Mrs. Karin Enders. Thank you for everything! From beta reading to proofreading, we appreciate your time, effort, and camaraderie!

We'd also like to thank our cover designer and formatter, Juliana. Thank you for making the photo we love work and for making it even better. We love your creativity and attention to detail!

Also, a huge shout-out to our pimp team—Pamela, Lynette, Megan, Shannon, Candace, and Laura. Thank you for always putting your two-cents worth in and giving us a safe place to bounce ideas! We love y'all!

Thank you to everyone in Jiffy Kate's Southern Belles. All of you make our days better.

About the Authors

Jiffy Kate is the joint pen name for Jiff Simpson and Jenny Kate Altman. They're co-writing besties who share a brain and a love of cute boys, good coffee, and a fun time.

Together, they've written over twenty stories. Their first published book, Finding Focus, was released in November 2015. Since then, they've continued to write what they know—southern settings full of swoony heroes and strong heroines.

You can find them on most social media outlets at @jiffykate, @jiffykatewrites, or @jiffsimpson and @jennykate77.

Made in the USA
Middletown, DE
07 September 2018